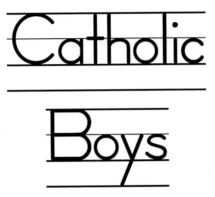

Catholic Boys

a novel

Philip Cioffari

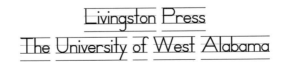

Livingston Press
The University of West Alabama

isbn 13:   978-1931982-98-6 trade paper
isbn 13:   978-1931982-97-9, library bind.
Library of Congress Control Number 2007932135
Printed on acid-free paper.
Printed in the United States of America,
Publishers Graphics
Hardcover binding by: Heckman Bindery
Typesetting and page layout: Angela Brown
Proofreading: Brittany Lovette, Genesis Brooks,
Lynestra Baldwin, Alexius White, Shelly Huth, Tim Edwards
Cover design and layout: Jennifer Brown
Cover photo: Louis Phillips

author's acknowledgements:
With gratitude, for their thoughtful readings of the mansucript: Dorian Dale,
Patrick Friel, Angela Himsel, Bill Petrick, Peter Selgrin; and Joe Taylor and
the staff at Livingston Press

This is a work of fiction.
Surely you know the rest: any resemblance
to persons living or dead is coincidental.

Livingston Press is part of The University of West Alabama,
and thereby has non-profit status.
Donations are tax-deductible:
brothers and sisters, we need 'em.

first edition
6 5 4 3 3 2 1

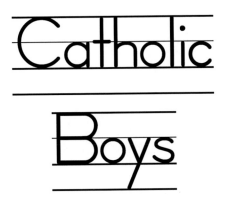

Catholic Boys

Prologue

The Bronx, 1960

The air smelled of rotting fish.

The girl, breathing through her mouth to avoid it, heard the river gurgling at the edges of the mudflats, and beyond that the whoosh of cars on the parkway towering on cement buttresses above the swamp grass.

In the firelight she began to undress—her top first, a white jersey that fit tight, and then her shorts, hooking her thumbs inside the waistline and pushing down, first one side then the other, a motion more jagged than she intended. She had done it before and they liked it, even though she wasn't yet graceful like the women in the movies. From the shadows at the fire's edge, they cheered her on.

Baby, baby! Sweet baby!

Her shorts fell to her feet and she kicked free of them. Naked now, she stood waiting. She was thin with small breasts that she apologized for by hunching forward. The heat of the fire warmed her back. Damper, cooler air from the river tingled her arms and legs. Usually they played these games in the hallways but she liked the thrill of this, outdoors, only several hundred yards from the housing project, swamp grass and mud sucking at her toes, boys calling to her from the shadows.

A song played inside her head: *come to me baby, whisper in my ear. . . .* She closed her eyes and let her body drift with the music, this way and that, far across the river and the swamp grass that in her mind went on and on forever—until hands wrapped around her arms, thick and calloused hands that squeezed through to her bones. It hurt a little but she kept her eyes closed while the hands brought her down to the grass and mud.

Spread 'em, honey, a voice said.

She did as she was told, opening her legs and lying back so that the grass tickled and the rank smell of mud bloomed around her. Her boyfriend, the leader, tall and hard in his black leather jacket, shoved a boy toward her. She didn't know his name but had seen him around: playground, candy store, wherever. He was pale, thin as she was, shaking like he was cold, like it wasn't hot-as-hell June.

Faggot here's got something to prove, her boyfriend said. He shoved the boy again. *Don't cha? Don't cha?* The boy stumbled but regained his balance, bent double, arms flailed back. Her boyfriend grabbed his neck and squeezed, the boy making gurgling noises like the river, her boyfriend squeezing tighter, shaking him harder as she watched the kid's eyes bulge like they were filling with air; for a moment she thought they might pop, spitting blood and membrane all over her.

Don't cha?

The boy was kneeling now, his narrow face wagging between the knobby posts of her knees, her boyfriend forcing him down until his face was flush against her, wiping like a rag across hair and the folds of her crack, the boy coughing and choking.

He a faggot homo pole-sucker, or a man? Which one? Which one?

A man, the boy said, choking, barely getting the words out. *A man like you.*

Prove it then.

Her boyfriend let go of the kid's neck and the others came forward. Two of them held the boy while the others ripped open his belt and yanked his shirt and pants off. He crawled to his knees and cringed like a dog. And then the kick came: her boyfriend's black shit-kicker on his butt, sending him sprawling on top of her. *Prove you're not a faggot. Prove it!*

She watched him prop himself on his hands like he was going to do pushups over her, his eyes focused on her throat or

Philip Cioffari

neck, anywhere but her face. He froze there propped like that: soft between his legs, shriveled up. Her boyfriend shouted, *Prove it, homo fucking pansy.*

The boy's eyes shut tight. Lips clenched, neck veins taut, he began to move: slow at first then faster, up down, up down, up down: crying now, but faster faster, his soft flesh squashing against her thighs. He held her tighter and tighter and she squirmed to free herself, sliding side to side; but he clung to her, sobbing and pumping harder than ever, too hard, way too hard she was thinking—*What kind of a freak are you anyway?*—and then he was pushing his face between her breasts like he wanted to crawl inside through flesh and bone to somewhere deep and dark and quiet and then he quit everything except the sobbing, louder now, too loud she thought for such a skinny kid.

She tried to push him away—he was disgusting, no man at all, not like the other guys, strong and hard before she even put her mouth there—but she didn't have to push very long because the other boys were dragging him to his feet, pulling and shoving him. He was spinning between them, between punches and kicks, words and groans, *faggot faggot faggot faggot,* spinning spinning, a thin lithe shadow colliding with the larger shadows of the older boys, *get him get the little faggot.* No chance—he had no chance at all—and for the first time that night she felt both fear and sorrow rise inside her like trapped birds. There was something helplessly soft about the boy: for a moment against the river's dark motion his body seemed to glow, the firelight like a fading sun setting on his skin.

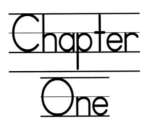

Chapter
One

MONDAY

On the path to the river Ramsey stumbled once, but kept from falling by bracing himself on the cement buttress of the draw-bridge where someone had scrawled JFK FOR PRESIDENT. Two members of the Crime Scene Unit stood downriver and he picked his way toward them over muddy ground. In the year he served as the housing project's Chief of Security he'd never ventured down here. There had been no serious trouble.

A short distance from the river's edge, the boy hung from the branch of a dead tree. His skin was astonishingly pale except for his face: dark red and misshapen, bruises around his swollen eyes, cut-marks and dried blood on his lips. *It was Evan hanging there*: a trick of the mind—and Ramsey blinked the image away. When he looked again he saw this boy's hair was darker, his facial features—bruises and cuts aside—more symmetrical, his legs and arms longer, thinner than Evan's. He hung from the rope of a swing, the braid twisted several times around his neck. The bench seat, a grey and jagged piece of driftwood, angled earthward between his shoulder blades like a broken wing.

The remnants of a homemade ladder, split and broken now,

were nailed to the river side of the trunk—from the tree's better days when its branches were used as a perch to view the sweeping arc of the bay.

At the base of the slope the remains of a wood fire blackened the tall grass; the area around the fire had been flattened. He stepped closer to the dead tree, its trunk as skeletal and naked as the body. He waved his arm to scare a fly that crawled across the face—a child's face, really, the boy couldn't have been more than twelve or thirteen. The age Evan would have been.

He moved around the tree's bifurcated trunk. Whoever had beaten the boy did a thorough job, back and front. He flinched and looked away, following the river's flow beneath the draw-bridge: past high walls of cattails, past mudflats and dense mats of cord grass and, beyond that, wet fields of yellow thistle along the bay.

From the service road, jammed now with Emergency vehicles, Tommy Morales came walking toward him. They had worked together at the 4-7 where they'd been partners briefly, before Ramsey left the force.

"You know him?" Morales asked.

"No." He'd made it a point to avoid the playgrounds, the ball field, this grassy slope alongside the swamp—anywhere he might see children at play.

"He one fucked up son-of-a-bitch, or what?" Maybe it was the tone in his own voice Morales didn't like, or something in the crushed look of Ramsey's face that made him add: "I've seen maybe two hundred DOA's, bodies carved up, stuffed in sewers, you name it. But there's nothing worse than seeing a kid."

"You might want to keep an eye out for the underwear and socks." Ramsey nodded at the clothes strewn near the fire. "They're missing."

"Yeah, I noticed."

"And you're going to have a helluva time keeping this place clear."

"I'm trying, man. I'm trying. 'Specially these paths to and from the site. I'm hoping to get a print out of one of them."

"Grass is too thick. Maybe along the river."

Morales yelled at one of the CSU assistants who tripped on

Philip Cioffari

a rock and fell heavily against the tree. "Hey, numbnuts, we got a crime scene here."

Ramsey pointed to the tree limb. "You've got traces of blood and mud on the bark up there." When he lowered his eyes against the sun something glinted in the grass and he moved toward it: a tiny gold cross with an arrow inlaid in place of the body of Christ. It hung from a broken chain. He held it to the light, then dropped it into a plastic bag Morales shoved at him.

"You shoulda stayed on the force." Morales' broad grin lit up his face. "Your brains, my personality. We woulda made some act."

"Yeah. In Vaudeville," Ramsey said. "You got activity here, Tommy. Flattened grass all over the place."

"We got someone coming in from the trees there—"

"And going *back* into the trees," Ramsey said. "The grass is crushed in both directions."

"Yeah, I checked it out. Nothing in there except an old Studebaker and some abandoned tires."

"You question the fisherman yet?"

"Says he don't know anything."

This section of the riverbank was on company property so it would be Ramsey's case, too. They'd work out the jurisdictional issues later. "I'd like to talk to him."

"Sure," Morales said. "I'll take all the help I can get."

Ramsey trudged through weeds and mud, his shoes squishing with each step. Sweat beaded on his neck. The sun hadn't been up an hour and it already felt like mid-afternoon.

Beneath the bridge one of his own men, Peterson, a tall gawky rookie, all arms and legs, stood guard with a precinct cop. The fisherman, a blue cap covering all but a fringe of his white hair, sat hunched on the platform edge. His legs dangled over the black water of the river, a fishing pole braced between his thighs.

"Name's Karl Elmore," Peterson read aloud from a pad. "Fishes here two, three times a week. Spotted the body after dawn. Says he went right to the Boulevard to make the call."

Ramsey crouched beside the old man who stared at the abutments supporting the bridge as it arced over the swamp.

"What do you catch?"

"Not a damn thing. Too much commotion."

"On an ordinary day."

"Depends. Upriver or down."

"What about right here?"

"Carp, mostly. Pickerel or bass, if I'm lucky." The old man spat into the river.

"What's in the bait can?"

"Lugworms, clamworms. Dig 'em up from the flats out there." He nodded downriver, past the wall of cattails. "Most people can't stand the stink."

"Can you tell me what happened this morning?"

"Already told them."

"I'd like you to tell me again." His knees hurt so much he had to shift his weight and kneel on the platform. He liked to think, at forty, he was too young for his body to go south. Instead, he blamed those years catching in the sandlot leagues: the constant crouching, the hits he had taken blocking the plate. Now the ridges of the cement bit his kneecaps through the cloth and he shifted position again. "Case you forgot anything."

The old man scowled. "Got here the usual time, four, four-fifteen, fished a while. Once the sun come up I took a stroll across the platform here, noticed something funny downriver. Went right up and phoned the police."

"What time was that?"

"Don't wear no watch." He held out his arm to prove it. His hand smelled of fish. Dried blood caked beneath his fingernails.

"Anyone else here?"

"Most folks fish City Island, from the bridge."

"You noticed anything unusual down here lately?"

"Like what?"

"I don't know, you tell me. Illegal hunting along the river, maybe? I hear they're taking rabbits, muskrats, things like that."

"Don't know nothing about it."

He stood and brushed the dust from his pants. "When you went to make the phone call, Mr. Elmore, which route did you take?"

Philip Cioffari

The old man hesitated before pointing a bony finger to the path along the bridge wall. "Right there."

Gotcha, Ramsey thought. It was an instinct he had, a built-in lie detector, and the old man with his hesitation had just failed it. "And when you came back? When you waited for the police to arrive?"

"Stood right up there on the road."

"You didn't cross the riverbank, take a closer look at the body?"

"Scared they'd get me. Whoever done him in." The old man spit another stream of tobacco juice into the water's black drift. Eyes narrowed, head lowered, he looked like a guilty dog.

"Clean your own fish, Mr. Elmore?"

"Right over there." He nodded to the far end of the platform where the cement ledge was discolored with red and yellow stains.

"Mind if I look in your tackle box?"

"Don't go messing things up."

"You have my word." His father had taken him fishing just once in his life. The Bronx River near 225th. They had nailed a string and hook to a broomstick, chunks of Wonder bread for bait. The bread kept dissolving in the river's current and floating away. When they did hook a baby sunfish his father held it dangling from the makeshift pole as if he had shocked himself with the catch.

He crouched next to the box and struggled to snap open the rusty clamps: a double tray of hooks, sinkers, floats—and resting in the bottom of the box were two fillet knives, one old, one new. He held the ancient knife to the light, its surface dull and pitted.

The old man grinned. "I keep it around. For protection."

"From who, Mr. Elmore?"

"Them kids, maybe." He glanced around, craning his neck apparently to check the billboard at the far end of the service road: a nymphet on her knees. The White Rock girl with her simple message: *have a soda, feel this cool.*

Chasing the old man's logic was making his head hurt. "What kids?"

"Hooligans. With their orgies. Girls and such."

"You've seen them? Down here?"

"Ain't said I seen them, but I know."

"Can you describe them?"

"Never look 'em in the eye."

Ramsey shifted his weight again to ease the pressure on his knees. "Help me out here, Mr. Elmore. Would you be able to pick them out of a line-up?"

"Ain't seen nothin', but in my heart I know."

He returned the knife to the box and lowered the lid. "Thank you for your help."

From the platform edge, Ramsey watched the body being carried to the coroner's van on the service road where a crowd had formed. Photographers flocked to the van; their flashbulbs' greedy eyes winked in the early light.

He hung a cigarette between his lips and flicked the top of his Zippo. He'd sworn to give the damn things up, but there were moments—with Helen, or on the job—when drawing smoke was the only comfort. His eye caught some movement above him and he looked up to see two boys in school uniforms standing on the walkway of the bridge. One of them was chubby—a carrot-top, the other thin and dark-haired. They watched the dead boy being carried to the van.

As Ramsey stepped off the platform, he caught sight of his own reflection in the river: broad face and shoulders, dark hair combed back, body beginning to look overweight now. But it was what he could see of his face that most disturbed him—the hollows of his eye sockets, the grim set of his mouth and jaw—the look of grief even a river's murky image couldn't conceal.

*****

From the Farrell's eleventh floor apartment Ramsey watched the crime scene unit form a line across the slope then move unevenly in the direction of the bridge, sweeping the tall grass with vacuums and metal detectors.

He had come to the window seeking relief but no breeze stirred from the wide vistas of marshland. Even the river seemed stalled. Behind him, Morales questioned Mary Farrell,

Philip Cioffari

the dead boy's mother. She had no idea why her son would have gone into the swamp at night. He'd been to the movies alone. A John Wayne double feature. Eight o'clock show. He *often* went alone, she said. He'd promised to come right home.

If she had been standing here at the window, he thought, if there had been enough light, she might have witnessed the end of her son's life.

He turned from the window, half-expecting to see Helen's face: the template for all sorrow. This woman, several years younger than his wife, sat hunched on the sofa, a fistful of Kleenex pressed to her eyes.

"I didn't think there was any harm in it," she was saying. "He always came straight home."

"Was this your son's medallion?" Morales asked, showing her the gold cross and chain.

"Saint Sebastian. It's a club—at the high school. They meet every week."

When she began sobbing, her sister—Miss Dorothy Campbell—leaned closer. Both women were in their thirties, Ramsey guessed, though Mary Farrell looked older than that: eyes veined with grief, her face ravaged. Her blond-grey hair was pulled back and wrapped in a bun, which gave her face a more austere look than her sister whose hair fell in bangs.

"I tried to raise him a good Catholic boy. God forgive me—" She broke down sobbing again and left the room. Her sister rose quickly and followed her into the bathroom.

He glanced at his former partner who stared uncomfortably after them. Dorothy Campbell reappeared, saying that her sister would return shortly. In the meantime would they like coffee?

Morales joined her in the kitchen, inquiring about the boy's father. Ramsey, waging a losing battle with his memories, only half-heard the isolated phrases: "missing in action . . . Korea . . . the boy never knew . . . not quite a year old when his daddy was shipped. . . ." Through the opposite wall came the sound of Mary Farrell's sobbing, then a faucet was turned on and he couldn't hear her tears.

The living room's heat pressed against him like a wet hand. He wiped his forehead and held the cloth there.

"He read a lot," Dorothy Campbell was saying in response to Morales' inquiry. She carried a coffee tray into the living room. "Mysteries, thrill-type material. Junk, if you ask me. If it wasn't a book, it was the movies."

Ramsey held the cup she offered him, but the thick steam made his stomach turn and he set it down. "I'd like to see your nephew's room, if that's all right."

The bedroom's scrupulous neatness bothered him. Evan's room had been as orderly as this one, though not because of Evan. Helen picked up after him, arranging his toys on the built-in shelves, returning his clothes to the closet. After the funeral she had gone immediately to that room and closed the door behind her. In his dark suit he'd leaned against the wall and smoked, listening for some sound of her, hating the restless beating of his own thoughts—until at last she stood in the doorway, staring at him as if he were an intruder. "We'll leave it like this," was all she said, pulling the door closed and walking past him in the dim hall.

From then on Evan's room was a closed door on the second floor. *We'll leave it like this.*

He sensed a presence behind him. Mary Farrell stood in the doorway, frail shoulders drawn tight.

"Did your son have a girlfriend, Mrs. Farrell?"

"He was much too young," she said quickly and emphatically. "He was still developing."

On the closet floor he found a dozen or more coiled posters: Dick Tracy, Tom Mix, John Wayne, The Shadow, the Green Hornet.

"I didn't think they belonged on the same wall with Our Savior." With a handful of tissues she blessed herself and murmured, "God forgive me, but I've nothing to live for now."

"You've got your faith, Mrs. Farrell."

"What good is faith now?"

His face flushed. The way she stood there with her shoulders collapsed, her eyes lost and unfocused, he was reminded of something the nuns had preached: *God never bestows upon us more burdens than we can bear.* Even as a boy he had his doubts about that; as an adult he found it laughable. "Your husband—" he said, getting to his feet.

Philip Cioffari

"He never came back. We buried an empty coffin."

"Your son—did he have an uncle, a teacher—"

"A father figure, you mean?"

"Yes."

"My family's in Pennsylvania. My husband was an only child. Except for my sister, we were alone." She drew in her shoulders to shore herself against that aloneness. Her grief brought a beauty to her face that surprised him. He took a step toward her and opened his arms. For a moment she seemed stunned then she fell against him; his arms clamped clumsily around her. The sweet fragrance of shampoo lifted from her hair; instinctively, he tightened his grip to stop her trembling. Before he could find words of comfort, she broke free, turning quickly and leaving him feeling foolish and useless.

He turned his attention to the bookcase with its shelf upon shelf of pulp magazines: *Comanche Fury, Showdown at Dry Gulch, Apache Wars*. Tucked behind them were more books, with racier covers: *Dead Man's Alley, Blind Lust, City of Sin*. In the dresser he found a rabbit's foot on a chain, a "Flying Fortress" B-17 bomber model airplane kit unopened, a chemistry set, a deck of cards for Canasta. No chestnuts, though. Evan had collected chestnuts. He had polished them against his shirt.

Behind the closed door of the adjacent room he heard Mary Farrell crying softly. He was thinking, it's true, the most dreadful fate of a parent: your child dying before you.

In the kitchen Dorothy Campbell washed coffee cups. "A boy can't have a normal life without a father," she was saying.

"Why's that?" Ramsey asked, leaning in the doorway.

Her face pinched tight as a prune. "He can't, that's all."

In the hallway, Morales slouched against the wall while they waited for the elevator. Half Italian, half Puerto Rican—or as he put it, half-guinea, half rican—he had the kind of deeply tanned, Mediterranean good looks Ramsey might have envied in the days when he cared about such things. Now Morales popped a piece of Double Bubble in his mouth and chewed like a hungry man. He showed Ramsey a page from his notebook. There was one name written on it: Donald Seward. "What the hell kind of kid's got only one friend?"

*****

The day fell upon Ramsey like a burden: a blur of heat, dazzling brightness, questions. Do you know this boy? Did you see. . .? Somewhere in the course of his travels he misplaced his sunglasses and he was forced to squint against the hard white glare.

Off the record, he and Morales had discussed procedures. Legal jurisdiction, for this belonged to the NYPD, but it was understood that as Housing Security Chief he would pursue a parallel investigation. They would share information. Where possible, Morales would give him access to police department files. This would be a high-profile case and he was happy to have Ramsey on the team. Unofficially, they would be partners again.

At noon, when he called Helen from the Rexall on Metropolitan Boulevard, the phone rang endlessly. He'd grown accustomed to her refusal to have her grief interrupted by small talk, though he worried about her just the same. Were these the hours she spent inside Evan's room, locked in a happier time?

He ordered a root beer in a carry-out cup, then stood outside to watch the throng that spilled back from the swamp and filled both sides of the Boulevard. These were decent, hard-working people—second generation Irish, Germans, Jews and Italians—without the means to move to Westchester or the Island. Overnight they'd watched their neighborhood change. No one stood in front of DiMetriano's to watch Sal D braid his homemade mozzarella, nor did anyone stop to gawk at the skinned rabbits hanging in the window of Vinnie's Meats; and outside Krumfeld's no line had formed for the penny candy machine. It was another trick of the mind, he knew, but the buildings seemed darker today, shabbier, their brick a sullen shade of rust.

Draining the last of the root beer, the cold liquid burning harshly in his throat, he stepped out from the awning's shadow and blinked against the white assault. A child's death seemed so unnatural on such a bright summer day.

Philip Cioffari

Chapter Two

Smoking was forbidden at St. Jerome's except for faculty, but Brody didn't care. From the library steps he watched the activity in the yard. His grey eyes looked as though they'd been staring for days and nights without rest, seen too much. His fingers pinched the cigarette so hard the tobacco bled through.

It was lunch half-hour—fifteen minutes to eat, fifteen minutes outdoors to blow off steam—then back to the grind. Classes were bad enough, but today they'd been hit first thing with a memorial service for the dead faggot. Brothers and priests with their eulogies. Arthur this, Arthur that. One of our best. One of our brightest. A terrible loss for us all.

Brody couldn't bear it. *Gimme a break.* Arthur was a faggot. Arthur sucked dick. Why didn't anybody say that? When O'Malley started in with *let us pray for Arthur's immortal soul*, Brody clomped his way down the steps of the risers and headed for the gymnasium's rear exit.

Shannon stopped him at the door. "Father Tobias hasn't excused you yet."

"Gotta take a crap, Father. Real bad." He kept walking. Shannon didn't say a thing. Not about his leaving, not about his black leather Brando's jacket or his shit-kickers—both of which were strictly forbidden on school grounds. A weird duck, that Shannon. Hot and cold. One day's he's badgering you to death, next day he's your buddy.

Kiss my ass, Father.

Inside the john, first thing, he lit up. Who gave a fuck whether Shannon smelled smoke? Fourteen days till graduation. Who gave a fuck? Worst of it was, even with the door closed and the windows open to the parkway, he could still hear the prayers. Let us pray. Let us pray. *Our Father who blah blah blah. . . .*

The hypocrisy. That's what got Brody. Hadn't they been shoveling it down his throat since junior high? No dirty thoughts, no dirty pictures. Keep your hands *to* yourself but not *on* yourself, yeah, yeah, ha-ha. What it came down to, plain and simple: cocksuckers went to hell. Canon law, or whatever. Of all the sexual sins, licking dick and taking it up the wazoo were the worst. Unnatural, unholy, un*fucking* acceptable. And now they were praying for the skinny little perv's immortal soul. Brody had to laugh. The one true church, who're they kidding? Holy of Holies. *Yeah, right.*

From the library steps he surveyed the yard. Where was Seward? He'd been eyeballing for him all morning but here, now, was his best shot. Lunch half-hour the whole school was thrown together. Guys banded together by age and class. Seniors got the best spot, near the library, which meant they didn't have to walk far to the classroom building. Freshman were exiled out by the fence.

He took in the wide straggly-grassed yard, side entrance, bus stop, parkway. Nowhere to hide. Scores were settled here, disputes resolved. At least five, six fights a day. Stand up and be counted. Take it like a man. Between fights, guys stood around in groups, yakking it up. A few diehards played hardball. Vicious games: fastballs thrown at the head, line drives ripping into the crowd, scattering guys left and right. Occasionally a power shot cleared the fence, rocketing across four lanes of traffic, cars veering this way and that. Disruption of any kind brought him a grim satisfaction.

There he was. Finally. The Seward rat. The little faggot's friend. Sneaking in through the front gate. *Look at him. Look at him.* Faking that cool walk, *trying* to. Who's he fooling? A pansy's a pansy, no way around it. *Look at him:* slipping into the crowd, head down, eyes low, lifting his collar to hide his face, standing with his back to the library steps. Thinks he's

Philip Cioffari

smart, thinks he's sneaky but you can always spot a pansy. Thinks he's safe. Who's he kidding?

No use, buck-o. Gotcha.

*****

Donald Seward had been ill all morning. He'd always been a sickly child, frail, slight of build. Today it was stomach cramps. He'd begged his mother not to send him to school. *Not today, not today, please.*

You say that everyday.

Today's different.

Yes, she said, that poor boy. What happened last night?

I told you, nothing.

That's all you ever say. Nothing. Nothing.

I told you. Nothing happened.

You go out, you do things. How can it be nothing?

I told you.

What did you tell me? What?

He said he was going to the movies. I came home. I told you.

That's all?

Yes.

You're such a secretive boy, you know that?

I told you. Nothing.

You can't run away from problems.

I won't. I promise—

You can't live in a shell.

I'll go tomorrow. I promise—

That poor boy.

I promise—

But later in the morning she changed her mind. *You can't mope around all day. It's not healthy. School will take your mind off things. School will—*

Brody flicked the butt in Seward's direction, came down the steps toward him. He was halfway across the yard when Seward turned, saw him coming. Then he was moving, too: zigzagging between groups of boys, walking on the first base line, head down, hands jamming his pockets.

Someone hit a looping fly to right. Before it dropped,

Brody and his friends had arranged themselves in a horseshoe around him, shoving him across the section of yard where the grass had quit growing. Seward pushed back like he usually did but one guy's no match for five, and they got more vicious the harder he fought.

Behind the maintenance shed, in view of the river's ooze, Brody said: "Hey, Sewer rat, you a pisser or a piss-on?"

Seward kept his eyes lowered on the silver stones that glittered in the dirt.

"I'm talkin' to you, piss-head." He swung. Seward's head snapped hard against the shed's metal. Then: fast jabs at his belt line that dropped him, head swaying like a crane out over his knees, over the hardscrabble ground of the river bank, hands clawing his stomach. Then: a pointed-toe boot knocking him flat. He tasted dirt.

"Piss-*on*." Brody's stream hissed first on the dirt, then warm across Seward's legs, soaking his pants. Laughter. Brody's the loudest.

Brody *knew*.

Dirt road behind the Drive-in—Brody had come by with his girl. His car headlights slashed across the tall grass, caught two boys with their arms around each other, kissing. He jerked the car to a halt, his girl flung hard against the windshield. Seward and Arthur Farrell were running fast, but he'd seen them, *seen*.

"What makes a faggot?" Brody said. His buddies stood in a loose circle around him and kept their mouths shut. It was a statement, not a question. He had gone down the list a dozen times before: the way they stand, the way they giggle, the way they fight. Like Arthur. Brody remembered the first time he beat up on the kid. The little faggot tried to bite him. *Bite* him!

Seward was on his knees in the dirt, crying.

"You don't want to end up like your friend, you keep your mouth shut," Brody said. "Remember, *I* know what you are. *We* know."

Someone said, "Yeah, yeah." Voices and footsteps faded.

In the dirt, Donald Seward was sucking air, but not fast enough to fill what felt sick and hollow inside.

Philip Cioffari

In the basement washroom he spit dirt and blood into the sink, soaked tap water into his uniform pants. Mud speckled the St. Jerome's insignia on his tie: AD ASTRA PER ASPERA. To the heavens through hard work. He rubbed it clean.

On the stairs Father Tobias said, "What happened?"

"Hurt myself sliding into base."

The Prefect stood on the step above, grey-haired and overweight, a double chin hiding his Adam's Apple. "You're late again. Report to me after school."

In history class he stared at the abandoned orphanage with its turrets and jagged-toothed roof line. Across the yard, in a jungle of thorn bushes, the outfield dead-ended against the highway. The voice of Brother Ignatius droned about the dreams of the Spanish explorers when they entered the new world. At fourteen he already felt beaten, his life not worth much, maybe nothing at all.

When the bell rang he waited while his classmates filed out, while Ignatius packed his briefcase and waddled from the room. No one seemed to notice he wasn't rushing to get out like the rest.

The stairs to the tower creaked even if you walked on tiptoe. This was where you went when you were bad, the torture chamber, the Prefect's *other* office. Guys got beaten here, that was the rumor. Out of sight, away from witnesses, the priests could go wild, knock the shit out of you.

From his desk Father Tobias, still as a statue, watched him enter. The Prefect's hair rose in waves from his wide, over-sized face, eyes delivering a pale and cold judgment. At that moment the clocks erupted in the bell tower above: the half-hour chimes, shaking down through walls and windowpanes. The statue moved ever so slightly, made a sound that was somewhere between a grunt and a wheeze.

"You've been here since January. Almost five months now," the priest said when the sound waves settled. He held up a folder, shook it in the air. "You were failing in public school and you're failing here. Don't you think you owe it to your parents to show an improvement?"

"Yes, Father."

He lay the folder flat, adjusted the corners until it was perfectly straight, and stared uncomfortably across the desk. It was not the boy's grades he wanted to discuss. "You were friendly with Arthur Farrell, were you not?"

"Yes, Father."

The priest pushed himself up from his chair and he thought it would come now, the beating. Because of his sin. Because, some way, the priest must have found out. But Father Tobias remained in the narrow space behind the desk, deep in thought, walking the length of the bookcase and back again.

"Did you—were you—?" He pulled forlornly on the folds of his double chin. "Arthur had been with us since . . . he began at our grade school across the river. He was . . ." His voice trailed off and his pale eyes looked for help. "You were together on Saturday here at the Disciples' retreat."

It was not a question, but Donald Seward nodded his head yes.

"Because of your association with . . . because of your *proximity* to Arthur, the police may want to question you."

The boy shifted noisily in his seat. "I don't know anything— I—"

"Is there something you want to tell me, my son?"

"Yes, Father. I mean no, Father."

"Perhaps in the privacy of the confessional?"

He sat forward in the chair, looking down at his hands clasped tight between his legs. "I don't think so, Father."

"You don't seem certain of that."

"Yes, Father."

"Yes what, son?"

He shifted his gaze toward the narrow windows with their view of the school grounds. There were two routes home: along either the river or the parkway. On one of them, Brody would be waiting. It was a game of who could out-guess who. But even if he won today, there would be tomorrow, and the days after that. "I don't feel good, Father. I feel sick."

"Do you want to see the nurse?"

"No, Father." It was Arthur he wanted to see, alive, alive. So

　　　　　　　　　　　　Philip Cioffari

he could talk to him and not feel sick.

"Anything, anything at all that pertains to—" Father Tobias was saying. He leaned forward with such earnestness that the desk creaked. "I can't tell you how many hours, days, nights, how much of my life I've devoted to . . . St. Jerome's is my heart and soul. If anything should happen that—" Tears welled in his eyes and his lower lip quivered. "It would grieve me inconsolably if—am I making myself clear?"

"Yes, Father."

"I want you to come to *me* first with anything that troubles you. Promise me that."

"I promise, Father."

"The police may not always be our friends in matters such as this. You don't have to say anything to them that makes you uncomfortable. Simply refer them to me."

"Yes, Father."

"I'll answer all their questions."

"Yes, Father."

"One more thing. I want you to stay away from those older boys during lunch break."

"I will, Father."

"In the meantime, I'll arrange special tutoring for you. I'll speak with your teachers. You can excel like Arthur. I'll help you. Everyone on the staff here will help you." The Prefect came around the desk and stood behind him, thick hands resting on his shoulders and the boy thought at first the priest was about to give him a massage, the way Arthur sometimes did; but the hands only tightened their grip on his shoulders, clamped hard on flesh and bone, unyielding. No hint of affection. A pressure so strong it hurt.

*****

The project with its twelve-story brick buildings cast a dark, imposing shadow over the grassland. Coming down the embankment to the service road, Donald Seward felt sick again. Police lights, barricades, cops everywhere. The grassy slope, the dead tree. *Arthur*

His apartment on the ground floor looked out on cat-tails

and mud flats. Sometimes the smell was so bad they had to shut the windows, even in summer's heat. When he came in his mother was in a mood, over-worked and worked-up, washing clothes in the sink one minute, chopping carrots and shucking peas the next. "That friend of yours," she said, without looking up. "His poor mother. I can't imagine—"

He cleaned the bathroom, took out the garbage, vacuumed the living room, his daily chores, performed without enthusiasm or concentration as he worked around his brothers and their rowdy game of Cowboys and Indians. Bad enough at night with all of them asleep in those cramped rooms, but during the day, with his brothers fighting and yelling, it was hard on the nerves. At night he would overhear his mother complain: the kitchen's too small, we need another bedroom (she and his father slept on a pull-out couch in the living room), we need a yard "for the boys." Above the sound of the TV, her voice would carry on about moving to a higher floor, to Westchester or Connecticut.

Once she said, "I should have stayed on 161st with my mother." His father worked days in an office: nights and weekends he drove a cab. Usually he just kept his mouth shut, but that night he'd said, "I wish you'd go to church, Sundays at least, set an example." But she came back quick with, "You gave me five kids. You took away any time I might have had for God."

"What happened to your face?" his mother asked when he had dismantled the vacuum and stored it back in the closet.

"Fell."

She held wet socks in her hand, pulling more from the sink. He moved toward the door, face turned away.

"Where you going?"

"Out."

"Where?"

"Just out."

"Why?"

"Why what?"

"Why can't you ever give me a straight answer?"

"I do."

"If everyone had as many secrets as you, there'd be no need

Philip Cioffari

for language in this world."

"Going out for a while."

"From now on I want you home early. Till we're sure it's safe out there."

He rode the subway. It didn't matter where: Far Rockaway, Coney Island, Pelham Bay, the Mount Vernon border. Sometimes he got out, walked around. Sometimes he just rode and rode: Simpson Street, Hunts Point, Rosedale Ave. He knew the station names by heart, his litany of escape. This was his life: riding away from what hurt: feet hissing on gravel behind the maintenance shed, punches that made him kneel without breath. Branded now, he'd live with the smell of blood in his nose, the river's sour breath, the dampness of stone. He was doomed as Arthur.

He stood in the first car, tracks sliding silver-slick below him. Ahead: the black hole of the tunnel, the rush into darkness, the wheels' ratcheting pulse dulling the memory of voices raised like fists, fists shouting like voices.

Floating through darkness, floating through light.

Like creatures beneath the sea, faces watched him from platforms dimmed and dulled and dreamless, passing fast, no threat at all. He was safe, he was safe, and somewhere ahead there would be sunlight breaking over tunnel walls when he made it through.

*****

Half-past six. Ramsey was late getting to the morgue at Jacobi. Morales, already inside, nodded with grim formality. There were few occasions when his cynical wit wasn't poised to pounce at the first opportunity; but he stood by the table with his head bowed, his body stiffly reverent, hands clasped in front of him. Beside him, equally grim-faced, was an A.D.A. named Benson.

Carlisle, the coroner, was finishing up. "So then," he said and cleared his throat. "What we have . . ." With his silver hair, his rimless glasses, his tall and slightly stooped frame, he looked ancient and wise. It seemed to Ramsey he'd come to confess something to this man, to seek counsel on matters that went beyond the death of the child lying on the table.

Washed and cleaned, Arthur Farrell's skin was as white as Carlisle's lab coat, which made the contusions on the boy's body even more pronounced. Though he had prepared himself for this, the inert and bruised body stunned Ramsey.

"Cause of death . . ." Carlisle was summing up for Ramsey's benefit. "Asphyxiation by hanging, and shock secondary to traumatic hemorrhage of the lungs. In other words, his neck wasn't broken. The drop was too short for that. He choked to death from lack of air." He pointed out small bleeding sites on the boy's lips. "Petechiae," he said. "The rope compresses the veins, but arterial flow continues. Pressure inside the head causes these small bleeding sites on the soft mucosa of the lips as well as inside the mouth and the eyelids."

He drew his finger along the collarbone where the skin was red and abraded. A thin dark line creased one side of the neck. It had been concealed when the boy was hanging from the tree, Ramsey realized, by the coils of rope. "These chain marks. We matched skin indentations with the chain found at the site. We also found gold traces on the skin around the neck. Most likely the chain was ripped from his neck during the beating." Carlisle lifted the boy's arms: first the right, then the left. "Contusions on the wrists and dorsal areas of the forearm."

"On the underside like that," Ramsey said for Benson's benefit. "Kid must of had a hell of a time fending off the blows."

"Let's just say it probably wasn't a fair fight." Carlisle lowered the arms gently until they rested against the dull sheen of the table. "The beating—"

Here he stopped and took a breath. He joined his hands together and pressed his fingertips to his lips in what seemed a prayerful gesture. "As you can see, the beating was brutal. It appears, for the most part, the blows were delivered by fists but there are several places where the weapon was less blunt, pointed toe boots most likely." He indicated several bruises on the boy's legs. "A lot of boys wear them these days. Shit-kickers, I believe they're called in teen parlance."

A door opened and one of the assistant pathologists came

in, adjusting his gloves. He crossed behind the table and positioned himself at a microscope along the far wall. Ramsey knew something of the procedure: the removal and sectioning of the internal organs, the minute examination of each organ's weight and condition. He had witnessed the disfigurements of age—the yellow fatty enlargement of the alcoholic's liver, the granularity of the diabetic's kidneys—he could accept that. But the disfigurement of youth, in any form, was harder to bear.

"Time of death," Carlisle was saying, "between one and four a.m."

"Was there blood on the boy's clothes?" Ramsey asked.

"None," Morales answered for Carlisle. "The kid's clothes were off before the beating."

"We haven't finished checking for hair and fibers under his nails. We have verified, however, the blood on the tree limb was his own." Carlisle stood with his arms folded, his face a mask of composure, directing his remarks now at no one in particular. "We did an anal swab. At some point last night the boy was sodomized."

*****

He let himself into his house and stood listening to the silence. The TV's light glared across the cushions of the sofa. Uncle Milty in a dress and a blonde wig pranced across the screen. It was Helen's practice of late to leave the set on, without sound. She would rarely sit and watch it, but relentlessly the characters moved in pantomime through a world quiet as dreams. He turned the set off, then climbed the stairs.

At her door, he listened first then knocked. He leaned in to find her curled on her side. The curtains had been drawn tight across the windows. Only a night light offered relief against the blackness. She wanted light when she slept, but not the silver-blue light from the street lamps—the color of grave stones, she said—which gave her a cold feeling. He didn't argue with her when she made judgments like that, just as he hadn't argued when she decided that it might be better if she slept alone "for a while." She had suffered so much already he wanted to give her whatever she asked, whatever she thought she needed. In the shadow of his grief, it had been easy to conceal his disappointment at not having her beside him through the night.

She slept with her right hand pressed to the center of her chest. The way the small fist rose and fell with her breathing made Ramsey think of the words from the Sunday prayer *mea culpa mea culpa mea maxima culpa.* Through my most grievous fault. He pulled the door closed against the gin's bitter smell.

In the kitchen he made himself a sandwich but when he sat down he left it on the plate and lit a cigarette instead. He was lighting his second cigarette when he heard Helen's slow, unsteady step and he rose immediately, crossing the living room to stand at the foot of the stairs—in case. We begin in hope, end by adjusting. Where had he read that?

He knew enough to turn the living room lamp on rather than the overhead light, just as he knew not to reach too quickly for her arm. When Helen emerged from her room she liked to do so in stages, without harsh light, with a minimum of intrusion. As she descended in her nightgown, her eyes blank and unblinking above her high cheekbones, she managed to look regal, as she often did despite her drinking, and he could not easily read her mood, the distance he would have to travel. When he offered his hand she smiled and let him guide her to the kitchen, but once there she disengaged herself. "That awful smoke," she said.

"I'm sorry, dear. I thought you were in bed for the evening." He waited for her to sit but she seemed contented where she was, leaning against the counter. He took his seat and snuffed out the cigarette.

"You haven't eaten your sandwich." Her tone was mildly reprimanding, almost playful. He thought for a moment a glimmer illuminated her blue-grey eyes that were dreamy in an unsettling way.

"There was a death last night."

"Yes, I know. It's been on the news all day."

"A child—"

"I don't want to hear the details." The flat stare she wore like

Philip Cioffari

a mask drove the light from her eyes.

"You know I'll have to be involved in the investigation."

"After what you've—we've—been through?"

"As Chief of Security—"

"You can't. You simply can't."

Ramsey's eyes met hers. "We've got to move on, don't we? At some point?"

"Where?" she said so softly, so helplessly that he came to her and put his hands on her shoulders. She turned away but he held her firmly.

"Look at me, Helen."

She stared at his shirt or maybe her eyes were closed, he couldn't tell. Then her head fell against his shoulder. "We've got to move on," he said gently, "the both of us. Together or separately. But we've got to."

She fought free of his embrace and stood at the sink, staring into the empty basin. "When you left the Department, you should have gone back into law, not Security work. You're too good for that."

She was moving into familiar territory. Normally he would have changed the subject but tonight he said, "What makes me *too good*?"

"You know that as well as I do."

"No, tell me."

He knew what she would say—she had been reminding him of this ever since he joined the PD ten years ago, reminding him of it again when he left the Department last year—but he listened to her recital in the kitchen's silence as if hearing it for the first time. Maybe he would believe it this time, maybe it would help him sort through the confusion and figure out where he was heading. He was educated, she told him, he held a law degree from Fordham, he knew that man was capable of higher things, of yearnings nobler than anything the lowlifes and criminals he chased could even imagine. He'd been a valued member of the City Council legal staff, not someone who hung back with the apes.

The long hours of the day ganged up on him and he leaned toward her, shoulders sagging, hands stuffed in his pockets. "You know I was never satisfied being a lawyer."

"That's something I'll never understand."

"And something you'll never forgive, either."

Tears clouded her eyes. "How can I?"

Ramsey wanted to explain, as he'd tried to so many times, that in committee meetings, in paneled offices, he had felt locked away from the world, out of touch: a bit player in a massive legal team. He'd come from a line of practical people— his own father had been a refrigerator repairman—who held jobs with a measurable effect. A man is someone who gets things done, that's what he believed. Someone who moved in the world of real and ordinary people and who managed to make a difference in that world. Keeping the streets in order was such a job. *That* had given him purpose. But she knew that. So he said nothing.

"*How can I?*" She turned to the cabinets, opening and closing doors until she found what she was looking for: an unfinished bottle of gin.

"Please," he said. She hesitated, gripping an empty glass. Then she reached for the bottle and filled the glass—no ice, no lemon—and took it with her, climbing the stairs without looking back.

He slid open the door to the porch and propped his arms on the rail. The yard, a double lot situated on a corner, afforded him a sense of privacy unusual for this section of the Bronx, this neighborhood of one and two-family homes south of Gun Hill Road.

The air smelled of basil and parsley, though in their own garden the grass had grown meadow-high. The hedges had to be trimmed, the flower beds replanted. One of these days he hoped Helen would get back to it. *One of these days*—he'd been saying that for nearly sixteen months now, as he watched her lose interest in everything: the garden first, then her crocheting, walks in the neighborhood, the poetry discussion group she belonged to at the library, the woman's club at church.

He smoked a cigarette halfway through, before following her upstairs.

She sat on her bed, her back against the wall, the half-finished glass of gin in her hand. "You didn't call today."

"I called four times, dear. You didn't answer the phone." He had arranged for Mrs. DeLorenzo, one of the neighbors, to look in on her and he told himself again that he had adjusted to her habit of not picking up the phone when she didn't want her grief violated. He took the glass from her hand and set it down. "Maybe you're right. Maybe I should think about going back into law."

He waited for Helen's voice to break the silence. It was easier when she was blaming him. Then he could blame himself as well. It seemed the simplest way to explain what happened to them. If he hadn't become a cop, she wouldn't have been left alone so much, especially at night. She wouldn't have had to drink to take the edge off her loneliness, even during her pregnancy, *especially* during her pregnancy when he was out collaring petty thieves and juvenile delinquents and she was left alone with her fears and her depression. If she hadn't started drinking maybe Evan wouldn't have been born the way he was. And if Evan had been normal, he might be alive today, he might not have acted so heedlessly. And if Evan hadn't died she wouldn't have had to start drinking so heavily again, would she? The rationale went on and on. It was Ramsey's fault. It was the lie that kept them from moving on.

He took her hand and held it, examining the pale skin crossed with blue veins, the thin nervous fingers and perfectly manicured nails. What had become of the woman he'd fallen in love with? She let her head fall against his shoulder and the smell of her body lotion quickened his senses.

She didn't stop him when he slipped his hand inside her robe, her skin cool beneath his touch, his hand rising from her belly and the contours of her ribs to feel the fullness of her breasts. For so long now she had refused to come to their room but sometimes it would happen like this, weeks or even months apart, on the narrow confines of a single bed. Always with the light on, always with the smell of gin on her breath.

There was no room for invention. He lifted the gown from her and she lay beneath him, gripping his shoulders. Her cry was loud and terrible as if he had reached inside her deepest wound to tear it open end to end. One of her hands settled on his face, fingers splayed like a mask, and she pushed hard in a way that forced his face sideward while her other hand, around his neck, pulled him closer.

She moved against him and cried out a second time, a wailing sound that made him shudder. It filled the silence and she cried out again and again. It seemed to him one continuous sound, rising and falling and rising again, gathering in this one place, this one act, all the accumulated sadness of his life. He closed his eyes against the yellow glow of the night light that reminded him of his room as a child, the nights he was sick with fever, with chills, nights so long he thought he would never see real light again.

Philip Cioffari

Chapter Three

TUESDAY

In darkness he stood at what appeared to be the center of a circle of children, dim figures occasionally stroked by light, moon-white and cold. They appeared to be crying out to him: mouths opening soundlessly, lips twisted, tongues lolling or too thick to be of use, eyes watching him with hope. Each face, in turn, was revealed by the light, but before he could reach out, the face had fallen back into darkness and he was forced to wait for the next glimmer of light, the next face that would turn its eyes upon him.

He awoke breathless and disoriented. This was the second night in a row he'd had the same dream.

Helen stirred beside him on the narrow bed. "Is it morning already?"

"Not yet."

In his own room he dressed slowly, bothered by the dream's mute and solemn faces. He strapped on his shoulder holster; the worn leather fit snugly across his chest. He hadn't worn it since resigning from the department.

Helen's hand waved away his kiss as if it were a bothersome fly. "I'll call later," he said.

"Promise?"

"If you'll promise me you'll pick up." He waited for her answer. No words came. Only the uneven hum of her breathing.

*****

At the Housing Security offices he tore open a pack of Viceroys—he had long since taken for granted the irony of his choice of brands—and thought about making himself a cup of coffee but decided against it: he was already too edgy, as if he'd reached the end of his day, not its beginning. This was supposed to be an easy job: nothing more serious than teenage rowdiness, domestic squabbles, an occasional purse-snatching. It was supposed to be a job he could handle blind-folded.

On the wall, beneath a map of the project's sixty buildings, was a smaller engineer's blueprint of the sub-basement network of hallways—the hundred halls, the neighborhood kids called them—built as a fall-out shelter in the early 50s and then abandoned halfway through construction. It was Security's responsibility to keep the doors to that level locked and to keep people, usually teenagers, from going down to explore. That would have been the more likely place for murder and rape, he was thinking, when the phone rang: E. Murray Albright, the President of Majority Life Insurance company, the owner of Baychester Housing. He knew the man by name and reputation only.

"We all know what a personal tragedy this is for the boy's family and friends," Albright said, his voice a rich baritone, the kind of voice a trained actor might own. "But there are other concerns as well, different concerns, *corporate* concerns."

Ramsey forced back his disgust. *If you say so, you old buzzard.* Through his window he could see reporters already gathering in the alley. The early birds. But who then was the worm? Himself? His assistant, Eddie Falcone, already hard at work in the outer office? He didn't care much for the analogy.

"Our reputation has been built upon the fact that we offer clean, safe, affordable housing for the middle-class," Albright was saying. "Something like this, well, I don't have to belabor the point. I've already spoken with the Commissioner. I want you to cooperate with the investigation in every way possible."

"Of course."

"I'm having a letter sent to each and every resident assuring them no expense will be spared in guaranteeing the safety of their children. And, Mr. Ramsey?" He paused before continuing what was an obviously prepared agenda. "It's come to my attention that there had been some difficulty in your previous position with the New York Police Department, as a consequence of your unfortunate personal circumstances. I trust this will not be a problem in the present situation."

"My staff and I will be working side by side with the PD on this."

"Good. Good." Another pause. "I'll be leaving for Nantucket this morning. When I return next week, I want all this behind us."

Ramsey stared at the phone resting in its cradle. The phrase *some difficulty in your previous position* brought back his last days at the department when he was told flat out by Moriarity, his precinct chief, that he was washed up as a cop, too crippled by his grief.

One of his theology professors at Fordham had advanced a theory that circles lay at the heart of God's design of the universe, and that man's emotional and psychological development assumed a circular pattern as well. By our own design or by fate, things come back around. We will always be offered a second chance.

And things *had* come back around, hadn't they? With a vengeance.

*****

From the top of the slope he saw them fighting in a clear space between the trees, the taller one swinging hard. The shorter one—younger, too, his head lowered behind raised arms—took the blows as he backed against the abandoned Studebaker with its windows busted out, its chassis sinking into the dirt at the swamp edge. The four teenage boys who lounged against the car and watched the beating stood up as he approached. They ranged in a loose line and squared their shoulders. The one getting the beating took advantage of Ramsey's sudden appearance to run in the direction of the service road where police vans were parked in tandem, the crime scene unit still at work combing the grass.

The tall boy, Brody, stood near the Studebaker's hood, breathing hard. With his tight T-shirt and jeans, slicked-back hair and hulking stance, he looked like any of the tougher kids in the neighborhood, though according to Falcone, this kid's mean streak ran deeper.

"I want to talk to you."

"Maybe I don't want to talk to you." Brody had a broad, solid-looking face, sharp cheekbones, eyes too haunted for a kid his age. The others formed a circle around Ramsey who flashed his Housing Security shield.

"I'm impressed." Brody held his ground but the circle broke up, his buddies drifting back toward the car, leaving him on his own. He had a tic, a twitch beneath his left eye, which gave a comical aspect to his otherwise grim expression.

"How old are you, son?"

"Twenty. Almost."

"Too old to be beating up on a kid that size, wouldn't you say?" He glanced at the other four, settled back against the rusting car. They called themselves the Brando's. All of them had been in trouble with the housing police—fighting, petty thievery, bothering girls. He turned back to Brody. "Or do you like beating up on little boys? Maybe doing dirty things to them?"

"I'm no faggot."

"Word I hear is you liked pushing Arthur Farrell around."

"I push around a lot of people."

"Why is that?"

"It makes me happy."

"You don't look happy."

"That's my business."

Beyond the trees, feathers a brilliant white in the sunlight, gulls dotted the long stretch of mud flats. Ramsey watched one lift above the water. It shimmered bright as glass in the cloudless sky before turning in a long arc toward open water.

"What about your buddies there?"

"Nobody here's a faggot."

"What'd you have against Farrell?"

"Nothin'."

"That why you liked to beat him up?"

"I don't like faggots, all right?"

Morales had already verified their alibis. All of them, home by midnight. It was the hours before he wondered about, the cut-marks and bruises on Brody's knuckles. "Sunday night. You didn't come down here?"

Brody kicked at the dirt with the pointed toe of his boot. "Told ya, we were riding around. We might a seen Farrell. Big deal."

"Your hands—"

"Punching bag. I work out."

Ramsey dug in his pocket for his car keys and wound the chain around his fingers, tight—anything to deflect the anger he felt for this bully. Maybe it was true about the good dying young, while punks like Brody lived on into old age, growing more bitter. Or was it he himself who was bitter? If he knew more about Brody's life, wouldn't he find something to pity?

"Mind if I take a look at your knife?"

"Who says I got one?"

"You want me to call some of my pals at the precinct, have them come help you find it?"

Brody spit close to Ramsey's feet, then slid his hand to his back pocket and drew out a small switchblade the length of a pocket comb. The tic started up, a non-stop winking.

"Open it."

He raised his hand. The blade snapped skyward.

"Lay it flat."

Grinning, Brody brought his hand down and held the knife across his palm: standard-issue for punks—pearl-handled, thin five-inch blade. Over the years Ramsey had confiscated dozens of them.

"Handle first. Give it to me." He took the knife and held it up to catch the sunlight, then approached the car.

The Brando's watched him with sullen faces. They wore their belt buckles on the side: tough-guy fashion statement of the day. Like a drill sergeant he made them go through a roll-call: Brian Murphy, Sparky Donohue, Richard Frankel, Joey Doyle. He told them, "Just flat in your hand, like your buddy. And hold them out so I can get a look." They each had the same model switchblade.

"You boys ever hear of the word *individuality*?" They looked at him with blank faces as he collected the knives.

He stood in front of Brian Murphy, a wiry kid with a bad case of acne. He knew from Falcone that Brian had a softer streak than his pals. "Maybe you've seen someone hanging around down here, somebody who might want to do some harm."

"Nah. Not me."

"Check out the faggots," Brody said.

"And where might they be?"

"Everywhere, man."

"Thanks for the tip." He checked his watch. "You boys gonna be late for school, aren't you?"

"That's our business," Brody said.

He glanced at each of them, his gaze lingering on Brody. "Yeah, well, I hear you're beating up on anyone younger, smaller or weaker than you, tough guy, that's *my* business. You're going to wish you never met me." He began to turn away then stopped. "By the way, you boys have a patron saint?"

They looked at him dumbfounded. "What the fuck, man?" Brody said.

"I was in school we each had to have a patron saint. Somebody we admired, somebody we prayed to. Help us be better people, you know? And seeing as how you're all good Catholic school boys I thought maybe you had one, too." He looked at their incredulous faces one last time. "Guess not."

Before he climbed the slope he hurled the knives, one by one, into the deepest part of the river.

*****

The place might have been ripped out of a medieval landscape. Brick, fortress-like walls rose on both sides of the entrance road, turrets jutted above the jagged roof lines, the air

Philip Cioffari

smelled of ancient trees and stone. He parked in the circular drive outside the classroom building. Inside, gleaming marble floors, mahogany walls. A gilded Christ hung from a gigantic crucifix. In the window's light, the crucified Savior took on a life-like appearance, his skin luminescent with a raw and savage nakedness.

Father Tobias O'Malley, whose ample girth and fleshy jowls suggested a comfortable life, was awaiting him. In his paneled office, he greeted Ramsey with measured cordiality. He was anxious to help, he said, but the police had already investigated and this was the second day Donald Seward had to be called out of class. "The boy is struggling as it is," he made a point of saying.

"I'll try to be brief, Father."

The priest stood at the window and smiled tightly.

"You told the police that Arthur Farrell had no enemies here at St. Jerome's."

"That's right."

"Is that possible? I went to a boys' academy myself. I know what kind of disagreements arise. And in the past, St. Jerome's has had a reputation—"

O'Malley winced. "That was before I was brought in as Prefect, Mr. Ramsey, that was in the days when it was an orphanage—"

"Is that the old orphanage building out back?" Visible through the glass was a nearly identical version of the building they were in: dark red-brown stone, arched windows, elaborate scrollwork on the facing.

"We're using it as a storage bin for the time being," the priest said tersely. "Or a museum. I'm not sure which image is more precise." He turned abruptly back to the matter at hand. "I assure you our boys behave properly when on school grounds."

"Off-campus then, perhaps. Have you heard anything—?"

The priest waved his hand in dismissal. "I can't speak to that, of course, but I can assure you we instill in each and every one of our students a sense of respect for, and tolerance of, one another. This is a Catholic school after all and the Christian values of compassion and good will are fundamental to everything we teach here. Arthur was an Honors student. He was well-regarded by faculty and student body alike."

"I'd like to speak to some of Arthur's teachers."

"Today is not a good day, Mr. Ramsey. The faculty has all it can do with counseling our boys through this crisis, and exams are coming up. I'm sure you understand."

"Perhaps later—"

"Or, perhaps better yet, you can consult with the police who have *already* spoken to them at length. A Detective Morales, I believe. He was quite thorough." He gave Ramsey a dark, pointed stare. "I believe Donald is waiting for us. If you don't mind, I would like to keep his absence from class to a minimum."

He led Ramsey briskly down the hall to a small reading room. "Our Theology library," he said in a tight voice.

Amid the shelves of leather-bound texts, Donald Seward sat at a table facing the window. The priest, absently pulling at the flesh on his neck, remained in the doorway and regarded the boy as if he were deciding something.

"If I might speak with the boy alone, Father—"

The priest continued to stare across the room at the boy whose eyes, when he finally turned toward them, would not meet his. "I'll be right across the hall," he said finally. "In my office." It was a threat addressed to both of them.

Ramsey loosened his collar and introduced himself. The boy wore his blonde hair brushed flat and parted on the side. Leaning forward, slight and nervous, he looked as though he might bolt from his seat. "It's all right, son. I just want to find out who might have wanted to hurt your friend."

"Michael Brody," the boy blurted out, then bit his lip. His eyes darted away from Ramsey and he shifted his weight in the seat, leaning toward the window.

"Michael Brody," Ramsey repeated. Yesterday, Seward had told Morales he knew nothing about what happened Sunday night. "Why would Michael Brody want to hurt Arthur?"

"Because he's mean. He hated him." Again, the boy spoke in haste and looked as if he wanted to withdraw what he'd said.

"How do you know?"

"He hates everybody."

"Did you ever see him do anything to Arthur?"

The boy hesitated. "No."

"Sunday night. Was he with Arthur?"

"I don't know. I went home. I—I didn't see."

"You went home after you had a soda with Arthur? After he left you to go to the movies?"

"Yes."

"So you never saw Michael Brody hit Arthur?"

"No." Donald Seward had sunk lower in the seat, lost in himself now, the way Morales had described him: tight-lipped and unresponsive.

"The last time you saw Arthur was a few minutes before eight?"

"Yes."

"Was anything troubling him?"

"He didn't say."

"Did he *ever* say he was very upset about something?"

"I—I don't remember."

"How could you not remember?"

He shifted in his seat. His hands rested in his lap and he played with his fingers, interlocking them and drawing them tight. "I don't know."

"Donald, is there something you're not telling me?"

The boy stiffened. "Like what?"

"Like . . . anything."

"He thought nobody loved him," Donald said finally.

"His mother, his aunt, they seem to love him very much."

"He just said it. I don't know if he really meant it."

"Did he tell you that Sunday night?"

Donald shook his head. "He just said he was going to the movies and he wanted to be alone for a while."

"And you don't have any idea what made him feel that way—unloved?"

"No."

"Was there a reason why you didn't tell me this right away? Or why you didn't tell Detective Morales yesterday?"

Donald looked out the window, his thin face pale and drawn.

Ramsey studied him. "I think there's something else you

want to tell me. Am I right?"

"No, sir."

He watched the boy fidget with his hands, locking his fingers and pulling them apart. "Is there anyone else who might know things about Arthur that could help us?"

Again, the boy waited to respond. Finally he said, "Nobody I know." He folded his arms and stared again through the window at the orphanage which was, Ramsey observed this time, in the same condition as its former occupants: abandoned, and in need of repair.

*****

He drove his aging Packard Clipper along the north edge of the swamp. From this distance the buildings of the project appeared dark and sullen. They fell out of view as he turned into the beach parking lot. He had come to see Fritz "the whiner" Weinstein, a felon he busted several years back for peddling porn out of a run-down beer and shot joint on City Island known as the Shack. The D.A. had cut a deal: probation, if Weinstein would finger the distributor he worked for. This job with the Parks Department was part of the deal. The whiner needed a legitimate income, and the D.A. hoped the fresh air might clean out his dirty mind.

At the Parks Department office he was told by the head supervisor that Fritz had been re-assigned last week to Pelham Bay Park.

Pelham Bay Park.

His first impulse was to let Morales handle this, but his own words to Helen challenged him, *We've got to move on, don't we? At some point?*

He drove along the Shore Road slowly, his face rigid behind the wheel. To avoid the park road he traveled two miles out of his way to the south entrance where there was a wide swath of grass with paths running off into the trees.

A tractor-mower sat idle in the middle of the lawn. No sign of Fritz. On a wooded path he came upon a girl stretched out beneath her boyfriend on a picnic table, the top piece of her swimsuit undone.

Philip Cioffari

Things happened quickly. The boy's head shot up; the girl let out a sharp cry.

Ramsey saw motion through the trees. Someone running.

He gave chase, following the path until it petered out and he was forced to battle low-hanging branches and vine-like bushes, his heart heaving against the wall of his chest. He stopped for air, to rest his knees. That's when he noticed Fritz Weinstein directly ahead, in worse shape than he was, crouched and wheezing against the trunk of a large tree.

"You late for a lunch date somewhere, Fritz?"

"I didn't do nothin'."

"You like the breeze blowing through your fly like that?"

Fritz, zipping his green uniform pants, kept his eyes on Ramsey. Small and mole-like, shifty-eyed, he stood with his upper body pulled in on itself in a perpetual cower. "I don't know nothin' about that dead kid, if that's what you're after. I never even been near that swamp."

"Take it easy, Fritz. I just thought you might have something I should know."

"Where would I hear that kind of stuff?"

"Your old cronies, maybe."

"Ain't seen them."

"That's not what they're saying over at the 4-7. They're saying you're back to your old tricks."

"Who's saying that? Morales?"

"Maybe."

"It's a lie."

"Your word against his. Who's going to win, you think?"

"He hates me. He's out to get me."

"Maybe I can put in a word for you." Ramsey stooped to pick up the man's cap from the dirt. "But they bust you again, you're going to do time. You know that, right?"

"I don't know nothin' about that kid."

Something fluttered high in the branches and Ramsey saw a bright yellow bird perched directly above Fritz. If he didn't know better he would have thought it was a canary. Who could say? Maybe it was. And even if it wasn't it was a magnificent sight. Unlikely outbursts of beauty amid the daily grind never failed to fire the ashes of his hope. He almost felt a shred of compassion for the man cowering before him. Almost.

"Find me something, Fritz. Who's asking for kiddie porn, pictures of under-age males, that sort of thing." He brushed the dirt from the cap and handed it to him. "Twenty-four hours. Then I let Morales loose. That's the deal."

The dark line of the park road looped around the ball fields. He had to move forward, he told himself. So he forced himself to drive the entire length of it, stopping the car two hundred feet from the north entrance where a sign erected too late, black letters on a bright yellow background, read:

SLOW
CHILDREN
PLAYING

Philip Cioffari

Chapter Four

"You don't look good," Eddie Falcone said when Ramsey reached the office.

Ramsey blamed it on the heat. He was trying hard to keep his mind off his son. Sitting heavily on his Assistant's desk, he reached for his handkerchief. "So what do you have?"

"Nada. That's what we have. We've gone through the buildings along the swamp. Couple people saw the fire. Thought it was fishermen. They'd seen fires down there before." He got up and walked to the coffee machine. "High octane?"

"No, thanks."

"How you get through the day?"

Falcone filled the over-sized mug to the brim, no milk. Usually he was a seven-to-eight-cup-a-day man but in times of stress he could hit twice that. He was smaller and thinner than Ramsey, hard and wiry, with movements quick as a cat. His hair, cut in a flat-top, gave his forehead a squared-off shape but it was his deep-set eyes the color of tar that bestowed a brooding intensity upon an otherwise ordinary face.

"The Brody kid," Ramsey said. "What else you find?"

"Nothing we didn't already know. A few drunk and disorderlies. Nothing on this level."

From his own office, the door partially open, he watched Falcone check his daily log book, then in his left-handed scrawl make a notation on the bottom. The man had been in security work almost twelve years; if he'd felt bitter at being passed over for the chief's position he didn't show it. Ramsey had always respected him for that and for his attention to detail, the way he threw himself whole-heartedly into each new assignment. This past year he'd been a life-saver.

The phone in the outer office rang. "Yes," Falcone was saying, "yes, yes." Then Ramsey's door swung open and he stood there, minus his coffee cup, his hawk eyes burning with news.

*****

On the door to the roof of building 5 someone had written:

a child

      a day

            keeps the doctor

                    away

Ramsey and Falcone stared at the glistening red letters scrawled in a backward hand. Despite the hall's dim light the words had a garish, neon-tint. In two or three places the blood hadn't dried.

Ramsey turned to Peterson, the gawky rookie who on his rounds had made the discovery, and who now stood at attention near the stairwell door. "You seem to have a knack for being in the right place at the right time, Peterson."

"Thank you, sir." The patrolman smiled unabashedly, then thought better of it and tightened his lips. He forced a cough and covered his mouth with his hand.

"You didn't notice anyone entering or leaving the stairwell?"

"No one, sir."

"You can relax, Peterson. No need to stand that stiff."

"Thank you, sir." He took a deep, noisy breath but kept his shoulders forced back. "Sir?"

"Yes, Peterson?"

"Is it possible this could be a prank, sir?" He seemed pleased with himself.

"It is possible, yes."

"That was my thought, sir."

"But even so, Peterson, anyone with a sense of humor like that ought to be forcibly taken off the streets and locked up, wouldn't you say?"

The patrolman shifted his weight and cleared his throat several times while he searched for a response.

"It's all right, Peterson. I was teasing you."

When Morales arrived, he stared at the words as if he'd just been made the butt of a joke. "What is this? Fucking peek-a-boo?"

"I wouldn't take it personally," Ramsey said.

"Not a thing in this world ain't personal."

"We've had this argument before."

"And you never let me win."

They moved floor to floor, top to bottom, ringing doorbells. When they reached the lobby Morales stuffed another stick of bubblegum into his mouth. He chewed slowly, his mouth filled to near-capacity. "Either Shakespeare *lives* in the building or he's got some unbelievable disappearing act."

"Or he used the tunnels," Ramsey said.

Morales looked like a kid left out of a game. "What tunnels?"

"This building has an entrance, doesn't it, Eddie?"

"Right below us."

"What tunnels?"

"Fall-out shelter."

"Why didn't you tell me this yesterday?"

"It wasn't a factor yesterday."

Falcone led them down to the basement where a series of storage rooms opened one into another. Bare concrete walls, dull yellow light. Overhead a maze of pipes cast crisscross shadows on the bicycles, scooters, wagons and hula-hoops chained to a metal bar. In the last of these rooms he opened a locked door. A metal grate served as a landing where they were able to look down into the lower level.

The smell of dead, trapped air lifted toward them.

"Goddamn tomb," Morales said.

This time Ramsey led the way down, their shoes resonating on the metal steps. His knees ached badly, but he crouched to examine the ground. What dust there was in this windowless hall seemed to have gathered closer to the base of the walls. No trace of a print.

The tunnel was built of concrete. Naked bulbs hung from the ceiling at random intervals, leaving long sections of shadow. He remembered a vacation, years ago. Caverns in Virginia. The same timeless feeling. A stillness eternal as death. He left the caverns feeling ill. Never had he been so glad for the light of day.

"Who else has the keys?" Morales asked.

"Nobody but Ram and me should have a key. I mean, some of the handy men have them when we do light bulb repairs down here and engineering inspections, but they're returned to me each time."

"They're locked away?"

"Safe and sound."

"Eddie will check who's worked down here lately. We'll get you a list."

They climbed the steps to the basement level and worked their way through the warren of storage rooms until they reached the street.

"There's no way we're going to be everywhere we should be," Ramsey said. "Not with sixty buildings and twelve miles of walkways and roads."

"And that's only what's *above* the ground." Morales leaned over the curb and spit his wad of Double Bubble neatly between the rungs of a sewer grate.

From his office Ramsey called Helen. She asked how his day was going in such an offhand way he simply said, "Fine, dear, just fine." When he told her he was running late, that he would take her to the cemetery later in the afternoon, she said in the same flat, off-hand voice, "If you have the time, dear."

He hung up, feeling angry. This past year, no matter how busy his schedule, he had never missed their monthly visits to the grave. Why would he miss today?

*****

Arthur had lied about the movie. The John Wayne westerns

Philip Cioffari

had played the previous week. Now playing: two Grade B re-runs. Orson Welles in *Touch of Evil*, and a more obscure film about female prisoners called *Behind These Walls.* Ramsey had seen the Welles' movie years before so he sat through ten minutes of the prison movie, enough to witness its preoccupation with women in various stages of undress punching, clawing and scratching each other.

If the mind was the last refuge from the dullness of modern life—he had read that somewhere—then movie palaces were the portals, the dark relief from a day too bright and clear for invention. He figured Arthur Farrell had found his refuge early in life. The portrait given by his aunt seemed, thus far at least, accurate: when he wasn't in his room, he had spent his time in libraries and movie theaters, feeding his fantasies.

Morales couldn't fathom how a kid could lock himself away like that, but Ramsey understood. There had been periods in his own life when he felt alienated. During the war, for one. Those nights hunched in the bowels of a tank, no light anywhere in the world it seemed: not from stars or towns or the farmhouses along their route, not from the tip of the cigarette he so desperately craved. He spent entire days and nights in silence, no interest in the small talk of his fellow soldiers. After the war when he returned to Fordham, he brought with him not only a dread of cramped places but a sense of alienation as well, feeling cut off from the neighborhood, a stranger to his friends, none of whom were even *thinking* of going to school, their plans for the future stalled at racing their chopped and blocked Chevies under the El on Jerome or chasing women and chug-a-lugging beer late into the night. Loneliness either drove you to others or pushed you deeper into isolation. The Farrell boy, he figured, fell into the second category.

He came out into the intermediate light of the lobby and spoke briefly to the gum-clacking manager who doubled as ticket seller. She hadn't been much help. No memory of Arthur buying a ticket. Or leaving the theater, either. The crowds, you see, she had told him. People coming, people going.

He asked if there wasn't a code, some system for determining what movies a minor could or couldn't see.

She snapped her gum hard and narrowed her eyes, as if she

might be taking the matter under consideration. "We don't sell tickets I'm out of a job." She reached up to scratch her head, her fingers lost in thick orange hair. "Tell you one thing, though. Ain't no hanky-panky goin' on inside there. I run a clean house."

*****

Past the Church of the Precious Blood with its walled gardens and grottoes, the neighborhood deteriorated into pre-war tenements, dim alleyways and courtyards, and the Shimmy: a bar he had once dropped into occasionally.

If Arthur were feeling adventurous this might have been his route leaving the theater. He might have peered through the Shimmy's curtains at shadowy dancers moving deep in the room's recesses.

He walked to the swamp a long block ahead, re-playing scenarios: *Arthur stands on the grassy slope. Normally he would turn around and go home; he knows his mother's waiting. But tonight he's restless—the movies, the sultry air; he craves some excitement of his own. Below him the swamp waits dark and mysterious. He's thinking of the river, cooler air beneath the bridge. He takes the path down along the highway wall where the shadows deepen. He's free, no longer visible to the buildings behind him. On his own. Afraid and excited, unsure what lies ahead. He doesn't know he's being followed, or maybe someone's already waiting at the bottom of the path.*

But then there was the matter of the makeshift paths: one from the river going *toward* the tree; one from the grove of trees going *to* and one going *away* from the fire; another one leading up the slope, *away* from the fire. And who lit the fire? And why?

A half dozen reporters prowled along the cordoned-off grass. Tabloid coverage had been gruesome: blurred photos of the boy's naked body, endless images of the dead tree, the fire's charred remains.

One of his own men had been assigned to the area, keeping his eye on the reporters *and* a handful of children who played a sluggish game of punch ball near the service road. At a sewer grate a boy using a coat hanger fished for lost Spaldings.

Ramsey lit a cigarette and noticed, farther down the road, two boys coming from an alley. One shouldered a baseball bat like a rifle, the other carried a leather mitt; they were the boys he had seen on the bridge the morning of the murder. They moved slowly away from him, down a walkway leading to the ball field.

When he had first taught Evan to catch a ball, his son's hands would move, much too late and too slowly, *after* the ball went past him, his small white hands with their short fingers making a circle, one of the few forms he understood, blessing the air with their innocence.

*****

The memory drove him to the Shimmy where a vacant-eyed blonde swayed on the platform, keeping time—barely—to the music pumping from the jukebox. She stared without interest at the handful of men watching her.

It was a shabby place, old and musty, but he noticed some improvements. The mirrors had been cleaned and polished. New lights lined the rim of the platform where the girls danced; the platform itself had been extended to reach above the entire length of the bar. Even the darkly private tables in back where he found a seat had been spruced-up with black-and-white checked tablecloths and sleek new smoked-glass ashtrays.

The waitress came toward him from the bar, face in shadows, long-legged stride light and graceful. Some note of familiarity registered dimly in his mind before he read the name *Krissie* on her shirt; then her face—partly obscured by the low light—became the face of the woman who killed Evan.

"Oh my God," she said, "it's you."

Ramsey stared back, speechless.

She looked toward the bar as if she might return there, but the barkeep had gone into the men's room and Leo, the Shimmy's owner, was nowhere in sight. No one could help her. "Would you? . . . Should I? . . . there's no one else on duty," she said by way of apology.

He thought about getting up to leave but said, "That's all right," the words garbled, the voice unrecognizable as his own. He struggled to form the phrase, "Just a beer." When she hesitated, biting her lip and looking uncertain, he said: "Any kind will do."

He watched her walk to the bar, her step less quick and assured. She was different than he remembered. Her hair had been lightened, cut short, she seemed thinner, paler, her face softer and more delicate. But then he had seen her only when she was horrified, grief-stricken. He had seen her as inseparable from the car she was driving: an object of assault. At the funeral he'd noticed her at the church, though he said nothing to Helen.

Afterward he declined to press charges. He didn't see her again except in memory, a member of his private collection of pain and anger: on the park road, her shoulders shaking convulsively; on the curb when the ambulance arrived, her face cupped in her hands. Fixed images seared into his consciousness. And now she had been sprung into motion again, bringing him a beer on a plastic tray.

She set two dishes down next to the bottle of Rheingold. "I didn't know whether you liked peanuts or pretzels. So I brought you one of each."

"Thank you."

"Is there anything else—?"

"No, no, thank you. This is fine."

She stood close to the table. "Would you like me to pour your beer?"

"I'll do it." She lingered there, so he forced himself to break the silence. "Gun Hill Manor. You were—"

"Yes, I was." She looked down at the table. "I'm surprised you remember."

"Some things—"

"Of course. How stupid of me."

"Some things remain," he finished.

"Forgive me. I didn't expect . . . I didn't think . . . I mean I knew, I knew you worked here at Baychester. I read it in the paper."

"Almost a year."

Philip Cioffari

"Is it that long?"

"Yes."

"It seems—"

"For me, too," he said.

She lowered her eyes. "I should leave you alone. If you need—"

"Yes," he said, but she had already turned away. He wrapped his hand around the cold bottle but made no effort to pour it.

*****

From the start Helen had been against getting the dog—she didn't want to clean up after it, didn't want the bother—but Ramsey had argued that a pet would be good for Evan, give him something to love and care for, teach him responsibility. She maintained Evan wasn't capable of that kind of responsibility; he had more than enough with learning how to take care of himself. Ramsey persisted: he loves animals, look how he responds when we take him to the zoo, he needs a friend, can't you see that? Besides I'll clean up after him, I don't mind, really I don't. Eventually he took Evan to a pet store where they picked out a brown and white beagle, six weeks old. And Ramsey had been right, his son fell in love with the dog, followed him everywhere. So of course they brought the dog to the park. Why wouldn't they?

In the past he'd always thrown the ball *under*hand—it was easier for Evan that way—but *that* day he thought his boy was ready for a new challenge.

Tragedy is a matter of timing, a confluence of details. A rubber ball thrown too hard. A puppy acting on instinct. A line of trees that kept Evan hidden from the road. A blue Plymouth Fury moving too fast. *Afterward: Buckey panting hard on the far side of the road, ball in mouth, waiting for the game to resume.*

He closed his eyes against the images, hearing the voice of Kristen, *Krissie*, telling him between choked sobs she'd never before taken this shortcut through the park. Just this once, because she was late. This one time.

Catholic Boys

*****

Above the bar two girls danced, a chesty brunette having joined the blonde who showed more enthusiasm now that a group of businessmen had filled the seats along the mirrored wall. One of the men began shouting for service. Krissie was nowhere in sight.

Perhaps it was the commotion that drew Leo from his office. He was a large bearded man with solemn eyes. Already dressed for the evening in a suit and tie, he seemed oddly out of place in his own establishment. He leaned forward in heated conversation with the bartender. They took turns throwing glances at the door to the ladies room.

When Krissie finally emerged, Leo motioned to her and she stood with her head bowed, wiping her eyes with the back of her hand. It was obvious that he was speaking harshly. Ramsey was about to leave, but at that moment Leo noticed him and came across the room.

"It is so good to see you again, Sergeant." He spoke a formal, sometimes stilted English, his accent vaguely Middle Eastern, though no one seemed sure of his exact origins.

"I'm no longer a Sergeant."

"Ah, yes," he said as if just that moment remembering. "I do recall reading about your change in position."

"Thank you for the flowers. Very thoughtful."

"You have long ago thanked me in the gracious note from you and your wife."

Of course, Ramsey thought. He had forgotten: one of many details buried in that blur of days following the funeral. He had written out several hundred notes of thanks, signing Helen's name and his own.

"My wish would have been to do so much more in your time of grief," Leo was saying. "You are closer to us now. I hope that means we'll be seeing more of you."

"Not likely."

"I do hope it is not business that brings you. The unfortunate—"

"No, Leo. Not unless you have some information for me."

"It would give me the greatest pleasure to assist your investigation in any way possible. If I learn of anything—" With his solemn face, his ministerial bearing, he might have been overseeing ceremonies at a gravesite. "Is there something wrong with the beer? Perhaps another—"

"The beer's fine. I'm a slow thinker *and* a slow drinker these days."

Leo's response was all business. "The waitress was satisfactory?"

He searched the man's eyes for some hint of mockery but found the same flat stare. "The waitress knows her job. You have nothing to fear there."

"I pursue the highest expectations." Pride broke like a rash across his face. "Do you like the improvements?"

"High class, Leo. Definitely high class."

"You are joking with me."

"No, no, I mean it." He didn't intend to hurt the man's feelings. "Very . . . tasteful."

"Jimmy let the place go, but I have plans." He stood with his arms folded as he surveyed the room. "Tomorrow, there will be great changes."

"Don't change the place too much."

"I will give it character."

"It already *has* character."

"I will introduce acts of sophisticated erotic fantasy. I will make it so that a man, especially a man like you, feels it is an honor to come here. In the meantime, if there is anything you require, we will provide it." He bowed gravely and walked to the table of businessmen where he introduced himself and began talking.

His mind drifted with the music, something slow and sentimental, a newer version of a song Helen and he had danced to at Roseland, after the war.

The dancers swayed in and out of blue light. From across the room Krissie glanced at him and he lowered his eyes. Only when he could observe her unobserved did he follow her small journeys, afraid of what she might lead him to but curious also, not quite sure of everything he was feeling: shock and disbelief, yes, and somewhere deeper, less visible than Helen's, pain and outrage waged their war of attrition. He was struck with an odd kind of wonderment: how a woman so light and graceful on her feet, could have been an instrument of such savage death.

She came over and asked if he wanted another beer.

"I'll just settle up."

"You're Leo's guest today. No charge."

When he was a cop, he would have insisted on paying. Now it seemed to make little difference. "Thank him for me, will you?"

There was a question in her eyes. In the silence he shifted in his seat. What had made him stop here?

"I know if I don't say something I'll hate myself later."

"There's nothing to say."

"I think there is."

The certainty in her voice surprised him but her eyes, a striking hazel-brown, seemed far less assured. "I've wanted to write you—"

"There's no need—"

"How many times I've tried—"

"What good would it do? You, or me?"

"Sometimes," she said, "I wonder why God gave us such complicated emotions and such a simple language to express them." She stared at the table between them. "I want you to know that I pray for him every day. For you, too. And your wife."

He thought if he stayed longer in the dark confusion of his emotions, he might say something foolish or hurtful. He stood up abruptly. "Thank you," he said, then adding, much to his own surprise, "God protect you," before excusing himself and hurrying head down toward the door, desperate for the hard bright clarity of the day.

Philip Cioffari

Chapter Five

There was a stand of trees near Evan's grave and an open field that one day would house row upon row of the dead; now it lay fallow, thick grass and wildflowers, white and yellow butterflies fluttering in the light as, separately—Helen kneeling, Ramsey standing beside her with his head bowed—they paid their respects as they did the sixth day of each month.

At one time he had tried talking to Evan as if his child were somewhere nearby. Now he simply let an image of his son flood his mind: Evan, arms raised, running through the yard in pursuit of fireflies, never remembering to close his fingers or watch his step, so that he would end up empty-handed and falling, unprepared as he was for this world of danger and light.

Helen used the trowel to loosen the soil around the flowers she'd planted in the spring. Ramsey walked to a spigot, returning with a water can that he tilted above the semi-circle of the flower bed. He filled the can a second time because Helen wanted to wash the dirt from the dates, January 2, 1948—March 6, 1959.

They sat near the grave in the shade of a willow. "Have you thought any more about quitting your job?"

"Something's happened." How would he explain without sounding foolish? "I've had these dreams."

Helen stared at him without comprehension. "What dreams?"

"Of children."

"I don't understand. You dreamed about some children?"

"Yes. Several times." He explained as best he could, the darkness, the circle of boys, the shifting light, the anguish in their faces.

"Many people have recurrent dreams," she said.

"But *I* don't." He waited before going on, hoping she would understand. "There's something—"

"So what are you saying? This is some sort of sign?"

"Maybe."

"From who? From what? You don't even believe in God."

"I feel a responsibility, that's all. To the children of the project—"

"You have *other* responsibilities."

He met the hard, stinging glare of her eyes, then looked away at the line of tombstones shaped like a fence along the field. He imagined walking there with Evan, taking his hand, guiding him through the tall grass, around stones, across the uneven terrain. "What is it that I'm not doing?"

Her lips stiffened in a stoic's smile. "I shouldn't have to tell you that."

"You want me at home more, Helen? When I'm there it doesn't seem to matter much."

"It's not just the time. You never ask anymore about *my* dreams."

"You never want to talk about them."

"Well, no," she conceded, "not now. They're too awful. But you could still ask. I liked it when you used to ask. When you were grieving with me." Her hands rested in her lap and he reached to cover them with his own. "This case," she said with a mixture of affection and concern that seemed to Ramsey to belong to another lifetime, "it's consuming you."

"I feel useful again. I . . . can't sit around and brood anymore."

"Like me?"

"I didn't say that."

"That's what you were thinking."

"I was thinking about the children—"

She leaned forward and began crying softly. He drew her

Philip Cioffari

closer. "We can have another baby. It's not too late."

"It is. It is too late."

He rocked her in his arms. A child's voice lifted in the air, then a dog's bark, fast and yapping. It sounded so much like Buckey that his heart raced. But it couldn't be Buckey, he knew that. They'd given him to one of the desk sergeants at the 4-7. And that man had moved to Miami six months ago.

She was still crying in his arms and he surprised himself with what he whispered next, to coax her back. He was staring at the grey marker of their son's grave. "Don't let Evan hear you crying," he said.

*****

They had just been seated for dinner: their table on a patio with a view of Rye Beach and Long Island Sound. Directly behind them the pink lights of the Dragon Coaster glittered above the midway. Helen had been quiet—lost in herself—so he was surprised when she said, "You're so far away from me tonight."

"I thought *you* were the one who was far away."

"Thinking. Just thinking."

"Me, too.

"About what?" She had smiled with an innocence that brought him back years. *Our dream-time*, she'd once called it, the time before the world pointed its jealous finger and turned their lives upside down.

Moments ago they had slipped briefly back into dream-time as, arm in arm, they strolled the midway, past the Fun House and the arcade, then the long stretch of boardwalk to the band shell where four women in white-sequined dresses sang: *say you're, say you're gonna miss me, like I miss you, say you're gonna . . .*

He'd leaned against the railing to light a cigarette and Helen leaned close to him. The upbeat music and the lights seemed to brighten her mood. She began to hum along with the song but had to stop after a few bars, laughing at herself in the process, Ramsey laughing with her, the song too new, too unpredictable in its rhythms.

Catholic Boys   57

The moment of lightness passed when he looked toward the pier where they had once taken Evan to watch fireworks. That night Evan wouldn't sleep when they returned home. He wouldn't lie down, wouldn't stay in bed, instead talking non-stop about the midway's lights and motion and noise, the burst of colors turning on and off in the sky.

Over-stimulated, Helen had called it. She didn't want to take him to the amusement park again.

"We can't isolate him from the world," he remembered saying. A familiar argument.

"We can protect him."

"From what? All we did was take him to an amusement park. He had fun. We *all* did. What's the harm?"

"I'm going to save him from wanting what he can't have."

"And what's that? What does he want that he can't have?"

"A normal life!" she screamed and threw her glass of gin at him. "As if you didn't know!" Then she was sobbing and hugging Evan, nearly smothering him in her embrace as the boy babbled on trying to describe the motion of one of the rides, something circular and spinning, and Ramsey went for a towel. She knelt beside him to collect the glass. "Forgive me," she said. "I—" He could read the terrified child's look in her eyes, the emptiness stockpiled over the years, the longing for what *she* couldn't have: the *normal life* that had been denied *her*.

He said he didn't mind staying up until Evan fell asleep, he didn't mind staying up all night if he had to. And he *had* stayed up all night, Helen falling asleep in his arms, Evan finally calming down and getting to sleep an hour or so before dawn, Ramsey carrying on the debate in his head until the first light. If he couldn't give her the life she wanted, he could at least give her the smaller things she asked for, couldn't he? So he had given in. They didn't bring Evan to the amusement park again.

"So," she asked now, smiling across the table, "is it a secret? What you're thinking."

"I have no secrets from you, dear. You know that." He wanted to tell her about Krissie, but there never seemed a right time.

"The children in your dream. You're thinking about them."

"I was thinking about the time we brought Evan here."

There was no visible change in her expression, which made him unsure whether she had erased the memory or was calculating her response to it. "He loved it here," she said. A half-smile flickered across her lips.

Had she forgotten how the night turned out? Or was she finally beginning to sort the good memories from the bad?

The waiter appeared, asking would they like a cocktail before dinner. An eternity hung in the wake of his question, a voice screaming inside Ramsey *No, they would not like any goddamn cocktails*, then Helen's voice sweet and coy in the real world, saying yes maybe I would, just one, gin with a splash of tonic, just a splash.

"And for the gentleman?"

"No, nothing. A glass of water, that's all," the phrase *just a splash* still nagging at him. He heard it as she tried to smile playfully at him, as she chattered on, as she raised her arm to bring back the waiter. "Make that a double, *just a splash.*"

The waiter turned to leave, Helen chattering in the void about the view, the tablecloths, the waiter's hairstyle, anything to ease the transition from what might have been to what *would be.* He stared dully at the grey waters of the Sound where small boats turned on their moorings in the evening light.

"You've gotten so quiet, dear. Don't you know it's impolite to ask a lady to dinner and then not speak to her?"

"I'm sorry. I—"

To soften his anger he reached into the past again: to her childhood on Pelham Parkway, the large brick house with the Tudor trim they had driven by many times, the stucco wall enclosing its backyard; to her stories about her father who died on her seventh birthday, leaving Helen a sickly child who suffered from nausea and dizziness, a general nervousness for which the doctors found no material cause. "I spent most of my childhood in that yard," she once told him, "listening to children playing in other yards. Sometimes, in the white dress my father liked, I'd climb onto the wall to watch them play and they'd shout 'Come down, come down and play with us,' but I didn't feel well enough and I was afraid, I didn't know how to have fun, I didn't know how to become part of the games they played; and besides I was waiting for my father, that's why I had my dress on. My mother said I was wasting my life on foolish thoughts and idleness and that one day I would regret it. She said I should be with children my age, take part in things at school. But she was lonely too, she needed me there, how could I leave her alone?"

A fairy-tale. Not quite real but in its way hinting at some truth: Helen as the helpless heroine. He had always been drawn to the young and needy; he couldn't refuse a call for help. It was the little girl in the white dress he'd fallen in love with. *But she's no longer a child, she's a woman now. Look at her:* the handsome face with its high cheekbones and angular nose, blue child-like eyes that seemed not to belong in such a serious face, hair swept back in an elegant wave that was always flawlessly in place for these monthly anniversaries.

"Alex?"

"Thinking," he said. "Just thinking."

"You used to like this restaurant. You used to think it was so romantic, remember?"

"Because I was with *you*," he said. Yes, he had thought it romantic with its outdoor tables overlooking the water and its ballroom where they had danced to the Glenn Miller orchestra. It was still romantic. Okay, the bands had been replaced by a jukebox and the food probably wouldn't be as good, but the new owners at least had maintained the atmosphere, with the checkered tablecloths and the white candles and the freshly cut flowers. And the leaves of the beech tree at the edge of the patio still threw their shadows across the flagstone floor. And it still smelled the same, that mix of salty air and cotton candy, that same warm breeze blowing off the water.

Nostalgia nagged at him like a stubborn child. Come with me, he wanted to say to her, back to the dream-time; but he was stopped by the waiter arriving with her drink. She sipped it steadily, finally setting it down when she became aware of the way he was watching her.

"Honestly, Alex, I don't know why you bother to keep up this charade." It was the pleasant, light-hearted way she said it that unnerved him. "Why don't you simply go back to your office? At least when you're at work you don't have to *see* what a disappointment I am."

"Stop it, Helen."

"Why should I?" she said in the same sweet, forced voice.

"Because you hurt me when you say things like that."

"I'm a burden to you."

"You're not a burden."

"You don't have to lie."

"I'm not lying, dear." He knew the difference—or thought he did. A burden was something imposed without your consent. A responsibility was something you chose willingly, *kept on* choosing.

"I'm a burden to myself these days. So I *must* be one to you."

Here it was again: the early evening parade of insights like soldiers marched out for his inspection, defeated by morning. He patted her hand. "We'll get through this."

"Do you believe that, Alex?"

"I have to believe it. We both do." Even as he said it he realized how unconvincing he must sound.

"Maybe you think I'm another case to be solved. If you can just figure *something* out, if you put *this* together with *that*. But no matter what you think, some things simply don't have a solution."

"You told me once you had enough hope for both of us. Don't you remember?"

She raised her empty glass to get the waiter's attention. "You're mistaken, Alex. You must be confusing me with someone else."

"Stop it, Helen. Stop it." His voice was stiff and hacking, almost a cough. Then there was no voice at all, only air. "*Help me,*" he said. The words lifted between them thin as smoke.

She shook her head sadly. "How can I, Alex?"

For a moment he thought she really wanted to help. He thought the hurt in her eyes was for him, *his* hurt that she was feeling with him.

"I've decided to leave—for a while," she said in a voice without accusation or self-pity. "I'm going away."

"Where?" He didn't understand.

"My sister's."

He studied her to see if she was baiting him. "Why are you doing this?"

"It will make things easier."

"For who?"

"For both of us. You won't have to take care of me. And I can think about going to law school." That had been their plan, before they were married and sometimes, when she was drunk enough, she still talked about it, speaking as if they hadn't married yet, as if Evan had not yet been born, referring to the children they were going to have, the home in Westchester, how when the children were older she would go nights to law school and they would one day share a practice, how above all she wanted what she didn't have as a child: the comfort of a family, a *complete* family. She usually stopped short of actually blaming him, but he would finish the job himself. He had chosen *his* dream over hers, theirs. He had made promises he didn't keep.

"You can go to law school *and* stay with me. We can start over. People *do* start over."

"I can't go through this again," she said. "This . . . investigation. It makes *you* feel important, but I feel my heart being ripped out. *Again.*"

The waiter brought her another gin. "I'm not a weak person, Alex, no matter what you might think. I know I have to do something. We can't go on like this."

He was distantly aware of conversations from other tables, the buzz from a speedboat in the distance, the clinking of ice in Helen's glass. He remembered their first night here, a New Year's Eve after the war, a frigid night but they had wanted a better view of the water so they had stepped out on the patio just before midnight. She pressed close to him and he no longer cared about the bitter cold, and she kissed him not for the first time but with such abandon that he knew he could never return to the solitary life.

Maybe it was wrong to have come back here, he thought, where they once had been so completely in love. This was a place for the young and hopeful. To his surprise, Helen reached for his hand and he looked for something in her face, her eyes,

Philip Cioffari

to help him through this moment.

It didn't seem fair. But maybe that was the point. All his life he had believed hope was the governing emotion, that it was hope—false or not—that got us out of bed in the morning, kept the knife from our wrists. But maybe the proof of love was that it could survive everything: you could still feel it even when there was not a hope left in the world.

Chapter Six

Notebook in hand, Donald Seward walked fast down the Boulevard, head turned, eyes averted to avoid the Brando's who watched from the corner.

Where ya goin', sweetie?

He crossed the street in the direction of the service road. They fell in behind; their metal taps scratched the pavement. *Whatsa matter, Donnie honey? No wanna talk tonight You inna hurry, huh? You got a date?*

The word 'date' got them laughing. He tried to walk faster without appearing to. No good. There was a stiffness to his walk, an awkwardness he couldn't hide. He tripped on a lip of pavement; they laughed. *Donnie cool*, someone said. *Hey, Donnie cool.*

Brody wasn't with them, thank god for that. Then he saw him a block ahead parked in his Fairlane with a girl. You couldn't miss that Fairlane: two-tone, bright red and white. Silver pipes, dual exhaust.

One of the Brando's called out behind him: *What's ya got in the notebook, honey? You got some love poems? Who's the lucky guy? Huh? We wanna meet him.*

On the service road now. Almost running, *almost*. If he crossed to the other side, it would be the same as running, giving off the smell of fear, and they would be on him. So he kept straight, skirting the edge of the grassy slope.

As he passed the Fairlane, the engine exploded into life, the car rumbling, keeping pace, Brody leaning past the girl to shout *where's the fire, sweetheart?*

A block past the Shimmy, he darted down an alley. Fear made him fast and he knew the alleys well. He was small enough to whirl around corners, squeeze through holes ripped in the fence. He knew the no-dog yards, knew where fences were low enough to jump or gates had broken locks. Up the weed-choked incline to the parkway and down the other side. Behind him their silhouettes rose on the berm. One by one they jumped the railing, picking their way down the hill. He sprinted along the river path where the tall grass opened in one long blur ahead of him, the refinery storage tanks round white ghosts squatting in the dusk. The light from the Drive-In lifted as blue mist from the river.

His chest heaved and his stomach cramped and a pain kept shooting up one side of his leg but he ran until he passed through the St. Jerome's gate. Safe this time.

From the bottom of the hill, outside the gate, the Brando's watched him, spitting in his direction, calling him *pole-sucker* and *pussy dick.*

*****

From the priests' residence, Father Martin Shannon watched dusk settle over the fields of marsh grass. In recent days these had been his moments of greatest anticipation, waiting for dark, for the boy to come walking up the hill. His heart beating out of control, he would pace the narrow room end to end. No place, no space could contain his desire. Certainly not this room, certainly not the fit, well-proportioned contours of his body. At these moments he had felt alive in ways he never thought possible. Now he stared at the window as if the greying sky, the murky river might yield, in memory at least, something of what he had lost. *How could a love so pure and beautiful turn so ugly?* In the blink of an eye, it seemed. In the blink of an eye.

When darkness fell, the room's damning silence drove

him out, down the back stairs, the route he always took on his nightly ventures. He crossed the yard and entered the orphanage through the basement door, walking the long hall to the abandoned chapel with its stone walls and arched ceiling, the air grey and cool and damp as a tomb. Absurd as it was, he half-expected to find the boy waiting, kneeling in the first pew, head bowed, hands clasped; but the room's emptiness, and the warm wind gnawing at the windowpanes, left him with a disappointment close to despair.

He stood there uncertainly, staring down the narrow aisle. The nearly naked Savior on the altar cross seemed to mock his grief. He had sinned grievously. He was one of those for whom Christ suffered and died—worse, a fallen priest.

Yet he had loved the boy. Surely an omniscient God would know that. Surely that would be a factor in any judgment against him. "I loved him," he said aloud in the darkness, his words ringing hollow against the stone, the eyes of the statuary watching in noncommittal silence from the shadows of the side aisles.

This chapel, despite its state of disrepair—the chipped and pock-marked ceiling, the years of accumulated dust choking the air—had always been a source of mystical beauty, of refuge, for him. He was a lover of ceremony—*secret* ceremony, above all—because it evoked the early days of the Church when the faithful gathered in hidden places away from a hostile world. To feel the raw, primitive, fear-defying devotion of the early Christians was the purest form of worship, faith as elemental as flesh and bone. He had explained that to the boy, used it to justify their meeting here, away from the eyes of those who would not understand.

But he would find no sanctuary now. With his head bowed he stood before the altar. To ask for forgiveness, that was his intention. But standing there, as he had so often with Arthur, he was overcome with yearning. As if entranced, he found himself lighting the single candle at either end of the altar, and kneeling on the damp floor where he felt the boy beside him like the spectral presence of a missing limb. Out of habit he began murmuring the prayer he recited at the beginning of their ceremony, asking that divine grace fill him with the strength to resist temptation but knowing in his heart that no amount of grace would keep him from the boy beside him. Eyes closed, he would reach for Arthur's hand, feel it trembling inside his own.

He could feel that tremble now, his own hand's tremor as well, and he saw them together that first night he had brought Arthur here, a cold rainy wind rattling the basement windows, the boy's turtleneck not thick enough to keep him from shivering, the candle flames sputtering wildly in their glass dishes as he pulled the boy closer to warm him, only to warm him.

"O my God, I am heartily sorry," he began but he was distracted immediately by a memory of the boy in the schoolyard, the first day of the school year, in his starched white shirt and blue blazer, standing apart from the others. Too fragile. Too unprotected. No trace of the requisite tough guy cover up: no hunched shoulders, no hands jammed indifferently into pockets, no slouch, no sneer.

He had befriended the boy to help him, that's all; gave him books on the lives of the North American martyrs, Catherine Tekawitha and Father Joliet: pioneers in the search for the spirit in a cruel and unforgiving world. By night, he read the boy's book reports word for word as if they were a private conversation between them.

"—and I detest all my sins—"

Again he was interrupted by his memories. Saturdays in the gym. Giving the boy fight lessons. The basics, at least. Arms up, protect your face and mid-section, weight forward on the balls of your feet, jab from your shoulder, put your body behind it, keep moving, keep moving. *Hit me*, Shannon hears himself saying. *Hard! Hit me hard!* The boy swings at him listlessly. *Harder! Hit me harder!* Shannon circles him, jabbing, egging him on, the two of them shirtless in the heat, skin glistening in the light from the gymnasium windows, *Hit me hard!* Arthur drops his arms, gives up all pretense; something in the helplessly indifferent look in his eyes makes Shannon feel even more kindly toward him. He rubs Arthur's face and shoulders hard with a towel. In the residence kitchen he makes American cheese sandwiches which they eat on a

Catholic Boys   67

bench overlooking the river.

"—because I dread the pains of hell, but most of all because I have offended Thee, my God—"

Arthur squints at him from behind the webbing of the confessional screen.

I had these feelings, Father.
What kind of feelings?
You know. Feelings. At night, in bed.
What do you do then, when you get these feelings?
I—I touch myself, Father.
Where do you touch?
My stomach, my legs. Between them.
How many times?
I don't know. I didn't count.
I have to know, child. A few times? A dozen?
A lot, Father.
Are you sorry for that?
I want to be sorry, Father.

It was his mission to help the boy, he told himself now as he had then, it was God's will that they help each other, Christian warriors battling the beast of lust. How many nights when the world outside was so quiet he heard the river's murmur, he lay in his bed feeling aroused at the words of the boy's confessions.

I was with someone, Father. We did things.
What kind of things?
Touching.
What kind of touching?
Fun touching. We took off our clothes.
And?
We played hide 'n' seek in the dark.
Who with?
Someone.
Who?
A friend.
A girl?
No, Father.
I see—
Not a girl.

Where—?

In the stairways, Father. In the basement.

You know that's a sin, don't you? A serious sin.

Yes.

Are you sorry for what you did?

I don't know, Father. I'm not sure. I liked it. I liked it a lot.

We can like something and that something can still be a sin, a grievous sin. Do you understand that?

I don't know, Father.

I want you to promise me something. The next time you feel like doing these things, the very next time, I want you to come to me. Will you promise that?

Yes, Father.

You promise?

Yes.

He sees himself sleepless on his narrow bed feeling again, unmistakable as stigmata, the boy's sweat on his palms and he desires the boy as he has desired no one before him. Yes, there had been crushes on other boys, fleeting fantasies, day dreams. Nothing like this. Nothing.

"—and I firmly resolve, with the help of Thy grace, to do penance—"

He opened his eyes in the dark chapel, his stare fixed on the glow of the candles behind red glass, the color of a sanctuary light. But there was no comfort in the words he had spoken, no absolution.

"O my God, I am heartily sorry—"

When he left the building he searched the grey fields for some sign of motion, half-believing he would appear as he so often did on the path from the river: a shadow moving across the hill. For a moment he did think he saw movement, a young boy's figure toiling on the path, a shadow crossing the tall grass. The persistence of his longing sickened him: desire so blind it was impervious to all things, even death.

O my God . . . I meant to help him. My Christ, my Christ. You know I did. You know . . .

Staring beyond the fields at the black and fouled river he blessed himself, remembering something the boy had said not long ago on a night like this: *I feel safe when I'm with you,*

Father. I feel so safe. . . .

* * * * *

Dirt road behind the Drive-In. The Fairlane's front end parked off the shoulder, nudged into the weeds. Brody pumping his girlfriend, hard. Sweet Nina. So small and skinny and agile there's no position she can't get into, front seat or not, her skin a soft white against the dark red vinyl. Like a wind-up doll she wiggles and shimmies. Sometimes too fast, too mechanical. But right now when he's hot like this, when they've just revved up, he doesn't mind, doesn't mind at all, he's crazy about everything: the feel of her small tits in his hands, the tight skin across her belly, her soft yelping cries, wet sloppy kisses. Moments ago she stripped for him without his having to ask, pulling off her T-shirt soon as he shut the engine, wriggling out of her shorts, bare to the bone in a matter of two, maybe three seconds. Now, sprawled back on vinyl, she squirms and moans to his touch and he feels empowered at the thought he could do anything to her. If he wanted. Anything.

Not like those years when he had to take whatever he could get, when he would chase them into hallways, an upgraded variation on hide 'n' seek, and the unlucky—lucky?—girl that got caught was held down by two guys while the third pushed up her shirt and slapped her belly pink. She'd be twisting and straining in protest, pretending she didn't like it, but he knew they liked it and even if they didn't, hell, they liked the *attention* because this was the way it was, boys and girls, men and women. He'd already figured *that* out.

Then older, junior high days: having to coax a girl into an incinerator room or a basement for a kiss, never stopping at kissing though, not a chance, slipping a hand inside her pants or shoving a finger up her butt, not letting go until she threatened to tell her mother, and then laughing and pretending he hadn't done anything. When she'd calmed down, canned her act, he'd beg her to let him feel her up just a little bit longer, *Please just one more time, once more, just once more I swear I swear.*

With Nina he never had to beg. Not from the first time he shoved his hand between her legs. Not for a second did she fight off his tongue in her mouth. And that first time they did it she had her clothes off before he had even unbuckled his belt. Quick and slick, that was Nina. Sweet and petite. *His* girl, his baby love.

The fact she always put out for him, no questions asked, got him hard, kept him hard even now when her bouncing and jiggling was getting monotonous, predictable, and his mind was beginning to drift so that for the next few minutes, this middle section of the act, he would not so much be doing it as watching himself do it. Maybe this was what his General Science teacher meant by an out-of-body experience, his mind suddenly aware of what had gone unnoticed before: the looming shadow of the screen above them, voices from the movie garbled and agitated and floating in the air; a cramp in his leg where it kept colliding with the steering wheel; the pressure of his belt buckle against bone each time he thrust deep.

He was too hot, too sweaty, but he had this thing about getting undressed in the car. Okay for the chick, not for him. He had to be ready for whatever threats his imagination paraded out for him: cops showing up with flashlights and sirens or, worse, mean-ass bikers from the Paradise—*oo-wee lookee here, we got us a party*—dragging him from the car and beating the shit out of him and then one by one taking turns with Nina while he was forced to watch. No way would he be caught with his dick in his hand. Not this daddy-o. Ready to roll first sign of trouble. Pants buckled. Fly zipped. Car in gear. Outta here, man, outta here.

The voices on the screen seemed louder now, a man and a woman shouting at each other, love gone bad. He thought of Nina's sister, Krissie, where this had all begun a year ago: his first big score in a bar, this older chick ripe for the plucking. He smelled it on her right away and he plucked, man did he pluck and she dug it, yeah, yeah she dug it. On that he would bet his life. No matter what she said now. No matter how much she hated him. He'd given her what she wanted—a hard fuck and more—having had to slap her around a little bit whenever she got weepy, whenever she fell into one of her crying jags which was usually right after he'd humped her brains out, usually then, and he'd have to slap her out of it because the one thing he couldn't stand was a teary-eyed broad with regrets. Fuck regrets, man. Fuck 'em.

A piece of ass, all right, jesus was she a piece of ass and he cursed himself because he couldn't get her out of his mind no matter how hard he tried, not even now bonking her baby sister who was no slouch in the piece of ass department, who in her own skinny-slithery way could keep pace with the best of the local hua's he'd banged, who maybe—when you got right down to it—flesh for flesh, bone for bone, pussy for pussy was a better screw than her sister ever would be. Not even now.

Remembering her broke his rhythm and he pulled out. "Wait," he said.

"What, Mikey, what?"

He pushed himself up and blinked the sweat from his eyes.

"What's the matter? Wasn't I doin' it good?"

"It's hot. Fuck'n hot."

With her balled-up jersey she dabbed at his face and neck. "Wasn't I doin' it good?"

"You were great, baby. Just great." He stared ahead at the dark river grass where he'd caught the two faggots in the act. Jesus, that had made him sick, his stomach turning even now at the memory of them, tongue-kissing, their hands in each other's pants. *Jesus.* His stomach churned violently as ocean waves, leaving a rotten taste in his mouth. He turned to kiss Nina, kiss away that rotten taste.

Her tight little body made him pump hard, this time for keeps. No turning back. Just grab. *Grab!* Fistfuls of skin, tits, shoulders, arms, the firm meat of her ass. He wouldn't think of anything. Not her sister not the faggots not anything just her just her. She was slick and sweet with sweat. She was fucking so hard he thought his dick might snap. Oh yeah, he thought, oh yeah. Bend me shake me break me. Oh yeah oh yeah oh yeah oh yeah

He came in a hot blurred rush and saw again: bright lights, green grass, black river. Headbeams sweeping the marsh as he swung the Fairlane around. Finding the faggots, frozen as deer crossing a road.

Closing his eyes, he tried to squeeze away the vision of

Philip Cioffari

Farrell and Seward, thinking instead of her sister, the two of them the best lays of his short career—it would take him a lifetime to learn he would never find better—but even then he saw them, fairies in the grass, eyes wide with shock and fear, running to escape the high beams' reach. His stomach churned again and he pushed away from her. Light-headed and sick, he forced open the door. It was air he needed. Air. He took one step toward the grass and vomited.

Quickly she was beside him, clothes hastily thrown on. "Mikey—"

"I'm awright." He glared in the direction of the river as if he expected the two faggots to pop up, ready to chase them to kingdom come if they did.

"You scared me, Mikey."

He wiped his hand across his mouth, leaned back against the Fairlane's grill. "I'm awright, I said."

"I know, I know but—"

"I'm awright, goddammit!"

"You look like you seen a ghost."

"I'll kill the fucker."

"Who?"

"The faggot."

"He's dead."

"The other one, stupid. The one still standing."

"Forget about him."

"No way." He tapped out a Lucky. One-handed he flicked the Zippo, thumbed the flint.

She snuggled close to him. He held the Lucky to her lips but she turned aside. She hated Luckies. "Forget about him. He's got nothin' to do with us."

"He bugs the shit outta me."

"So what?"

"So plenty."

Murmur of the river. Voices from the movie. Kind of peaceful. Kind of nice. She tucked her head against his shoulder, ignoring the storage tanks with their rusted ladders and the rows of gravestones the other side of the river. "Mikey, you love me, right?"

"Course I do."

"You ain't gonna let him manhandle me, are you? Like you did with the other one?"

"He didn't manhandle you."

"I know, but he could of, if he wanted."

"Faggots don't touch girls."

"Yeah, but you didn't know for sure—"

"I knew."

"But he could of, if he wanted. You were gonna let him."

"Was a test, that's all." He flicked the Lucky into the weeds where it sputtered out. "I asked you to do it and you said okay, remember?"

"I know—"

"What's the big deal?"

She held him tighter. Her fingers played on the ridge of his belt buckle. "Don't seem right, is all. You loving me and that going on."

"You do for me, I do for you. Love, right?" He curled a fist beneath her chin and tilted her face. "I mean, he was a faggot, that's all. Anybody touches you I don't say okay first, I'll kill them."

"You would?"

"Course I would. Specially if he was a faggot."

She pinned her hair up, the way he liked it. She was his girl, Mikey's girl, and he ran his hand between her legs. No response. Nothing. She stared across the river. One of her moods. One of her goddamn girl moods.

"You're not still foolin' around with my sister, are ya?"

"Why you askin' me that?"

"Cause."

"Why you askin'?"

"Say yes or no."

He jammed his fists in his pants and spit. "Nah."

"You don't like her anymore, like you used to, right?"

"The fuck is this? What's eatin' you?"

Sad eyes. Pouty lips. "I don't know."

But he knew. Girl fucks you that good's gonna want something back. Gonna want you to hand her your balls on a silver platter.

Philip Cioffari

Donald Seward stood in the shadow of the garage, a low building with eight bays—near the priests' residence and across the lawn from the orphanage. He had something to ask Father Shannon. Something he needed to know. But the residence stood dark and quiet on the hill and he was afraid to climb the steps, afraid to knock on the door. Instead he kicked stones in the gravel driveway then wandered through the bays, empty except for a rusted pickup the gardener used, and a '38 Ford with flat tires. The garage smelled of motor oil and dust. Bats flittered between the ceiling beams. He sat in the Ford and turned the wheel this way and that like he was cruising cross-country, state by state. He thought about writing in his notebook, but there seemed no point now.

When Arthur told him he was seeing Father Shannon at night, he had wanted to come too; but Arthur got angry and said no, it was private and he couldn't come, he couldn't. Let me walk you there, Donald pleaded, at least let me walk you there. And finally Arthur said okay. But only as far as the gate. You can wait for me there.

That's when he first began filling the pages of his notebook, describing the orphanage, how it looked against the night sky; the river slow and heavy like black oil oozing; and Arthur, all kinds of things about Arthur: his face, his different expressions, the clothes he wore, things he said. To pass the time that first night, he sat with his back against the stone pillar of the gate and wrote pages and pages.

When Arthur returned an hour later, Donald asked what he did up there with Father. Arthur looked down; he wouldn't answer right away.

Talk mostly.
About what?
Things.
What kind of things?
Jesus. The Saints. Holy things.
We do that in religion class.
This is different.

Catholic Boys

Different how?
Just different.
How?
It's a secret. I can't tell.
Sure you can.
It's a secret. I can't.
Friends don't have secrets.
I promised Father.

On the way home Donald sulked. Arthur tickled him, tried to make him laugh.

What's in the notebook?
Thoughts.
Like what?
Stupid things. Nothing.
See, you've got secrets too.
They're not secrets.
Sure they are. If you won't tell.

The next night Donald asked again what Father and him did up there; he didn't want to be friends anymore if Arthur didn't tell him, and Arthur started crying, saying it was a secret and he'd taken an oath, he might die if he violated it. Friends come before oaths, Donald said, and we've been friends almost a year now. Best friends. Better than best friends. And Arthur said, yes they were. Better than best friends.

You have to promise you won't tell anyone, ever. You have to promise.
I promise. I won't tell anyone, ever.
You swear?
I swear.
Swear to God.
I swear to God.

They used a Scout knife to cut their thumbs, blood on blood. Then Arthur told him. About the meetings with Father Shannon. Like in the old days, the Dark Ages, when Christians were persecuted, when they had to celebrate their religion in secret, underground in the catacombs, when they were killed for their beliefs.

He teaches me things.
What kind of things?

Philip Cioffari

About suffering. The humiliation of the martyrs. We light candles and pray.

We do that in St. Sebastian.

This is different.

How is it different?

It just is.

How?

It just is.

What happens then?

I told you. We pray.

What else?

That's all.

What else do you do?

I told you, I told you. We pray.

What else?

Last Saturday night, Donald didn't have to wait long at the gate. Arthur came down the hill in a hurry, his face twisted like Christ's under the weight of the cross. He came through the gate without looking at him, and walked fast toward the river. On the river path he said he didn't want to go home, didn't want to go anywhere ever again. They sat by the water, Arthur was crying, saying it was because he broke the oath, that was why, he had known something bad would happen, it was all Donald's fault because he made him tell, because he hated him too like everyone else. Donald said that wasn't true, he loved him, *loved* him, and to prove it he kissed him on the mouth, their first kiss, and then Arthur was touching him and he was touching back and then it was like a lightning flash had hit them because everything was suddenly lit up and someone was shouting, running toward them, and they were slopping through mud and grass trying to hide, trying to get away.

When they got home Arthur turned toward his building without saying goodbye. Next day Donald couldn't find him, not until night time, at Krumfeld's: Arthur in a booth by himself, sipping a Coke. He wouldn't talk except to say he was going to the movies.

I'll go with you.

Leave me alone.

No, I—

Catholic Boys

Go away.

Please. Please let me—

But Arthur's eyes were cold and dark as the river. Then he was walking away without looking back. Not once.

That was the first time Donald ever followed anybody. That night, in secret. Because he didn't know what else to do with all the hurt inside.

That's what he wanted to ask Father Shannon. If he thought Arthur died because he broke the oath. Would *he* die, too, if he told the police about the secret prayer meetings? If he told them what he saw last Sunday night.

He worked up his courage and stepped out from the shadow of the bays. Turning the corner, he came face to face with Father Shannon. He stepped back in shock.

The priest, too, seemed shocked. "Donald, what are you doing here?"

"I—" He stood frozen.

"You frightened me. For a minute—" The priest wavered on the uneven ground, searching the boy's face. "For a minute I thought—" He stopped himself and said, "I guess I don't know what I thought."

The boy tried to speak but no words came out.

"Did you want to—are you here to—?" The priest ran his hand through his thick blonde hair and looked at the boy helplessly. "Is there something I can help you with? Anything at all?"

"No." The word came out sounding funny.

"Is this about your problems at school today?" He took a step toward the boy, holding out his hand. But the boy turned the corner and was running past the open bays toward the road, his footfalls quick hissing sounds on the gravel.

"These secret meetings of yours will destroy us," Tobias O'Malley said from the darkness above.

Shannon whirled around in surprise. His Superior, as if about to deliver a sermon, stood with his hands resting on the porch rail. Shannon felt himself cower inwardly; he had never gotten over feeling defensive around the man. Quickly he composed himself, drawing back his shoulders and climbing the stairs.

"Purely accidental, Toby, I can assure you. I thought he might be in need of help."

"Like the Farrell boy?"

Shannon spoke softly, refusing to rise to the bait. "Yes, like the Farrell boy."

The floorboards creaked violently as he moved toward the door. He would go to his room. A confrontation would only aggravate the situation.

"We have to talk," Father Tobias said.

"We already talked tonight."

"I hardly consider polite dinner chit-chat *talking*."

"Now even my dinner conversation displeases you." He stepped back from the door and regarded his mentor. Drinking again. He had smelled it earlier at dinner; here on the porch the older priest's whisky breath saturated the mild air.

"I expected you, Martin, to be more . . . forthcoming."

"To whom?"

"To me."

"Not to the police, as well?"

"Don't play with me, Martin. I'm not one of your students."

"My, but we're vicious tonight."

Even without his robes, even in his crumpled undershirt, he was an intimidating man, Shannon had to admit. He had put on weight and he had aged—not quite an old man but on his way—yet he still had the power to instill awe, or was it fear? He terrified the boys, even the seniors, though they made fun of his paunch, the often humorless stare with which he greeted the world. Silhouetted against the sky, his bulky frame seemed even larger and more threatening than normal. He moved slowly to a patio table where he poured himself a drink. Imported single malt Scotch. He would drink nothing less.

"I've been patient with you, Martin. I've overlooked your activities, even when I strongly disapproved. I think I'm entitled—"

"Entitled?"

"I don't think that's too strong a word. As your prefect, your mentor, your . . . friend." He seemed embarrassed by that last word and Shannon smiled, despite himself. A moment's weakness in the old fogy. A rare manifestation of vulnerability.

"You told me once to spare you the details of my activities. They caused you too much pain, you said. Don't you remember?"

"That was for purely personal reasons, under different circumstances. There's more at stake now. Even you can't be so self-absorbed not to see the difference, the consequences—"

Shannon shifted his weight, settling back against the door. "What is it you want to know?"

"Your responsibilities in all this."

"Ah," Shannon said, "responsibility. Such an elusive concept, especially in moral terms. You taught me that, remember?" He raised the inflection in his voice. "*The strength of our impulses can so destabilize our free will that the level of responsibility becomes at times almost impossible to determine.* Remember those words, Father?"

"You won't let me forget them, will you?"

"Quite heretical, in theological terms. I must confess, as a young seminarian I was shocked by such a view, especially from a pillar of the faith like yourself."

"You admired me for it, as I recall."

"How could I not? Rebellion has an irresistible appeal to the young, even in an institution as tradition-bound as the Church."

"That, I'm afraid, was another world. I'm not talking about theoretical ethics here."

"Nor am I."

The older priest coughed, then breathed in and out heavily to clear his throat. Despite his bulk he seemed unsteady on his feet, as if he were standing on a boat. "God knows, I have no intention at this point of intruding on the privacy of your relationships—"

Shannon laughed. "You've *always* had the intention of intruding upon my privacy. From the time I entered seminary."

The Prefect clutched the glass to his chest. "I've put that in God's hands long ago."

"Why don't I believe you?"

80   Philip Cioffari

"I've put that in God's hands. I wish you would, too."

"I can't absolve myself quite so easily."

"You can be cruel, Martin."

"You taught me well."

"I never taught you to torture a man for his weaknesses. We're all . . ." He drank deeply and turned toward the river. "Defective. One way or another."

"Whiskey makes you maudlin, Father. It's unbecoming," Shannon said in a gentler voice.

"I think I have reason to drink, don't you? Under the circumstances?"

"Perhaps I'm the one in need of drink." But alcohol was not his failing. It made him sick rather than drunk.

"Are you going to tell me then?"

"Tell you what?"

"What you're hiding."

"And what is that?"

"Were you with the Farrell boy Sunday night?"

Shannon thought he might, after all, need a drink. There were no glasses on the table. "Not very sociable of you, Father. You know the caveat about drinking alone."

"You never want to drink with me. We're like strangers living under the same roof. If it weren't for Father Benedict—"

"Ah, yes, the good-hearted Father B. The stabilizing—if dimwitted—presence in this home of ours. Aren't you afraid he might become privy to our little secrets? Talking frankly as we are, out here in the open."

"You know his habits as well as I. He's been asleep since sundown."

Shannon laughed bitterly. "That's one way of dealing with night's unruly demons, isn't it?" He reached for the scotch and drank directly from the bottle.

"Were you with the Farrell boy Sunday night?"

Shannon stared into the mouth of the bottle. If only escape were this easy. "What makes you think I was?"

"You were seeing the boy, I knew that. You were meeting him here at night."

He turned to the Prefect with an accusatory smile. "I thought you had no intention of intruding upon my privacy."

"How could I help but notice? I know you, Martin, no matter how much you prefer to think I don't." He rested his hands on the table and leaned toward Shannon as if he were begging. "I hear your pacing, I know about your nightly *walks*, I know when you're troubled—"

Shannon's eyes flashed at him angrily. "And when I'm troubled—?"

The older priest lowered his eyes. "I know there's a boy involved."

"You should have been born divine. With your powers of omniscience—"

"Observation, Martin, not omniscience. You can deny it all you wish, but we're alike, under the skin. It's what—"

"Brought us together? In the seminary?"

"We were both troubled in the same ways."

Shannon sneered at him across the table. "Speak for yourself, Tobias. What drew me to you was your wisdom, the nobility of your ideals and the eloquence with which you spoke of them: how the world was a place of hurt and desperate souls, crying out to be heard, to be understood; how we must offer to the most helpless and lost of God's creatures a gentle voice, a caring hand; how the young particularly needed our help and guidance, each on his own path to the Creator."

Without mercy his eyes searched his Superior's face. Hard to believe he had once thought of this man as his protector. "To this day, I remember your words. You were the living embodiment of what I hoped to become as a man, as a priest." He set the bottle down hard on the table. "Not your *troubles*, Tobias. Your holiness, your belief in your power to change the world for the good, that's what drew me to you."

The Prefect's eyes brimmed with tears. "And now you despise me."

"I despise your need to insinuate yourself in my life. To *know* me, as you put it. At first I thought it was coincidence that we received the same assignments, that I was constantly under your charge. Until I realized it was your influence with the archdiocese, not chance, that kept me like a prisoner under your prying eyes."

"How? How have I treated you like a prisoner? I've done

everything possible to leave you alone, once you made it clear that—" He reached toward Shannon but the younger priest moved to the edge of the porch. "When you came to the seminary I knew what we had—the special nature of our friendship—was a temporary thing, a gift I would one day have to give away. In silence I've endured each of your infatuations which, in my opinion, were your way of spiting me—"

"That's right. Everything has to do with *you*. There's no way I might have a life of my own, needs of my own—"

"If we only knew our needs, our true needs, we wouldn't be where we are now."

"More pearls from His Holiness."

"Stop it, Martin. Stop it." He stood behind Shannon, but the young priest kept his back turned. "I know more than you think I know. But I've kept it to myself. Out of respect for your privacy."

Shannon had turned toward the orphanage, its turrets jutting toward the half-moon rising above the river. "What is it you think you know?" he said quietly.

"I know you've hardly slept these past four or five nights. I know you've been sneaking into the orphanage to meet that boy. It's broken my heart to see you in such torment day after—"

Shannon turned abruptly to face him. "So why, as my Prefect, didn't you forbid me to see him?"

"So you could mock me? Call me a hypocrite? No, I suffered in silence for your sake, and mine. Even when I knew of these nocturnal rendezvous, your Gothic excesses, the candles, the incantations—"

"You *watched* me," Shannon said breathlessly and the Prefect lowered his head.

"Only once. Only because—"

"I should have known. You've always been an emotional voyeur. Why not a literal one as well?"

The older priest gripped the porch railing for support. His breath came heavily and he sipped the whiskey to calm himself. "Only because I had to know for certain. Only that one time—"

In the dim light his eyes looked grey and defeated. What

Shannon felt for him was more pity than disgust. Leering in the dark—the final refuge of the old and unlovable. For a moment he glimpsed his own future in his mentor's sorrowful eyes. He took the glass away from him and walked to the table where he filled it. He came down the porch, the floorboards creaking noisily, and handed back the glass. "If I say yes, I saw the boy Sunday night, what then?"

The Prefect set the glass on the porch rail and clasped his hands. He'd been prepared for this. He'd been thinking of nothing else for the past twenty-four hours. "Then we must decide what to tell the police. If they find out, if Arthur told anyone—" He hesitated. The consequences were too horrible to contemplate. His life's work flushed away in shame. "Your reputation, the reputation of the school, of all of us, hangs in the balance."

Shannon considered his response. Choices, he knew, were the bastard offspring of decisions made long ago. That he could choose freely now was an illusion. The door had already locked behind him. And it had been he himself who had thrown away the key.

Philip Cioffari

Chapter Seven

Exposed himself . . . fondled his genitals . . . masturbated openly . . . stalked his victim . . . repeated anal and vaginal penetration. Ramsey skimmed the review Morales had prepared of the borough's sexual assault cases. The child offenders in the group were minor players. Guys like Fritz. Guys like Vinnie Sensa who'd been picked up three times in the past two months for displaying his *pee-pee*—Sensa's word for it—outside the public bathrooms of a playground on Bainbridge. And Arnold Montrose who liked to walk around nude in the woods of Van Cortlandt Park and show himself to Boy Scouts or Girl Scouts, whoever happened by. And Allen Loder who'd been picked up for sitting in a tree and playing with himself in a section of the Botanical Gardens where men went to meet other men. How, Ramsey wondered, did such behavior fit the design of the universe?

At 8:30 Falcone handed him a list of children in building 5 where the message had been scrawled. He glanced over the names: twenty-eight in all, boys and girls, ages six months to nineteen years. There were six boys in Arthur Farrell's age range.

"But there are boys that age all over Baychester, Eddie."

"True."

"So why building 5?"

Why building 5? Ramsey was still pondering that question when the phone rang. Fritz Weinstein, twelve hours before deadline. His voice came over the wire thin and whining, as if the simple act of speaking caused him pain. Ramsey held the phone away from his ear. "What's that, Fritz? I can't understand you."

"Bartender. Name of Harold. At John's Paradise," Fritz said in a voice still whining, but easier to decipher. "He might have something."

*****

Building 5 was halfway between his office and the swamp, part of a cluster of buildings that faced the North oval: an open area of grass surrounded by benches and playgrounds. There was little to distinguish it from the other Baychester buildings with their twelve stories and plain brick facades, unadorned except for the terra cotta gargoyles hanging above the entrances. This particular gargoyle showed an eagle, wings spread wide, hovering above a reclining maiden.

From the roof he looked down on the grassy oval. The playgrounds had just closed. On walkways children ran ahead of their parents or dawdled in protest, their complaints thin and barely audible at this distance; farther off on the Boulevard, beyond Hanscom's Bakery and Rexall Drugs, the usual handful of men gathered outside Krumfeld's awaiting the morning edition of the *News*.

He watched the smoke from his cigarette dissolve in the darkening air. The children had vanished from the walkways; the benches were beginning to empty. An uneasy stillness settled over the wide oval of grass. Once his night patrolman came into view, he felt better about leaving his perch.

On the Boulevard a precinct cruiser pulled alongside him. Willie Metcalf, one of his old crew from the 47th, leaned from the window: "Hey, Ram. Morales left word at your office, but said in case I saw you tell you in person. That blood in the hallway? It's rat's blood."

Ramsey leaned back in surprise.

"Rat's blood," Metcalf said again, shaking his head. "Figure *that* the fuck out."

Four or five times a weekend the cops came in to break up fights or answer noise complaints, but even weeknights John's Paradise Inn was a powder keg: bikers and their girlfriends spilling onto the street, live music pulsating from the open windows. Word had it that since the Shack had been shut down, John's had muscled in on the local porn scene. According to Morales, Vice was just itching for an excuse to go in and bust the place up.

Ramsey pushed through the crowd of sweating bodies, stopped more than once by a wall of leather and denim. Girls in their skinny black pants and halter tops were as immovable as the guys. A leather jacket swung roughly against him. Brody.

"Polite thing to do is to excuse yourself," Ramsey said with a smile. Brody stared back, unblinking. Behind him the Brando's craned their necks for a better look. "Why am I not surprised to see you boys here?"

The face-off with Brody endured. "Well, I've certainly enjoyed the intimacy but duty calls—" Brody held his ground. Ramsey smiled again. "All right, big guy, I think you've made your point." Brody turned abruptly, leaving Ramsey with an eyeful of black leather: B-R-A-N-D-O arced in silver studs across his shoulders.

Once Ramsey reached the bar he managed to squeeze in between the wall and a pair of aging, boilermaker-guzzling biker buddies. Harold was easy to find. A six-foot-six bald black man with a hoop earring, he stood behind the bar with his arms folded, surveying with sullen ferocity the territory of the dance floor. He dressed like a biker: pegged jeans, denim vest over a bare chest. A rose tattoo highlighted each of his huge biceps.

Ramsey signaled for a beer. "You have some information for me," he said when the towering black man set the mug on the bar.

"Don't know nothin' about it. Don't talk to no cops, either."

"Oh? Why's that?"

"Against my religion."

Catholic Boys   87

"You can put your mind at rest, my man. I'm with Housing Security at Baychester." Guitar music assaulted his ears. The room was too hot, too noisy, reeking of beer and body odor. He was getting old; the world was already turning him out. "Fritz Weinstein says you know something about a child that disappeared couple of years back."

The black man stood with his arms folded, lips pursed. He was staring beyond Ramsey at the far wall, though *far* in a room so small was a relative term.

"You do know Fritz, don't you?"

The man remained immobile, indifferent.

"Cause he knows you. Knows you very well. Says you were asshole buddies when you worked over at the Shack. And you know what I hear?" Ramsey stared into the hardened profile. "*Police grapevine*," he said in a conspiratorial whisper, his voice low enough that Harold was forced to forego his rigid pose and lean toward the bar. "I hear the D.A.'s going to open a new probe into the porn rackets up here. My guess is he'd be mighty interested in your contributions to a Grand Jury inquiry. Catch my drift, Harold?"

It was only a hunch on Ramsey's part. He assumed from what Fritz told him, and from what Fritz *didn't* say, that Harold had at least his pinky in the smut pie. Harold, though, was one cool operator. His face gave away nothing. He turned and walked away to pour a double shot of Wild Turkey for a biker who'd been slamming his fist on the bar.

When he returned he planted his huge arms on the bar and stared past Ramsey again, his face cold and distant. He might have been speaking to himself or to the air. "All I know is this, man. Guy was in here a year, maybe a year and a half back talking 'bout his kid who'd disappeared over in Riverview. Seemed to think bikers had something to do with it. That's all I know, man."

"Riverview?" Ramsey knew the housing project, a postwar development not unlike Baychester, built along the Bronx River between Bruckner and the new expressway. He couldn't remember hearing about any child who'd disappeared there.

"That's what the dude said, man. Riverview." His eyes still wouldn't make contact with Ramsey. He straightened up and

Philip Cioffari

walked to the far end of the bar where he became a statue again, arms crossed, staring into the crowd.

*****

Bar music still battering the inner linings of his ears, Ramsey crossed to the cemetery side of the street. Graves stretched away in a long dark plain. Someone had once joked that this was a "bare bones" kind of cemetery. Treeless and flat, its headstones modest, it seemed squeezed as an afterthought between Bruckner Boulevard and the Hutchinson River Parkway: a burial ground for people whose death was marked as their lives had been, without pretension.

He'd gotten lost here—the first time he had come to visit after his mother's death—and had wandered in frustration for nearly an hour among the seemingly identical rows of markers. Now, entering through a side gate, he had his signposts: straight ahead the length of a football field to a stone in the shape of a small pink valentine. Turn right to the third water spigot. Four rows beyond the spigot, turn right again. The sixteenth plot on the left side was his parents': a modest stone, arched at the top, the names *Rita* and *William* etched in small letters next to their dates.

During these visits he sometimes saw his mother as a young woman: dark-haired and fair-skinned the way she looked in family photo albums; other times she was older, grey-haired, heavier, with wire glasses that always seemed out of place on her youthful face. Her death had come quickly but his father died slowly over eighteen months so that the images of him were more starkly contrasting: the rugged, thick-shouldered repair man with strong hands—and the pallid wisp of a man prostrate on a hospital bed, hands too weak to press the call button. Human life, it had often seemed to Ramsey, was far too short and fragile to bear such reversals.

When Evan died Ramsey assumed he would be buried here next to his grandparents, but Helen couldn't bear the thought of him lying on *this barren field* without the beauty of trees and flowers. She wanted a cemetery that was not in any way crowded by the hard edges of the city.

Catholic Boys   89

He turned his thoughts to the sacrifices his parents made so that he would have an easier life—his farewell ritual during these visits—but his concentration was broken by the sound of traffic that rose and fell like a strong wind. Blown away were the images of his parents. Helen had been right, in her way. At moments like this the city *did* intrude.

He blessed himself, a gesture performed out of habit, and turned to leave.

Finding his way back was easier. He had only to move in the direction of the fence, using the thumping music from the bar to guide him.

*****

On his desk he found a note from Falcone—the words *RAT'S BLOOD?* scrawled across a sheet of paper attached to a list of the project's children. The X's scratched into the margin next to the names of the boys in Arthur Farrell's age range disturbed him, as though these had already been marked for a bad end. He left a message for Morales to check out the disappearance of a child from Riverview.

He sat idly in the darkness. Pointless to call Helen at this hour. She would be asleep or lost in her own world.

In the outer office a clock ticked into the silence.

It was his habit to make time like this at the end of the day. Taking stock, he called it. Arranging random and miscellaneous details: a scavenger hunt for order. But what kind of order could he find in a day like this one? Finally the sound of his own breathing, heavy and isolated in the quiet room, forced him out.

*****

Headlights and engine off, he sat listening to the music coming from inside the Shimmy, softer and more melodic than the guitar ravings at John's. If he closed his eyes for a minute, he might gather the energy to go inside for a nightcap. Or he might simply drive home. *Close your eyes, take a deep breath,* his mother would tell him as a child when he couldn't

Philip Cioffari

sleep. *Tomorrow the world will be brighter.*

The music turned harsher because it was John's Paradise he was looking at, from quite some distance: what seemed like miles upon miles of gravestones. He'd been searching for Evan's grave and he was exhausted, his legs rubbery, his knees aching. How much farther could he walk? As far as we need to, Helen said beside him, *as far as death.* They had already found death, he tried to say, all around them, but she wasn't listening: she couldn't understand his hesitation, his doubt. This isn't even the right cemetery, he told her. *Of course it is,* she insisted, *of course it is. Evan is waiting, don't you see? Our boy is all alone waiting for us, the poor poor thing, he'll die if we don't find him.* She was weeping uncontrollably. Should he stop to comfort her or go on searching—because now the graves stretched to the horizon in every direction and all his signposts had been taken from him.

A voice cried out. At first he thought it was Helen's voice from his dream until he saw the woman on the opposite side of the lot swinging her fists at a man who held his arms open as if to gather her up. The man's gesture seemed gentle, protective, until he caught hold of her in a crushing embrace which she fought against, pushing at his face with her open palm, kicking at his legs.

Ramsey was running toward them, hearing their shouts now, Brody's "You bitch, you lying cheating bitch," Krissie's "Please please I don't want this anymore;" and then he had Brody in a choke hold, Krissie standing back, watching as he wrestled him to the ground. "Get the fuck off me, get the fuck offa me," the kid was shouting but Ramsey had his knees jammed into the leather-jacketed chest and he swung at his face until it was bloodied. Finally the face was still—Brody's arms outstretched and limp on the ground.

She stood above them crying, "You bastard, you bastard" in such a way that Ramsey wasn't sure to which of them her words were addressed. He'd come at the kid harder maybe than he needed to, blind instinct gone awry, and he stood back now leaving him battered and bloody on the ground. Maybe he'd interfered in a lover's quarrel, none of his damn business; he half-expected Krissie to berate him, ask what the hell he thought he was doing; but her eyes looked at him with gratitude.

From the back door Leo said, "I have called to the police."

"You hurt?" Ramsey asked her.

She shook her head no.

"You want to press charges?"

"No."

"You're sure?"

"He was my boyfriend." She looked at the man on the ground with pity and disgust. "You hear that, Mike?"

Brody stared sullenly and wiped the blood from his mouth. "*Was*. It's over now. How many times do I have to tell you I don't want it anymore."

The bar owner stood watching. His oiled hair glistened in the light coming from the door. "It's all right, Leo," Ramsey said, "you can tell the police everything's settled." He offered a hand to the kid. "Come on, Mike, time to go."

Brody pushed himself up on his own power and spit a mouthful of blood that narrowly missed Ramsey's shoe. He stood slouched in a movie idol way, his sneer part James Dean, part Elvis. "This's got nothing to do with you."

"It does now."

"The fuck it does."

"Let's just say I have a lot of friends at the 4-7. You come anywhere near this lady again, they're going to make your life miserable."

"It's over, Mike," Krissie said, her voice breaking. "It's just over."

"You're gonna regret this." He whispered something as he brushed past her.

"What did he say?"

She forced a smile and raised her head defiantly. "He said, 'Love like ours never dies.'"

"He should write a song."

"I don't want to talk about it right now." She watched the Fairlane roar from the lot, exhaust vapors hanging in the air.

"Detective Ramsey," Leo called from the doorway. "please, that I might express my gratitude, won't you join with me in a drink?"

"It's late."

"It would give me such pleasure."

"A short one, then."

"And Miss Varick," Leo said with a colder formality, "I would like a word with you in my office." He stepped aside as she hurried past.

Ramsey came toward him more slowly. "Don't be too hard on her. We all made mistakes at that age."

"I am a man of conservative values, Detective. I do not like unnecessary commotions."

"Without them, it would be a very different world than the one we live in."

"Perhaps so. But each man dreams the world to his own needs, does he not?"

"I'm not the man to ask about dreams."

"I do not believe you know yourself as others know you."

At the bar he poured Ramsey a beer and himself a lemon-colored liqueur from a squat, short necked bottle with Arabic lettering. He raised his glass in a formal toast. "To you, Detective Ramsey, a man who brings order and stability in a world of chaos."

"You flatter me, Leo. It would be truer to say that I'm still in search of those things."

"Perhaps we are saying the same thing."

"Are we? I wouldn't have thought that."

"A great prophet once said, 'A man is known by the things he seeks.'"

"I'm a man of the streets. The sayings of great prophets aren't meant for me."

"On the contrary. A man's actions can lift him above the limitations of his class."

Ramsey saw himself in the mirror—sagging face, sagging belly—and pushed his hand through his hair. He leaned hard against the bar. "I've got too many limitations. *And* regrets."

"You do not believe in the power of the human spirit?"

"I've lost my beliefs, I'm afraid, along with my dreams."

"And your hope as well?"

"Maybe not that. Not yet."

"Then perhaps in time you will see things differently. And

we will have a conversation like this one, and we will be in agreement."

"I wouldn't count on that."

"I do count on that. In my heart of hearts. And I pray that your hope will grow as a flower grows, nurtured by light and warmth."

"A pretty thought."

"I have many such thoughts for you, my friend." He downed the liqueur with one quick toss of his head and clenched his lips. "There are some who claim this nectar is much too bitter to give pleasure. But bitterness can sharpen our sensitivity to life, don't you agree?"

Ramsey laughed. "I hadn't really given it much thought, but I see I'll have to now."

"You are a very serious man, but I admire that you are able to find laughter in the dark wood."

"The dark wood?"

"Yes. From a poem I read by Robert Frost. It is a metaphor, no?

"Ah, *that* dark wood. Yes, it's a metaphor. We usually make it plural, though. Dark *woods*."

"The difficulty of this world."

"That's what it means."

"Dark woods," Leo whispered to himself, emphasizing the *s*. "Dark woods."

"Now you've got it."

Raising himself to his full height, Leo stood tall and erect, his face in the bar light the color of smoke. "Tomorrow the Shimmy will no longer exist."

"I don't understand."

"I believe that places, as well as people, are capable of rebirth. Tomorrow what was once the Shimmy will be known as the Wild Moon. A place of inspiration. Like the moon when it is full. Transporting our souls to acts of splendor and love."

"But in folklore and witchcraft, the moon is thought to inspire us to more sinister acts."

Leo waved his hand in dismissal. "In a metaphor there are many meanings. Like the world which is full of good as well as evil. We can choose whichever we prefer, no?"

Philip Cioffari

"In theory, yes."

"Therefore the serious man must continue to seek the light amid the darkness."

"The *serious* man?"

"The man of worthiness. He who would be taken seriously. Is that the more proper way to say?"

"Ah, yes. I see your point."

"I am so happy that we can agree, Detective, if only in brief." He glanced at his watch. "I must beg your indulgence now. I have some business to attend to. But I shall return promptly. In the meantime perhaps you would enjoy the company of one of the dancers." He motioned to a table where several dancers in street clothes counted their tips.

"I'll just finish this beer."

"As you wish." Leo bowed and walked past him to the office.

Ramsey sipped his beer slowly. With the lights on, without music, the room felt sadly ordinary. Even the girls at the table, pretty as they were, seemed ordinary: somebody's daughter or sister or wife, fallen from imagination's grace. He drained the rest of his beer and left.

He was crossing the parking lot when Krissie came running behind him. "I didn't get a chance to thank you. That was so kind. What you did."

"Habit. I don't deserve thanks."

"When you saw it was *me*, I would have expected you to walk away."

"I don't like to see anyone hurt."

"Even *me*," she said with bitter self-deprecation.

"*Including* you."

Something flashed across her eyes and she lowered her head, biting on her lip. "I deserved it."

"No one deserves being hurt."

"Even when they've hurt others unforgivably?"

"I'm not interested in punishing people. That's for the courts."

"I can't tell you how much—" She didn't finish and he found it hard to meet her eyes, as grateful and expectant as they were. "He's not always mean as that, you know."

"Your boyfriend?"

"*Ex*-boyfriend." She laughed. "*Most* of the time, yes, but not always. He had to act tougher, of course, because you were here."

"We should all be judged on our finer moments."

"Do you always give people the benefit of the doubt?"

"I shouldn't have hit him so hard—"

"He can be stubborn, and the fact that, well, that you're an older man probably hurt his pride. He likes to brag about what good shape he's in."

"Will he leave you alone?"

"I don't know. I've always gone back. When I left him before." She gave him a rueful, apologetic smile. "He's actually going out with my sister now. I want him to stay away from her, too. But we'll see."

He reached into his pocket for his car keys. "You have your car here, right?"

"No, I sold it. After—" Her face flushed and she bit down hard on her lip. "I don't drive now."

"You have someone to take you home?"

"Oh, yes. One of the girls."

"I should be going." He stood there without moving and then her body was pressed against him, holding onto him as if she were his child, her lips brushing his cheek; and just as quickly he was alone again, heart thumping hard against the walls of his chest, as he watched her hurry back toward the bar.

Philip Cioffari

Chapter Eight

WEDNESDAY

At first he thought he was back in the cemetery lost among acres of stones until he saw the boys in a loose circle around him, faces intermittently illuminated by the light of the moon or a searchlight. Again they appeared to be crying out, mouths opening soundlessly, eyes desperate with hope. As each face was revealed he strained for a closer look before the face fell quickly into shadow.

The shadows became the shadows of his room, the light—not occasional now, but constant—the pale cold glow of the corner street lamp. He was breathing as if he'd been running uphill. His wristwatch read 3:45.

He forced himself from bed and ventured into the hall. Even now, he had to stop himself from turning left to check on Evan. Helen's room was to the right. He walked softly on the creaking wood and stood in her doorway.

It took some time before he saw her clearly, thrust forward on her stomach, one arm flung—carelessly it seemed—off the edge of the bed. The empty glass and her books—paperbacks that she read by the dozens—were within arm's length on the floor. Her bags had been packed and stood side by side near the window.

"Alex?"

"Just checking on you."

She turned her head to see him better. "You all right?"

"Bad dreams, that's all."

"Me, too."

"Morning soon."

"Morning," she said in a faraway voice. "Such a beautiful word."

He wanted to tell her about Kristen Varick but there didn't seem any point now. "You won't reconsider, will you, about leaving?"

"Everything's arranged."

"I thought—"

Her eyes watched him flatly in the dark. "It's for the best, Alex. You'll see."

He thought she might want him to sit with her while she fell back asleep but she said nothing. "Call if you need anything," he said.

Despite his fatigue he slept only for brief intervals, as if vigilance was a punishment to which he'd been sentenced. When grey light replaced the streetlamp's light in his window, he felt relief that the night had passed without the phone ringing, without news that another body had been found. Then the phone beside his bed *was* ringing: Eddie Falcone, already in the office, reporting the discovery of a new message. This one on pavement in black chalk. In the North playground.

*****

The graphologist, a balding man with an unusually white scalp and dreamy eyes, knelt close to the words: *WHAT THE SHADOWS KNOW, DAYLIGHT WON'T REVEAL.* With his hand, as if he himself were the writer, he traced the shape of the letters in the air. "One of my own idiosyncratic techniques," he explained. "Not scientific by any means but it helps me get a feel for the configuration."

Morales rolled his eyes at Ramsey.

"Whoever did this," the dreamy-eyed man said, "probably saw the stairwell version and has a pretty good eye—but look. For one thing, the *a*'s and *o*'s aren't the same. They aren't formed the same way. In layman's terms, to put it simply, the loops this writer uses as connections are different."

He bent close to the message and pointed to the way the *a* and *t* of the word *what* were joined, and then he traced the *a* and *d* and the *o* and *w* of the word *shadow*. "See? The connective marks are much straighter here. In the stairwell inscription the dip of the loop is much deeper."

"So what does that tell us about personality type?" Morales said. "The bozo in the stairwell is looser?"

"Looser, freer, more uninhibited maybe. Even careless."

"And this joker?"

"Straight-laced. More controlled."

Morales gave Ramsey a hopeless look. "So what do you think? We got another joker here with a sick sense of humor?"

"I'd feel a hell of a lot better if he'd keep his jokes out of the playground."

It was past nine and children were already waiting outside the fence. One of them called out to Ramsey, "Hey mister, hey mister, we can't play here?" He had white hair; his ears, over-sized for such a small boy, stuck out awkwardly from his head.

"Not today, son."

"Not fair."

"The other playgrounds are open."

"Still not fair."

"Tomorrow you'll be able to play here."

"Did someone get murdered?"

"No, no. Nothing like that."

"All right," the boy said reluctantly. Ramsey watched him ride away on his skate box. The other children had already begun moving toward the playground on the far side of the ball field.

He lit a cigarette, keeping his back to the reporters on the walkway. Morales joined him, peeling back the wrapper from a jumbo Double-Bubble. "Moriarity's up my ass something fierce," he said. "Calls me into his office like ten, twelve times a day. Calls me at home. Last night, right, I get home 'round midnight, call up a friend, she comes over, we're at the 'Oh God, oh God' part, the phone rings. Moriarity."

Catholic Boys

He took a bite of the rolled gum and chewed noisily, mouth open. "Same old thing, you know? The Commissioner's on his ass because the Mayor's on the Commissioner's ass. And we got a new player now—the archdiocese. The *Cardinal's* on the Mayor's ass. Apparently the Farrell kid was inducted into some honor society the Cardinal founded to prepare the future leaders of the Christian world, or some such. Spellman's in a shit fit over what happened. He's threatened to withdraw his support if this case don't get resolved fast. And Wagner doesn't want to lose the Catholic vote."

Morales stopped chewing, his eyes turned inward. "Anyway, you can imagine what Moriarity's like these days."

"I don't know if I want to." Ramsey remembered the last meeting he'd had with his former precinct commander, several months after Evan's death. He'd overheard Moriarity making an under-the-breath comment to one of the other detectives about how he didn't know what the big deal was—*The kid was a retard, if it was me I'd be glad he was dead and out of his misery.* Ramsey freaked, hurling himself at the captain with such force he nearly knocked him through the window, hammering at the man's face and mouth and neck until he was pulled off. "That honor society," he said, "that the one Farrell wore the gold cross for?"

"Probably," Morales said. "Oh, I checked out that Riverview thing. No record of a missing kid there. But I did find something in River*dale*. Remember a few years back? Timothy Oster? Disappeared on his way home from school. Let's see . . ." He took out his notebook and found the notation. "June 5, 1958. Never found. He was at St. Jerry's, too."

Ramsey did remember the case. It had made the papers briefly and there had been an APB on the boy. Police investigation inconclusive. Oster was logged as a likely runaway. "You going to check it out?"

"Moriarity thinks it's too cold. Wants me to follow up on the rat's blood thing with the Department of Health's Pest Control Division. While I'm downtown he figures I should check out the faggot bars in the West Village."

"I doubt you'll find our man in one of those joints."

"Can't hurt to look."

Philip Cioffari

"Time," Ramsey said. "That's where it hurts." He ground out his cigarette against the fence and dropped it in a trash bin. "I'll follow up on the Oster boy. You might want to stop in at St. Patty's while you're down there, talk to someone on the Cardinal's staff. See what that honor society stuff's all about."

*****

When Katherine Oster opened the door, Ramsey announced himself as though it were an apology.

She was about his age, forty-ish, smartly dressed in a navy-blue serge suit: a small woman with reddish-blonde hair and pale blue, nervous eyes. Her Victorian home overlooked a broad sloping lawn that fell to the Hudson, dark blue under a strong morning sun.

In the parlor room, overshadowed by elaborate period furnishings, she seemed even more diminutive. "You'll find the love seat most comfortable," she advised him. "I adore antiques, as you can see, but I'll be the first to admit they're not always practical."

The room felt sacred as a museum: ornate lamps; intricate maroon and gold patterns on the Persian rug; tables displaying stone figurines, bronze pill boxes and other objets d'art he couldn't identify. On the dark polished wood of the walls, gilt-edged frames held scenes of the English countryside. A pair of formal photographs on the fireplace mantel caught his attention: one, he assumed, of her son—a boy of nine or ten in the picture—and one of her husband, a handsome man in his fifties.

"Collecting began as a hobby and became, well, something of a passion, you might say. Something to do on weekends. Browsing through curio shops—it's a game. You never know what you might discover." She appeared to have suddenly forgotten what point she was making. "May I bring you something, Detective?"

"A glass of water, maybe. The heat—"

Left alone in silence he became aware of a clock ticking, several clocks, their various tickings out of sync with one another, echoing in the high-ceilinged room. Through the lace curtains the sun was bright on the street. Elegant, expensive homes. Fine cars in the driveways. A place where a child would have all the advantages.

He was studying the boy's face on the mantel when she returned with a tumbler of ice-water. "When you called this morning I thought, at first, you might have news."

"I'm afraid I have only questions."

"Our Creator must be a lover of mystery, don't you think? Why else would he burden us with so many?" She sat stiffly in a straight-backed chair. "That poor child," she said vaguely. Her grief had settled at the edges of her eyes, in the tight compression of her lips, the difficulty with which she smiled.

"At this point we don't have reason to believe there's any connection to your son's disappearance. It's only that—it's come to our attention that your husband thought a motorcycle gang might have been involved with what happened to Timothy."

She bowed her head. "My husband developed many theories in the months after Timmy's disappearance. That was one of them."

When Ramsey had phoned earlier, she told him her husband wasn't home "at the moment." Something in the way she had used the phrase *at the moment* stopped him from inquiring further. Now, though, he was impatient to talk to Bruno Oster. He thought perhaps that would be easier, less painful, though why he thought so he couldn't have said.

"The police," Katherine Oster was saying, and he heard an edge of bitterness in her voice now, "seemed incapable of finding any leads themselves. They had *no* theories, except that he might have simply run away. So Bruno supplied some of his own. Look around you. You've seen what it's like here. Why would a child willingly give this up?"

"Were there problems that might—?"

Her body stiffened. "Our problems began *after* Timothy's disappearance."

"There was nothing else that—"

"Might have caused him to want to leave us?" She smiled resolutely. "Absolutely nothing that I'm aware of. Nothing." Her voice swelled with conviction. "Believe me when I say I've explored that possibility again and again, and I can find not one thing that would have caused Timmy to run from us. Not one." She leaned toward him with her hands clasped to her chest. "The police—they simply gave up. Perhaps they have as great a distaste for unanswered questions as I do."

"I lost a son once, too. Under different circumstances."

"Then you must understand." She rose from her chair quickly and stood with her back to him.

He listened to the ticking clocks, her quiet breathing. "Would it be possible for me to speak with your husband?"

"He's not here now."

"Is there a number where he works?"

"He's not working now. So far as I know."

"Then he's not living here?"

"Not at present, no." She was still facing away from him. Beneath the tailored blue serge, her shoulders quivered. "The Holy Light Mission on Westchester Square. That's the last address I have for him."

"Did he mention making inquiries at a bar called John's Paradise Inn?"

"He may have. His theories were complicated with details. Too many to remember."

"Did he ever tell you why he thought bikers might be involved?"

"My husband couldn't bear living in this house after Timmy was gone," she said, returning to her seat. "He was drinking a lot. His mind began to . . . slip. There were nights when he would go on for hours about his theories. None of it made much sense."

"Your son, Mrs. Oster, did he like it at St. Jerome's?"

She drew her head back sharply. "Why wouldn't he like it?"

"I don't know. It can be a tough place I hear."

"The priests are strict with the boys, if that's what you mean. I consider that a good thing."

Her eyes had taken on a guarded look and Ramsey said, "Of course, of course" in a gentle way to put her at ease. "So he never mentioned having any trouble with the other boys there, or his teachers?"

"On the contrary, he was very involved with the school. Clubs, sports. He was very well liked there."

Catholic Boys

"The police report indicated that he was seen getting on the bus in front of the school shortly past three o'clock."

"He didn't have any activities that day so he was coming right home—"

"And to get home he would take, what, three buses?"

"Four. The 29 to Pelham Bay Park station, the 4 to West Farms, the 9 up Broadway and then the 7."

"Quite a trip."

"He didn't mind it," she said quickly. "He did his homework."

"So he might have been intercepted anywhere along the way," Ramsey said, thinking out loud. "Mrs. Oster, was there anyone at the school he was particularly friendly with—someone on the staff perhaps who would remember him?"

She rested her head in her hands and thought a moment. "There was Father O'Malley of course, the principal. He knew Timothy well. And an English teacher, I think—a Father Shannon. Timmy spoke highly of him."

At the door she said, "It hasn't been easy for me—staying here, I mean. But I say to myself, what if Timmy comes back and he finds strangers living here? No matter how difficult it is to wait like this, *I* want to be the one to hear his footsteps on the porch. *I* want to be the one to open the door when he rings the bell."

*****

A blue neon cross burned outside the Holy Light Men's shelter. At the front desk a clean-cut young man wearing a ministerial collar rang Oster's room. "I trust Mr. Oster is not in trouble of any kind?"

"No trouble," Ramsey said.

"Perhaps this is in reference to something about which we here at the ministry should be informed. As you may know, we provide spiritual guidance as well as a temporary home to our residents."

"Thanks, but I'm interested in speaking to Mr. Oster himself."

"His peace be with you," he called in an aggressively cheerful voice as Ramsey crossed the lobby to wait in a linoleum-tiled room of card tables where several elderly men sat isolated from one another, staring into space. Against the far wall a younger man in a faded and ill-fitting blue suit sat at an upright piano playing—too loudly, Ramsey thought—a Tchaikovsky piano concerto.

The room depressed him—not only its stuffy, unpleasant odor, its drab-ocher walls the same color as the linoleum, but the faces of the old men as well with their vacant stares, their limp bodies as oblivious to one another as they were to the soap opera playing on a small black-and-white TV and the gushing, over-heated passion of the piano concerto. He drifted back into the lobby.

The clerk said, "He's awfully good, isn't he? How wonderful to be blessed with such God-given talent."

Ramsey mumbled a "Yes, it is," and asked him to ring the room again.

The smell of onions from the cafeteria door made his stomach turn; he would have lit a cigarette except for the red-and-white NO SMOKING signs. Instead he wandered into the chapel, a room unadorned by iconography other than the plain altar table and the Christ-less gilded cross that hung from the ceiling. He sat on a folding chair and leaned forward with his face in his hands, thinking of Helen traveling to Schenectady. She would be there by two, greeting her sister, her new life. . . . The smell of food, present even here, and the maudlin notes of the piano intruded upon his reverie. He returned to the lobby and told the young man that he'd just go on up to Oster's room.

"I'm afraid our policy—"

"Police business."

"Sir," he said with an ingratiating smile, "this is a *Christian* refuge. We answer to a Higher Power."

Ramsey slapped his Security badge brutally hard on the desk. "Give me the goddamned room number, boy." The badge looked enough like the gold NYPD detective's shield that the clerk barely glanced at it, his face already ashen, smile-less. "Yes, sir."

As always, he avoided the elevator—he couldn't bear tight,

closed spaces—and took the stairs, climbing slowly up the hot and airless shaft. On the seventh floor he leaned against a wall to wipe the sweat from his forehead. The hall stretched away from him: long and narrow, rooms on both sides. From behind a closed door came the muffled voice of a radio announcer, the sound of a chair scraping, an isolated cough. As he moved down the hall the death-like quiet became more oppressive. A white-haired man in a T-shirt and pajama bottoms emerged from the bathroom, carrying a towel and a soap dish. He shuffled past Ramsey without acknowledging him.

At 719 Ramsey listened first, then knocked. "Mr. Oster?"

Through the transom he heard a fan's whir. He knocked again. "Mr. Oster?"

He nudged the door inward. The room was narrow: a neatly made bed along one wall, a small writing table and chair, a three-drawer dresser. The window opened into the grey, trapped light of an air-shaft. An anonymous holding cell for the dispossessed. A long way down from a white Victorian in Riverdale.

He found Bruno Oster waiting for him downstairs. He recognized him from the mantel photo, though his grey hair was longer now, combed back flat and straight, and he had grown a close-cropped beard. Sitting across the room from the piano, his eyes lit by some intensely private light, he looked like a shabby and aging Jesus.

"You know where Timmy is? You know where my boy is?"

"I'm sorry to say I don't."

"Figures." He rubbed the back of his hand slowly across his mouth and watched Ramsey with a wary reserve.

"You don't mind if I sit a minute, do you? My knees had a hell of a time on those stairs." He pulled up a chair with a battered cushion and sat down. Oster smelled of whiskey; that smell mingled with the general unpleasant odor of the room. "You were at John's Paradise some time ago, making inquiries about Timmy."

"They wouldn't talk."

"Who?"

"The bikers. Who do you think?"

Ramsey raised his voice to be heard above the piano.

Something from *West Side Story*—too loud, too choked with emotion. "What made you think they had something to do with your son's disappearance?"

Oster's stare was directed somewhere into the room's middle distance.

"Mr. Oster? Was there something concrete behind your assumption?"

"Concrete enough for me."

"Can you be more specific?"

"My boy adored those creeps. Don't ask me why. He thought they were gods on their fancy machines. He'd drop everything to gawk whenever one of them rode by."

"All young boys have heroes."

"Heroes, yes. But those people are degenerates." Oster leaned toward the table and the reek of rot-gut whiskey was unbearable. "What gives a healthy boy from a good family such a craving for the sordid?"

"Isn't *craving* too strong a word? Perhaps it was more a fascination—"

"I knew my son," Oster said in a voice close to shouting. "It was a *craving*." His eyes glared with wild, indiscriminate hate. "Sunday mornings on their way upstate, they'd ride past the house. By the dozens. Timmy couldn't take his eyes off them."

"Are you saying your son went with them willingly?"

"I'm saying they abducted him."

"For what purpose?"

"Degeneracy."

Ramsey held his breath against the room's stale, rank, tired smell of urine. The man at the piano pounded heavily on the keys, oblivious—it seemed—to the indifference around him.

"It's in the nature of our society," Oster was saying, his hands spread wide and gripping the table as if he might hurl it across the room. "It's been coming for some time now."

"What has?"

"The laxity, the indulgence, the decay of our moral structure."

"I'm not sure I follow you."

"Since the war, it's been eating us up. The pursuit of the easy life. The obsession with pleasure. You see it in the movies all the time. And it's already all over the TV."

"I'm still not sure I understand."

"Outsiders, villains—all cast as heroes. No wonder our children are being seduced by the false promises of what is being labeled 'freedom.' Without a set of standards, without a moral code, freedom is a danger to us. Nothing but an excuse for irresponsibility."

Oster's knuckles turned white against the table; Ramsey had to keep his weight forward to prevent the table from sliding. "In the center of society there are those who are productive— and on the edge, there are the failures, the riffraff. The failures have nothing to lose so they eat away at what's good, grabbing here, grabbing there, stealing it right from under our eyes. Like vermin picking away at the foundation of a house. So secretive. So . . . relentless."

His eyes bore into Ramsey as if he, of all people, should understand. "One day we're going to wake up to find it all gone: everything we've worked so hard to preserve. This country we love snatched from our hands by sick degenerates."

The exclamatory notes of the piano reached crescendo after crescendo then abruptly ceased. In the silence that followed, Oster's shoulders slumped as though he'd traveled an enormous distance and suddenly realized how exhausted he was.

"Was there a particular gang you thought responsible for your son's disappearance?"

"The Devil's Disciples," Oster said with a contemptuous laugh. "That name. It says it all, doesn't it?"

"Did you tell the police about them?"

"They couldn't find anything substantive." He made the word 'substantive' sound like a sneer. "I hold my wife to blame for this."

"For what?"

"Sending Timmy to that school in the first place. He could have gone to Fieldston, a perfectly fine institution, but she insisted he have a *proper* Catholic education—way the hell over the other side of the Bronx where those creeps hang out. He comes home from school one day talking about how he wants to join them, become a Disciple."

"You say you tried to speak to someone in the gang?"

Oster laughed again, his eyes stalking Ramsey humorlessly. "Wouldn't give me the time of day. Businessman in a Buick. Like *I* was the scum of the earth—" He had worked himself up again to such a state of outrage that he simply fell silent.

"If I learn anything more about Timmy—" The man had crawled so far back inside himself it seemed useless for Ramsey to continue.

He was halfway to the door before he realized he had not once during their talk expressed sorrow for the man's loss. He turned back with the idea of saying something but Oster's eyes were so flat and vacant that he didn't have the heart to approach him again.

At the desk a different young man smiled at him: same clean-cut looks, black ministerial shirt, falsely-inflated smile.

"His peace be with you," the young man called out as Ramsey moved toward the street.

*****

What had Oster said? Something about his son's craving the sordid. *What we crave is the very thing that will destroy us.* Is that what he had meant? Or was that Ramsey's own interpretation of the man's words?

From a street corner phone booth he called Arthur's Aunt Dorothy. She was leaving later that afternoon for the funeral, she told him. Scranton. Where the Farrell side lived.

On her back porch with its view of the Whitestone Bridge, she served him tea and muffins. This was the neighborhood Oster had been talking about, the back roads squeezed between St. Jerome's and Ferry Point. Sal Mineo, the actor, had grown up here, adding an otherwise undeserved hipness to the collection of bungalow-style houses in run-down condition. When he asked her how sexually aware Arthur was, her face pinched around the mouth. She smoothed the hem of her dress and smiled demurely. "I'm not at all sure what you mean."

"I understand this isn't . . . easy." He held her gaze so intently that she stared into her lap like a schoolgirl.

"Oh, dear." Her face blanched. She brushed her bangs back, keeping her hands pressed to her head.

"When we first spoke to you, the day of Arthur's death, you said a boy can't have a normal life without a father. Did you mean a normal *sex* life?"

"God forgive me."

"For what, Miss Campbell?"

"Which is the more unforgivable sin, Detective? To lie, or to betray a trust?"

"That would depend upon the circumstances, I imagine." He waited while she set her cup down and rose with self-conscious deliberation.

"She made me promise," she said, standing at the edge of the porch, her back to him. "She didn't want anything to sully Arthur's name. She wanted—we both did—the boy to rest in peace."

Her thin frame stood in shadow against the screen. Beyond the netting bees hummed under the eaves, a dull and listless sound that made the heat seem more intense. "There was a man he saw," she said softly, addressing the marsh grass still and neon-green in the windless afternoon. "He met him in one of the stairwells. They played some game together."

"What kind of game?"

"He never said. Of course my sister forbade him to see this man. But whenever Arthur was angry with her, he'd taunt her by saying they had played the game together, alone in some secret stairwell."

"*Secret* stairwell?"

"That's what he called it. He had a vivid imagination at times."

"Would the boy have made this person up? To get back at her?"

"Possibly. But she—we—both knew Arthur already had . . . certain tendencies."

"What tendencies, Miss Campbell?"

She turned to him tearfully. "Do I have to spell it out? What you came here to find out, what you thought Arthur might be."

"Did he ever describe this man? Did he say anything about

him?"

"Something about his arms. I don't know. . . ." She hesitated. "I think Arthur told her once he liked looking at his arms."

"He said nothing else about them?"

"Nothing—at least that I'm aware of. And my sister and I have no secrets." She sat down, holding the back of her chair. Her tears had dried, leaving her eyes a cold hard blue. "That's what you came here for, isn't it? That's what you wanted to hear."

He stared at the coppery liquid in his cup. "Forgive me, Miss Campbell. I know how difficult—"

"We're a God-fearing, Catholic family." For a moment her lips formed words soundlessly.

"I understand. . . . When did Arthur first mention this man?"

Her eyes narrowed and she pressed her fingers to her lips. "Three years ago, maybe."

"Not recently?"

"No."

"Is there anything your sister may have held back from you, out of embarrassment or—?"

"My sister and I had no secrets—at least where Arthur was concerned. I told you that."

"Did Arthur ever say anything about feeling unloved?"

She flinched. "Of course not. We showered him with love, Mary and I. Why would you even *suggest* that?"

"It was something his friend said."

"Then he was mistaken." Her face pinched tight as a prune and she glared at him with contempt.

"I imagine he was." He set the cup down. He had never liked tea. It was what his mother had given him as a child when he was ill. "By the way," he said, getting to his feet. "Are there any bikers living in the community here?"

"Bikers?"

"Hell's Angels' types."

"Oh," she said. "Most of them have gone. There are two or three in that corner house on the way in."

He glanced through the curtain but there were no bikes visible in the yard.

Catholic Boys   111

Her eyes judged him harshly. "If you interrogate my sister, she'll deny everything. I guarantee that. And she won't forgive me for telling you. You'll take away the last thing we have. Our trust in one another."

A pressure, a heaviness, had settled behind his eyes. "I wouldn't want to do that, Miss Campbell."

But the rest of what he thought he left unsaid. *Unless I have to.*

That's what it came down to, after all. The desperation that makes us who we are. *Unless I have to.*

What was it Helen had said about him being better than the rest? At another time the humor of that might have made him laugh.

Chapter Nine

"Bad coffee, Eddie, or you're telling me the job sucks?" Ramsey said in response to Falcone's grimace. He had just told him to pull the files of the Baychester workforce: maintenance staff, landscapers, independent contractors, patrolmen.

"What am I looking for? I mean, we've got close to five hundred people on the payroll."

"Who was working here three years ago, for starters. Anybody with access to the tunnels."

"You really know how to lighten a guy's workload."

"What can I say? I don't know what I'm looking for. Somebody with unusual arms."

"Huh?"

"Muscles, maybe. Or tattoos."

"These files aren't going to be much help with that."

Ramsey lit a cigarette and stared blankly at the two secretaries, Gladys and Viola, typing yesterday's patrol reports. "Morales call?"

"Not so far."

The fans at the ends of the office were serving hot air. He felt warmer than he had outside. "You want to get some lunch?"

"Already did, thanks."

"The girls?"

"Them, too. You know it's almost three o'clock, don't you?"

He called Helen's sister in Schenectady who told him Helen was resting. She didn't want to disturb her right now but

Ramsey didn't have to worry, she'd arrived safe and sound; then he phoned the precinct and left a message for Morales to round up a few Devil's Disciples for questioning. On the way out he told Falcone he was going to grab some lunch at the Shimmy.

"I didn't know you hung out there."

"I don't really." He felt he should apologize. "In this heat, you know, it's dark and cool."

"I like it, too. Helps me get through the weekend sometimes. That and the movies."

He realized how little he knew about his co-worker. Only this, really: that he lived alone, had never married; once a week he visited his mother in Brooklyn. Beyond that, he could only make assumptions. On one occasion, rummaging through Falcone's desk in search of a file, Ramsey had come upon a 1957 Brigitte Bardot calendar tucked in the recesses of a bottom drawer. The discovery had made him feel bad for the guy. Maybe because it was hidden away like that. Or because he'd kept it around for three years. Or maybe because our fantasies were so damn far-fetched.

*****

Krissie stood in high heels smiling at him. In the new lighting her blonde hair looked white. Why had he come back? *Why?*

"Too late for lunch?"

"Kitchen's open all afternoon now. The *new* image," she said, hiding a smile. She glanced behind her at a mirror decaled with iridescent moons and stars. A system of shifting-blue-vaporous lights had been installed so that the dancers appeared to be drifting through unearthly realms. "I shouldn't make fun. He's trying, he really is. It's just that—"

"Some things are what they are."

"Exactly."

"Your boss is an ambitious man."

"Oh, yes." A silence fell between them. She smiled awkwardly and shifted her weight on her heels.

"You hear from Brody?"

Philip Cioffari

She hesitated in a way that made him think she was figuring how much to tell him. "He called me, made some threats. Nothing serious."

"What kind of threats?"

"The usual jealous guy kind. No big deal."

"Like what?"

"Oh, I don't know. . . ." She made it sound like the whole thing was routine. "I wouldn't make it on my own, he'd rather see me dead than with somebody else. That sort of thing."

"I don't like the seeing-you-dead part."

Her eyes were bright but noncommittal. "He still thinks I'm gonna come back, so he's not going too crazy yet." She drew her shoulders in resolve. "I'm more worried about my sister."

"I should talk to her."

"She's a good kid, really, though she works hard as hell to hide it. And I'm not much of a mother to her." She bit her lip and forced her eyes to meet his. "I'm surprised you came back here—"

"Just for lunch." Surely his lie must be transparent. But why *had* he come back? Seeing her like this, or even simply thinking of her, he was bombarded with difficult emotion: anger, resentment, outrage, and an odd kind of tenderness as well.

"Here I am blabbing away and you must be starving," she was saying. "Burgers are the best thing we do here. No matter what Leo says about our new *continental* specialties."

"A burger's fine."

"Fries?"

"I'm trying to keep my weight down."

He thought about canceling his order, saying he had to get back to the office—*What the hell was he doing? this woman killed his son!*—but he unfolded the paper Falcone had given him and read the front page headline, A KILLER'S POEMS, above side-by-side photos of the hallway and playground inscriptions. The accompanying caption read, "Within a few miles of Freedomland, the newly opened family entertainment park celebrating the highlights of American history, a violent and sadistic killer stalks a neighborhood at will. . . ."

When she returned with the burger there were four pickles

and a stack of sliced tomatoes on an oblong platter. He pushed the paper away. "Sometimes it's better not to know what people are saying about you."

She frowned as she read the article. "They talk as if the police could have prevented all this. Newspapers shouldn't be allowed to force their views on people. They're supposed to give the facts so you can make up your own mind, not be telling you *what* to think. Or what *they* think. They act as if this one crime will cause the collapse of civilization."

Her vehemence made him think she was talking about something more personal than the shortcomings of journalists. Guys like Brody, perhaps. Pushing her around.

"You wouldn't know it right now, but this case has been great for business. They go out to look at where the boy was killed, then they come in here to forget about it. Crazy, isn't it? My tips—they've doubled this week. I'm thinking, maybe I should give the extra to some kids' charity. I feel so guilty." She caught herself and added quickly, "About the tips, I mean." Then she corrected herself again. "About everything, really. Sometimes I just want to die."

Ramsey worked hard to keep his face free of emotion. She said, "Let me get you some coffee," and turned away quickly.

He pushed the plate aside. It took him a moment to steady himself before making his way toward the door, alarmed at the glimmer of hope he felt in this woman's presence and how absurd that was, under the circumstances.

*****

The sudden white glare blinded him. Hand raised against the sun, he tried to blink away what he saw: two boys running across the street, dodging cars. His heart beat mercilessly; he shouted a warning. They zigzagged through gaps in the traffic and reached the curb safely. These were the boys he had seen before.

"Hey mister, hey mister," the chubby red-haired boy said. "You're one of them detectives, ain't you?"

"That's right."

The boy stared at him wide-eyed, his mouth moving but no

words forming.

"You fellahs should be more careful crossing the street."

It was then, with an unnerving jolt of recognition, that he noticed the second boy. Up close like this, his face was strangely familiar: moon-white skin, large dark eyes, the long silence of his stare; and he realized it was the face of one of the boys in his dream.

"What's your name, son?"

The boy hesitated, then dropped his eyes. "Luke Hutchinson."

"Everyone calls him 'Hutch.' " The chubby one stood with his hands jammed into his pockets, listing toward his friend. "We're not in trouble, are we?"

"No, son, just be more careful. You could get hurt cutting across traffic like that."

"My name's Allie," the boy offered.

"All right, Allie. You two keep an eye on each other, okay?"

Then he was watching them run again, the boy from his dream faster than his overweight friend, until they reached the corner and disappeared around a building, leaving Ramsey alone and confused as if still blinded by the sudden brightness of the sun.

Chapter Ten

Father Shannon came striding across the yard, his wavy blond hair blowing in the breeze, his rugged face as troubled as it was handsome. Next to the bleachers, the track team assembled for their afternoon workout.

"All right, boys, start loosening up." He tried to inject a note of normalcy into his voice; he tried to inject some spirit.

It had been his style to run workouts with a military discipline: insisting they form a straight line, that exercises be performed precisely, enthusiastically. He abhorred sloppiness or laziness. The human form was a thing of beauty and in motion it was at its most beautiful. For two hours each afternoon he had devoted himself to being both custodian and admirer of that beauty.

"Rogers, keep that torso straight—"

"Williams, stretch those legs, *stretch* them—"

"Gunderson, suck in that bell—"

With the roar of parkway traffic behind him, he would pace slowly along the line: a grin of approval here, a scowl of disappointment there. For the thirty-one year old priest, afternoons were for the body, for keeping in shape with his team. At the moment, though, he took no pleasure in the muscled arms and legs of his boys. While they stretched and turned, he stood at the edge of the bleachers. Thinking, helplessly, of Arthur. Poor sad Arthur.

If only the boy hadn't been so willing, so needy. If only his

Philip Cioffari

pale tender skin had not been so irresistible. If only God had given his servant the strength. . . .

How he had tried to break it off. Lord Jesus knows, he had tried. Saturday night. Telling the boy they couldn't meet in secret again: that it was over between them. Over.

It's breaking my heart, he'd told the boy, *to do this breaks my heart. But one day you'll thank me. You will, Arthur, you will. For saving your immortal soul.*

He thought the boy understood, thought he accepted it, until he showed up again Sunday night: persistent martyr to Shannon's lust, standing so close, as if to say: *Do with me, Father, what you will. Do with me. . . .*

Thick clouds had moved in, cooling the air down enough to work the boys hard, work *himself* hard. If only he could ignore that face, the pleading eyes as he stood outside the residence Sunday night. He had taken the boy into the stillness of the orphanage basement to talk, only to talk: words, endless empty words ringing in the silence, explaining what couldn't be explained until it was no longer his mouth that was talking to the boy but his hands, his body—one last time.

"Father Shannon," a voice called from behind him. "Father Shannon. We gonna work out today, or what?"

In their gym shorts and jerseys, they stood around listless and dispirited, watching him. "Yes," he said, working hard to muster conviction in his voice. "Full workout today."

He stripped off his sweatshirt and joined them. What else could he do but forget and move forward? The Lord would want him to, surely. He had work to do, *God's* work. What was an occasional transgression amid a mountain of achievements? A man should be judged on the overall effect of his life, shouldn't he? Surely the good he had done more than outweighed the evil. Hadn't God, in His way, confirmed that fact? Why else would He have taken Arthur like that, sparing Shannon further opportunities to damn his immortal soul?

If only he could forget. If only forgetting were a function of will.

Simple stretching exercises first: touching toes, reaching for the sky, bending left and then right. Squat-thrusts, push-ups, sit-ups, leg kicks. He divided the team into groups—milers, half-milers, quarter milers, sprinters—then ran wind sprints with them on the straight-aways. Legs and arms pumping. The blur. The hiss of cinder flying from his shoes. He liked the quick, hard rush, heat rising from within, the smear of sweat on skin. Jog the curve, sprint the straight-aways. Jog, then sprint. Again. Again. Heart pounding, lungs screaming for air, Arthur's voice the faint but persistent whisper he was running from: *I feel safe with you, Father, I feel safe.*

*****

He stood near the bleachers, hands on hips, breathing hard from his final sprint and watching the new boy, Hutch, running with the milers. The boy had long, spindly legs; with his uneven, tentative stride he reminded Shannon of a frisky colt. Still developing, a long way to go, but a possible replacement for Reilly, who was graduating. Like many of the first year boys he hadn't quite accepted St. Jerome's yet, attached as he was to his old neighborhood, still spending most of his after school time there, but Shannon sensed a determination in him that, if developed, would serve him well as a distance runner.

He was drying himself with a towel when he noticed a man in a dark suit coming across the yard. A book salesman, a cleric, or a police detective. No one else would dress like that in this weather.

"How's the team doing this year?" Ramsey asked when he drew near, patting his face with a hanky.

The priest's defenses stiffened. He felt his anger flare. Arthur had, in the end, betrayed his trust. With Seward, most likely. And Seward had gone to the police. Or maybe he was jumping the gun. This might simply be a fishing expedition. "Our mile relay brings us some medals." He spoke with a cool reserve, his voice raised above the constant, rushing noise of traffic. "Our sprinters and middle distance runners, well, they're still developing."

"Did you know Arthur Farrell well?"

The Prefect had warned him about this man. *How much did he know?* "What do you mean by *well*?"

"Was there anyone here at school who might have had it in

120   Philip Cioffari

for him? Mike Brody, perhaps?"

"Brody is a bit of a problem," Shannon conceded.

"Did he ever threaten to kill anyone?"

"Not that I heard. Though it wouldn't in the least surprise me if he had." He was not good at this: thinking quickly, defensively. But why not at least raise the possibility? Anything that might turn the spotlight from himself.

"Were there other boys—or teachers perhaps—who picked on Arthur? Was there a reason he might have felt unloved?"

"Arthur was a . . . solitary boy." He considered his response. He would be truthful, to a point. Lies of omission, he believed, were less sinful than overt falsehoods. "And sometimes that provokes boys his age to—" He watched his milers come around the far turn. In a few minutes he would begin timing them. Soon as he could rid himself of this meddlesome man.

"To what, Father?"

"To respond with aggression."

Ramsey patted his face again. The sun glared off the hard-packed dirt beyond the track. He had been meaning to buy another pair of sunglasses but hadn't gotten around to it. "This Saint Sebastian thing Arthur belonged to. Is that affiliated with the Diocesan honor society at St. Patty's?"

"No relation. The Order of Saint Sebastian is a club here at St. Jerome's. For our more spiritually minded boys."

"You're in charge?"

Shannon blushed. "Yes. I founded it when I was assigned here."

"How does a boy get involved in the Order?"

"By invitation."

"Yours?"

"That's right."

"Are there certain criteria you use?"

"Naturally." He spoke more curtly than he had intended. Who was this man to grill him about sacred matters? "The boy must possess a certain level of spiritual awareness, a willingness to spend time in prayer and meditation. Not everyone—"

"Of course, Father. I understand." Ramsey held the hanky to his forehead. "Do you remember a Timothy Oster? Several years back—"

"Most certainly. He was a disciple, too."

"A biker?"

Shannon looked confused. "A Disciple of the order of Saint Sebastian. That's what we call ourselves."

"Oh," Ramsey said, squinting into the sun. "So you knew him fairly well then?"

"Fairly well."

"Was he an unhappy child? Did he say anything about not getting along at home or with his friends?"

"Not that I can remember. Why?"

"There was some talk that perhaps he had run away."

"Yes, that's what we thought at the time. There seemed no other likely explanation."

"Kidnapping, Father. There's always *that* possibility." He spoke more harshly than he had intended, but the priest's naïveté—or disingenuousness—irked him. That and his Hollywood looks. Pretty boys had an unfair advantage in this world; he wouldn't cut them any slack. He wiped his damp hanky across his brow to regain his composure. "Would you mind terribly, Father, if I attended one of your Sebastian meetings?"

Shannon's face blanched but he recovered quickly. "We don't allow visitors. Our meetings are more like small retreats—prayer and sacrifice. Our emphasis is on reflection, the internal life. We make every effort to eliminate—"

"I promise you I won't be a distraction."

The priest hesitated. His instinct was to insist on privacy. In support he might cite school tradition, church history, the sanctity of prayer. If he refused the man access, though, wouldn't it appear he had something to hide? He didn't like Ramsey at all. He didn't like his grim-faced scrutiny. "There's one this evening, if you're free," he said without the slightest bit of encouragement.

As Ramsey crossed the track he noticed Luke Hutchinson among the handful of boys running the straight-away. He stopped to watch him pass the way a motorist might observe with bewilderment a roadside accident. There was no plea in the boy's face as there had been in the dream; rather, it was contorted with physical strain as he struggled to keep pace

Philip Cioffari

with his teammates. He raised his hand in a wave but Hutch did not see him.

When he crossed the yard he found Father O'Malley, his broad face deep in scowl, waiting for him near the school building. "Our policy here, sir, is that all visitors must first register with the office. We enforce it strictly."

Ramsey offered a cigarette, but the priest declined. "My apologies, Father. I happened to see Father Shannon right there on the field—"

The priest's head bobbed mechanically. "Yes, yes, of course. But we have the safety of our students to consider, you see. If anyone could simply walk onto campus—"

"Apologies again, Father. And in advance, for tonight."

The Prefect stared at him as if he'd been made the butt of a joke. His eyes bulged in his fleshy face. "I don't follow you."

"Father Shannon," Ramsey explained, taking a childish pleasure in the priest's discomfort. "He's invited me to the Saint Sebastian ceremony this evening."

The priest's blue-grey eyes registered blatant hostility. "Well, tonight then—" He turned abruptly toward the building but Ramsey stopped him. "By the way, Father, you wouldn't happen to know if they cut up rats in your bio classes—"

"Rats?" the priest said. "They use guinea pigs and frogs for dissection, if that's what you mean. Never heard of anyone using rats."

*****

A believer in mysticism, Ramsey was not. He had never gone in for fortune tellers, card readers, that sort of thing. Nor did he believe in the prescience of dreams. But there were eighty-two hundred children in Baychester, why did Luke Hutchinson's face attach itself to his dream?

Coincidence, most likely.

On the way back to his office he nearly convinced himself of that. But when he scanned the list of children who lived in building 5, Luke Hutchinson's name was among them. Was that coincidence, as well?

He mentioned his name to Falcone but decided not to say

anything about the dream. "Same physical type as Arthur Farrell and Timothy Oster. I thought I might keep an eye on him." As soon as he said that, he felt foolish. "Along with all the others, of course."

Making the rounds, he passed the North playground where a TV crew was filming the scrawled message for the evening news. On the paved ball field he stopped briefly to watch a father teaching his son to pitch.

Someone screamed so sharply it lifted above the general din and he jerked his head around to see a girl on a skate box colliding with the fence, her screams tinged now with delight rather than fear; but her piercing cry had unnerved him, jolted him back to harsh reality: from any window in the long arc of buildings a killer's eyes might be staring.

Chapter Eleven

Outside Donald Seward's building, the Brando's waited. Mornings, afternoons. Before school, after school. He used the basement halls to travel building to building, so they wouldn't see him enter or leave. Sometimes he took the sky route, jumping roof to roof till he was far enough away to descend to the street unnoticed. At school he stayed away from the bathroom, never went into the schoolyard unless there was a teacher present. It was like living undercover, like the rat they said he was: hallways, basements, stairwells: sneaking place to place, shadow to shadow.

After school he came home, did his chores, told his mother he was going out. Be back for dinner, she said, but he had a St. Sebastian meeting at 7:30 and didn't want the Brando's to follow him, so he told her he'd eat at school, then left before she could protest. At the hall window he checked the street, decided which route he'd take to slip past his enemies.

Four hours to kill before the St. Sebastian meeting.

He rode the subway all the way to Coney—where he walked past rides that whipped and twisted and turned—all stalled in pre-season midweek suspension.

Killing time before time killed him.

The subway again. Motion was salvation. Dyre Avenue, Pelham Bay, Bedford Park Boulevard, Woodlawn, Wakefield/ 241st Street. But even moving fast like that, moving non-stop, he couldn't escape the images from his dreams: being chased through empty, lonely streets; being held under black river water where he couldn't breathe. Always he heard voices, whispers, someone close behind, gaining on him.

When the train crossed the river the clock on the St. Jerry's tower read seven o'clock. Half-hour to go. The meeting, then Confession—where he would ask God's forgiveness. Then he would confess again—to Detective Ramsey. Tell him everything.

Looking down right then at the black curl of the river he saw the tree where Arthur hung. Only it was himself hanging there, head jerked sideways above the noose, face bloated, eyes bulging and dripping blood. He blinked away the vision, but the truth remained.

There was no end to the ways he could die. Because sewer rats died as they lived. Like trash.

*****

"Martyrdom is the noblest sacrifice a mortal being can make for his God," Father Shannon said from the altar of St. Jerome chapel. "It is the way we become most like Him, He who martyred himself for all mankind." Behind him a near-naked and bloodied Christ with shimmering skin seemed to ascend above the altar.

Brutality breeds brutality. The thought came unbidden to Ramsey sitting in the rear of the chapel. If you thrust an image like this at young boys, you divide their world immediately into two camps, don't you? Victims and abusers. Bullies and pansies. Choose your sides, guys. What's it gonna be?

An oversimplification, to be sure, but he wondered if as a theory of schoolyard behavior it was not entirely without merit.

Shannon's eyes seemed lost and unfocused but there was no uncertainty in his voice, a theatrical voice, well-modulated and resonant. His hair fell in a perfect wave across his eyes and he brushed it back with a careful, self-conscious gesture. "We take our strength and inspiration from the sacrificial victims of all ages but particularly the early Christian martyrs, among

Philip Cioffari

them our namesake, St. Sebastian himself, born in Gaul three hundred years after the death of Our Savior, whose dying words were 'Let me follow the example of the suffering of my God.' As an officer of the imperial guard in Rome under the emperor Diocletian he was a highly visible public figure, a man whose life was rich with the comforts and blessings of this world. Nonetheless it was his private life that consumed him: the forbidden worship of the Lord God in hidden places, cemeteries and caves and secret gardens. It was his faith that he lived for."

Ramsey had expected something more along the lines of Leviticus: an eye for an eye, a tooth for a tooth. The harsh, old testament God had been the centerpiece of his own Catholic upbringing. Though the more he listened to the priest's rendering of Sebastian's life—how he was tortured for his beliefs, left for dead, resuscitated by a kindly stranger and eventually sentenced to death a second time—the more Ramsey saw this as a disguised version of the same penchant for bloodletting and pain.

Shannon moved along the altar rail, eying each of the five disciples before him. "What makes Sebastian unique among the martyrs of Christ," he said, his voice swelling to fill the chapel's dim recesses, "was that he was given the chance to die *not once but twice* for his God. Rather than try to escape, Sebastian offered himself to his pursuers willingly, so passionately devoted to Christ was he that he could not bear to miss the chance of dying a violent death for His sake. And this time his martyrers were successful, battering him to death with sticks and clubs."

It occurred to Ramsey that this was how the priest might see himself: a rescuer of lost boys, a nurse who would heal their wounds, restore them to the world that had rejected them. But once he had "restored" them to the world, what then? Did he find satisfaction in watching them suffer a "second death" for Christ? Did he leave them on their own to sink or swim? Or was he, Ramsey, simply pushing the analogy too far?

He watched emotion flood the priest's cheeks with color. He watched him blink away his tears. A wave of hair fell glamorously across his eyes again and he brushed it back with the same careful, self-conscious motion. "As true disciples of Sebastian that is what we must do: die for Christ over and over again, as often as we are called by the Lord.

"Though the cause of Arthur's tragic death is still a mystery to us," he continued, "there is no mystery about his devotion to Our Lord, the example he set as a young suffering Christian—" He interrupted himself, overwhelmed it seemed by his own words. In a quivering voice, he said, "Let us pray for Arthur's immortal soul. Our Father who . . ."

He raised his hand to display a shiny gold cross. He brought the cross with its emblematic arrow to his lips and kissed it.

*****

Ramsey's lie detector had gone off again and again. Surely the artfully falling hair and the mannered gestures seemed too stylized. There was something more, too. It was *what* he said, not just how he said it—the seductive appeal to the dispossessed and disenfranchised. If you're persecuted or abused, embrace your suffering willingly for Christ—instead, Ramsey thought, of doing something constructive to improve your situation. Sacrifice rather than initiate. The end result? A congregation of lonely, silent sufferers in need of help. Was that why there were only five disciples present? Or did that have more to do with Shannon's criteria for choosing them?

Shannon had already entered one of the confessionals. The Disciples—thin, brown-haired boys—lined up for confession with him or Father O'Malley. For the first time Ramsey could see their faces. Donald Seward was one of them. And so was Luke Hutchinson.

*****

"I didn't tell the police things I should have," Donald whispered during his confession a few minutes later. "I was too ashamed."

Father O'Malley shifted his massive shoulders and leaned toward the screen. Please Lord, he prayed, don't let this be what I fear it is. "What things, son?"

"Things I know, the night he died. Things I saw."

"What, son, specifically?"

"He didn't go to the movies like he said. He came here to see Father Shannon."

"How do you know that?"

"I followed him."

"Did you actually *see* him with Father Shannon?"

"In the orphanage. Through the window. They were holding hands. Then they had their arms around each other. Like they were dancing."

"Is that all you saw?"

"They moved away. It was dark. I couldn't see."

"You mustn't assume things, son. Father was most likely comforting your friend. He was a troubled boy in some ways, was he not?"

"I saw the Brando's too, in Brody's car. They were parked near the gate, waiting for Arthur to come out. But I was mad at him and I was jealous. I wanted to hurt him. So I didn't warn him. I went home instead. I knew they were going to hurt him, but I didn't warn him, I didn't—"

"All right, son, all right," the priest interrupted. The grim set of his mouth seemed locked in place forever. "I understand that you feel some responsibility, but this . . . information . . . is . . . general . . . and based upon nothing more than supposition. It's nothing that will help the police. And it may cause harm to others who are innocent, like Father Shannon. And even yourself. You don't want to hurt innocent people, do you? You don't want to hurt yourself or Father Shannon, do you?"

"No, Father."

"Because that would be morally wrong and I would have to deny you absolution for your sins. You wouldn't want me to do that, would you?"

"No, Father. But it was a mortal sin what I did. Not warning him."

"I will absolve you of your sins. All of them. If—*if* you keep these matters we spoke of between yourself and Almighty God. That's what the sacrament of Confession is for. Leave this matter in His hands."

Catholic Boys

*****

The school yard stretched away from Ramsey, eerily still except for the hum of parkway traffic. He wasn't sure why he was hanging around—maybe because the brevity of the meeting had surprised him, left him unsatisfied, though exactly what he had expected he couldn't say.

He walked along the tree-lined driveway and found Donald Seward sitting in his car. "I need a ride," the boy said.

He drove slowly down the hill. The boy sat with his arms crossed, turned away from him.

"Was there something you wanted to tell me?"

"Brody's gonna get me."

"The police are keeping an eye on him."

"He's sneaky."

"If he bothers you, tell me."

He swung onto the entrance ramp of the parkway; they drove in silence above the grassland and the river. "Why do you think Father Shannon chose you to be a Disciple?"

"He thinks I'm holy."

"Aren't you?"

"Sometimes."

Ramsey laughed but the boy didn't join him. When they reached his building, Donald said "Thanks" and left the car quickly. He had already disappeared inside when Ramsey noticed the notebook on the seat. It took him a moment to realize—he had turned off the engine and was about to go after the boy—that the book had been left there intentionally.

*****

He used the car's dome light to read through the twenty pages of scribbled notes. Dreams, he thought at first, the kid's describing his dreams; but he decided some of the stuff might actually have happened. Like the trips up to the school at night, waiting for Arthur at the gate—too many specific details for it not to be true. The long passages describing Farrell in minute detail revealed more of a secret obsession

130   Philip Cioffari

than a normal friendship. Seward clearly had a crush on the kid. The boy's account stopped with Arthur's Saturday night visit to Shannon. Seward wrote: "I see Arthur coming down the hill now. Walking fast, like he does sometimes when he's mad about something or very very upset. . . ." After that entry the pages were blank.

At the office he called Morales who rattled off the day's highlights from his end: *One:* the graphologist had officially determined there were two discrete message writers. *Two:* the Disciples' interrogation was a bust, as Ramsey thought it would be. In his disordered state, Oster had gotten his disciples confused. *Three:* the Catholic Honor society business, the Cardinal's pride and joy, failed to yield anything new about Farrell: he was a quiet kid, didn't say much at the meetings, no close friends, yadda yadda yadda. *Four:* No luck at the fag bars. And *Five:* The foreman at the Department of Pest Control said there wasn't much chance an employee could stockpile rats without being noticed, unless he was making midnight visits to the dump at Fresh Kills. As to draining their blood for an ink supply, he found it hard to believe one of his workers would bother. They hate the damn buggers too much, he told Morales.

Ramsey drew on a cigarette and wondered aloud if the man they were looking for was thinking sex or murder that night.

"Who the hell knows what a sick fuck like that thinks?"

"That's it? A sick fuck. That's our profile?"

Morales grunted in disgust, as if it was Ramsey's fault he had to scavenge the bowels of such a twisted mind. "Guy's full of rage, probably all his life. Doesn't know why. Something got fucked up a long way back. Hates himself, but loves little boys. Buys dirty magazines, anything with kids in them; hangs around parks, playgrounds, public rest rooms. Watching boys pee gets him hard. Maybe does himself in one of the stalls, thinkin' about some twelve year old's pole in his mouth. Sex is dirty, *real* dirty. Maybe he gets so disgusted with himself after he comes that . . . what? He pukes? Or maybe he doesn't come. Maybe he holds back until he can't take it anymore and it all comes boiling up, the sex, the rage, the guilt. He's got to get off by killing some kid 'cause that's the only way he can purge himself." He caught his breath and said, "How am I doing?"

*****

Ramsey worked side by side with his assistant, going through the files of Baychester employees. The place smelled of old coffee and dried-out pizza, the air—for all the fury of the fans—only marginally cooler than outside. Finally the names and the details began to blur, became one seamless fabric without beginning or end.

"Don't know about you, Eddie, but I'm starting to lose it here."

"You go," Falcone said, getting up for more coffee. "I'm gonna stay a while."

"You don't like to sleep like the rest of us?"

"*Can't* sleep. It's not that I wouldn't like to."

"Cut down on the caffeine."

"It's not the caffeine." He held up an orange packet of Sanka to make his point.

"You see a doctor?"

"Oh, yeah! I've got enough pills to keep me asleep for a year. Sometimes I take them. Trouble is," he said, coming back to his desk, setting the cup gingerly on the blotter scarred end to end with coffee rings, "they work on the symptom not the cause."

"So what's the cause?"

Falcone sipped from his cup, thinking it over. "Gets quiet like this, I don't have something to do, I start to worry—that's what. Weird stuff, you know, 'bout being alone and dying, about my mother, what's gonna happen to her, what's gonna happen to me. Maybe I'd be better off with a wife."

Ramsey took a long drag on his Viceroy, exhaling slowly. "I'm not the person to ask right now."

"Then I think, what if I turn out like my old man, beating up on her?"

"You're not that kind of guy, Eddie."

"That's what I tell myself, but who knows? Who really knows?" He stopped and studied Ramsey's face. "You ever think like that? You ever think maybe that's what keeps us

Philip Cioffari

going—the fact that we *don't* know, the *hope* that we're not the murderers or rapists or brutalizers we're afraid we might be."

Ramsey laughed uneasily. He'd figured Falcone was a pressure cooker, stuff boiling up inside, but he'd never seen the lid come off, even a little bit.

Falcone said, "I keep on like this you're gonna think *I* knocked the kid off."

*****

At the Shimmy he was surprised to find Leo on the back steps, lighting up a pipe with a curved stem. His hair was oiled and he looked particularly elegant this evening: black tux, shiny new shoes.

"Didn't know you smoked, Leo."

"Tonight, it is a special night for me." He nodded at the new iridescent-blue *Wild Moon* sign over the door, then at the real moon, nearly full. "A good omen, don't you think?"

"For us all, I hope."

"Forgive me for thinking so selfishly, Detective." He bowed in apology. "As always, your generosity of spirit exceeds that of a humble businessman like myself."

Inside at the bar Ramsey nursed a beer. Krissie had taken the night off—family troubles, according to Leo. The place, despite its recent make-over, seemed dull without her. On the platform a dancer in pigtails had undone her Catholic school girl's costume: white blouse and tartan plaid skirt. In a cotton bra and panties she slithered around the runway pole.

For a while his mind drifted with the music and the motion of the dancers. He felt vaguely aroused. Maybe it was the image of the Catholic school girl: ancient fantasies resurrected. Then, abruptly it seemed the music cut off and the dancers vanished; the platform went dark. Through the thinning crowd he noticed Krissie sipping a drink and his mood lifted.

"Everything all right?" he asked.

She forced a smile. "It was *that* kind of a night."

"What kind?"

"The kind you want to forget."

"You want to talk about it?"

"I'm nothing but trouble, you know that."

"We're both in trouble," he said.

She fingered the rim of the glass. "All right. Not here, though."

"My sister," she said in the parking lot. "She won't stay away from Brody. When she moved in with me, we had this agreement: she was supposed to do what I told her. But now I've become the mother we were trying to get away from—at least that's how Nina sees me." She leaned against the Packard and held a cigarette at her side. "Everything she does is to spite me."

"She with Brody Sunday night?"

"Says she wasn't."

He took a drag on his cigarette before flicking it away. "Let's talk to her."

*****

Ramsey made his way through the trees, saw the girl bent over the hood of the rotting Studebaker, Brody in the process of yanking down her shorts, her head turned back to him, her voice sounding like her sister's—slightly hoarse and sweet at the same time—saying, "Not that way, honey, not that way *please*." He flashed the light full in Brody's face.

"Fuck you doing, man?" Brody said.

Whimpering, the girl moved away from the car, buttoning her shorts. She was smaller than her sister, her hair longer, darker, curlier, her makeup heavier. Her tight clothes left nothing to the imagination. "Stay the hell away from me," she told Ramsey.

Brody, steely-eyed, his face still bruised, stepped between them. "The fuck outta here, man."

Ramsey shoved the flashlight so deep into the kid's neck the light was swallowed by the folds of his skin. "You don't back off, son, you're looking at sodomy charges with a minor."

"Mikey," the girl whimpered, "don't let him take me," but Brody stepped to the side and Ramsey grabbed her arm. "Chat time, darling," he said, pulling her with him up the hill.

Philip Cioffari

In the car she wouldn't give her sister in the back seat the courtesy of a look. "I knew it was you," she hissed between clenched teeth.

"It's *you*," Ramsey said. "The friends you keep."

"That's my business."

"Not anymore."

Nina turned halfway in her seat and sneered at her sister. "She's jealous that Mike wants *me* now."

"Were you with him Sunday night?"

"What if I was?"

"Were you?"

She smiled triumphantly at her sister. "A while, yeah."

"When?"

"I don't know. Early."

"Seven? Eight? When?"

"Eight, maybe. We hung out here."

"Then?"

"I went for a walk."

"Where?"

"The Boulevard. By myself."

"Anybody see you?"

"How should I know?" She dug in her purse for a cigarette, reached across the dash for the lighter then turned toward the open window and blew smoke into the warm air.

"So you never saw Brody with Arthur Farrell?"

"They were talking when I left."

"Just talking?"

"Yeah."

"Who lit the fire?"

"Some of the guys, why? Just havin' fun."

Ramsey gave her a long, disappointed look. The hard-shell of her face stared back with indifference. She turned away, drew hard on her cigarette and let the smoke curl from her mouth without exhaling. There wasn't much about her that inspired trust. "And when you came back from your walk?"

"They were gone."

"Farrell, too?"

She turned her small hard face to him and smirked. "I wasn't lookin' for *him*."

Catholic Boys   135

"Did Brody ever say he was out to get Farrell?"

"Not that I heard."

"You know," Ramsey said, "work farms aren't much fun."

She dangled her arm out the window, flicked her cigarette and smirked again. "Can't be worse than livin' with *her.*"

He looked back at Krissie, who raised her eyes and cocked her head in Nina's direction. Her expression said *See, told you.*

Before taking them home, he drove the streets of Baychester one last time.

"Putting the neighborhood to bed," Krissie said.

He liked the sound of that. Putting the neighborhood to bed. Turning out the lights for all his children.

*****

He stood outside his two-story brick house with its fenced yard, its crabapple trees and overgrown garden. He imagined the occupants of the house as if they were strangers to him, figures from a dream or some long ago past, as if he had wandered by accident onto their street, into their dream, the Ramseys' dream, a family he once knew but hadn't seen in years. Would he knock on their door? Or would he pass by, leaving them to their own devices, abandoning them to the past they no longer shared? The thought that he might simply move on in search of some other resting place chilled him, made him feel as remote and detached as the street lamp's cold blue light falling on the yard where once a child had played.

When he entered the house, the phone was ringing. He thought it might be Helen calling to see how he was and rushed to answer it, holding the receiver to his ear, Falcone's voice telling him Donald Seward was missing. He'd never made it home.

Chapter Twelve

THURSDAY

"Someone was here to see you." Father Benedict's words stopped the Prefect as he climbed the stairs to the priests' residence. He gripped the handrail for balance. It was as if the words had stopped his heart as well. *Someone was here to see you.*

"Who?" he managed to ask.

"Some fellow." Father Benedict sat on the porch, peeling potatoes. On the floor a metal bucket held the skinned results: pale, moist and quartered. Since his stroke his hair had gone white. His movements were slower, his memory for details—other than regarding his garden duties—far from complete. "Didn't say much."

"Did he say *anything*?"

"Not that I recall. Said you'd be expecting him, that's all." The old priest smiled his gracious, empty smile. "I invited him to stay, but he said he'd rather come back."

"When?"

"When *what*?"

"Did he say when he'd be back?" He spread his words out slowly, as if talking to a child.

"Later," Father Benedict said, dropping the quartered

sections of another potato into the bucket.

The word hung like a threat in the air. *Later*

"Thank you, Ben." The Prefect drew a breath as if to gather his strength, hoisted himself over the remaining stairs and crossed the porch. His heart had come back to life with a vengeance, pounding his chest hard; he felt an odd chill despite the heat. He knew it was not the police this time.

When the detectives had arrived early with news of Seward's disappearance, he held out vain hope the boy might surface, that his absence was temporary. But as the morning wore on, his hope gave way to dread. *It was happening again.* Arthur's death had been the warning knell—though he had tried to convince himself that a hanging death did not fit the all-too-familiar pattern. The others had vanished without a trace; secrecy, not public display, had been the key. Yet the first tremors of panic had begun to rattle his nerves. And now this: Donald Seward. The signs made it clear: the nightmare of the past *was* repeating itself.

In his room the stagnant air nearly choked him. He poured a double scotch and drew a bath. He was exhausted. . . .

All day it seemed he'd been defending either himself or Martin: first with the police, assuring them that his colleague had remained on campus all day Sunday, that he'd been in his room from ten p.m. on, he could swear to that, *would* swear to it in writing; then off and on throughout the morning, fielding questions from the press and after that at Diocesan headquarters where he'd been called to an emergency meeting. That meeting of the Diocesan Board had been like a tribunal—the gravity of the situation underscored by the Cardinal's presence. Questions were raised: about the school, *his* school.

In its orphanage days when he was a teacher there, the late 40s and early 50s, St. Jerome's was constantly running afoul of the state board of inspectors—health violations, low academic test scores and performance, high truancy rates. A close friend of the Cardinal, an inept monsignor named Cornelius Shea, ran things. In deference to the Cardinal, so the rumors went, the Diocesan Board voted to close the orphanage rather than replace the monsignor. The problem then was what to do with the campus and its buildings. A year later St. Jerome's rose from the ashes as a junior high and high school extension of the Church of the Precious Blood grade school. It would be a day school, no more dormitory students, with O'Malley as its prefect. He had called in every favor owed him to get that position.

At that time—six years ago—he'd been charged, the members of the Diocesan Board today reminded him, to make Jerome's a showplace for Catholic education in the Bronx. Events of the past several days were hardly what they had in mind. In his defense, he reiterated what he hoped was obvious: these were things beyond his control. There was nothing that he, personally, could have done to prevent them. Nothing.

On that point the Board members were noncommittal. They did, however, express interest in Martin Shannon. It had come to their attention, through various sources, that he grew overly fond of his students, that he became "entangled" in their private lives, perhaps to a degree that was not prudent.

He offered a blanket denial: Father Shannon was a dedicated and passionate teacher. He was involved with his students, yes, but for the best and most noble of reasons, because he cared deeply about them. He was, in fact, the most effective member of his teaching staff. In any event, he had already spoken to Father Shannon, stressing the importance, the *necessity*, of avoiding even the most remote appearance of impropriety.

Still, one of the Board members insisted it might be best "for all concerned," if—under the circumstances—Father Shannon were to be considered for transfer outside the Diocese.

Dread had descended upon him like a blackening cloud; he could not imagine life without Martin Shannon. He told the board he could handle the matter, he *would* handle the matter. He would gladly speak of the Board's concern. Father Shannon would understand. He was a reasonable man. An honorable man.

It was then that the Cardinal broke his silence, rubbing his eyes as if they caused him great pain, finally looking directly at O'Malley and speaking in a measured but unflinching voice. "I believe you understand the gravity of the situation. We cannot afford to have St. Jerome's again become an embarrassment, or worse. I don't want to jump the gun here but—" He stopped himself to remove his wire spectacles and rub his eyes again. "I'm counting on you, Toby. Let's leave it at that for now."

Certainly, Your Eminence. Most certainly. He had not labored so exhaustively these many years to throw it away now. He would not jeopardize his chances for advancement in the hierarchy. Not if he could help it. By God, no.

*****

He soaked in the tub until his fingers and toes turned white, his thoughts pitching like a boat in heavy seas. If every moment in a man's life can be reduced to a central dilemma, then his right now was the narrow path he would have to walk between his ambition and the sins of his past. *O Martin, how I've loved you. More than you know. So much more.* And his unwelcome visitor: how he had loved him, too.

The metal rail steadied him as he rose from the tepid water and he stood there wheezing, water dripping from the flabby body he had come to despise, his sex small and flaccid. Stepping from the tub he lost his balance, legs gone out from under him, hands reaching for and missing the rim of the sink, his over-sized body twisting and thrashing as it hit the floor, bringing with it the empty highball glass that splintered across the black-and-white floor tiles.

He lay on his side, heaving like a toppled rhino.

It took him another fifteen minutes to right himself, to dab Mercurochrome on both feet where the glass had cut him, and to dress himself. He took a new bottle of scotch from his cabinet and left the room. His feet hurt him as he walked; he wondered if he had cleaned out all the glass.

In the kitchen he informed Father Benedict that he would not be having dinner with them as usual, then he carried the bottle out to the porch and sat facing the river, waiting for his visitor to return.

*****

Morales found three missing children cases similar to

Philip Cioffari

Oster's: a twelve year old, Carl Nordstrom, last seen June 12, 1952 on his way home from Holy Angels Academy in Franklin Lakes, New Jersey; an eleven year old, Richard Rizzo, last seen July 20, 1955 in a park near Suffern, New York; and a ten year old, Lionel Hayes, missing from a playground in Garden City, Long Island, August 16, 1956. Each vanished without a trace, body never found.

To that legacy they could now add Donald Seward. Vanished. No trace. And he, Ramsey, was last to see him alive. The boy had been safe in his car, and he had let him go. Of course, he couldn't have known, but he beat up on himself anyway, frustrated by a morning of prowling the boy's building and coming up empty-handed. "Nada," he told Morales when he stopped by the station, mid-afternoon. "Nada por nada."

They left it that Morales would follow up with the local PD's. Ramsey would talk to the victims' parents.

He checked first on the New Jersey kid, Nordstrom, but ran into a dead-end. Six months after the disappearance his parents moved to San Francisco, and six months after that they split up. On the day their divorce came through, after a farewell lunch together, they were killed in a car accident. So Ramsey spoke on the phone with the only surviving relative, the maternal grandmother, a seventy-four year old woman suffering from some form of senile dementia. When he asked her about Carl, she rambled on about a house in the country with a white picket fence and a rose garden with long wooden trellises.

He spoke next to Thomas Rizzo, owner of a restaurant called La Bella Napoli in Suffern, who told him, "I have four beautiful children, I have a successful business, I have more than I thought I would ever have in this world, but I can't forget the one that's missing." His son vanished in the woods of Harriman Park, where he went every Saturday to play with friends: a soldier's game they called 'hunt down the enemy.' When it was Richie's turn to hide, he said, his friends couldn't find him. They searched and searched.

At one point in the conversation his wife, Angela, took the phone. "You think he was murdered like that boy in the Bronx. That's why you called, isn't it?"

"There's likely no connection at all, Mrs. Rizzo. More like leaving no stone unturned."

"She wants to buy a plot, have a service," Thomas Rizzo said, returning to the phone. His voice sounded even more helpless than when he spoke directly about his son. "But that's crazy, isn't it? We don't know anything for sure. There's still a chance, isn't there—?"

Ramsey had to make several calls before reaching Vernon Hayes, a history prof at L.I.U. In response to Ramsey's question about the playground where Lionel was last seen, the man began slowly, saying *yes*, he went there regularly, and *yes*, at the time there was a large tract of undeveloped woodland nearby which had since become a Sears shopping mall. *Yes*, he was a solitary boy; he often played alone. *No*, there was no older man he was friendly with, so far as he knew. "It was a rainy day," Vernon Hayes added before Ramsey hung up. "That's why there were no witnesses. Lionel shouldn't have even been allowed out that day, but he insisted"—and here the man's rich baritone voice broke momentarily—"so we gave in against our will."

"You don't look so good," Falcone said when Ramsey came in for coffee.

"This creep we're looking for. He's a stalker."

Falcone grunted. "Which just makes it a little bit uglier, doesn't it."

He sipped the coffee and grimaced. "I don't know how the hell you stand this stuff, Eddie."

"Hold your nose, swallow fast."

*****

Track practice was cancelled, so Luke Hutchinson left school after class at 3:15. The day had been filled with the commotion of photographers and reporters until Father O'Malley ordered them off-campus and locked the gates. In the yard at lunchtime there were all kinds of Seward stories. The main theory was: he'd run off because he didn't want Brody to get him. Guys were betting quarters he'd show up in a day or two. Hutch, though, thought he should go to confession in case he was next on the killer's list. "What's to confess?" Allie said in the hallway outside the chapel. "Let's just get the hell out of here."

At the bus stop Allie started in about how Drysdale was better than Ford any day. He came from Brooklyn and still liked the Bums even though they were gone to L.A. *Any* day, he said for emphasis.

"He is not," Hutch said.

"Is too. Nobody's got a better fastball."

"He plays dirty. He throws at the batter's head."

"Ford plays dirty, too."

"Does not."

"He rubs dirt on the ball, so the hitters can't see it good."

"Who says?"

"My brother. He's been to lots of games."

They sat in the front of the bus, though Allie kept turning to see what was going on in back where a crowd had gathered. "Come on," he said, getting up and making his way over book bags that clogged the aisle.

On tiptoe Hutch stood at the edge of the crowd of boys. He'd seen dirty pictures before, Allie got plenty of them from his brother, but the one being passed around was grainy and blurred, a black pit with wild grasses growing at the edges. When it was his turn he held the photo and tried to figure things out. He didn't get it. He was young for his grade and he felt stupid. "What is it?"

"A pussy, dickhead. Up close."

Hutch swallowed hard and blinked. Everything seemed out of focus. The crotch stared back at him, a smudge of shadow. Something turned over in his stomach, like before he threw up. Father Shannon talked about how our body was the temple of the Holy Ghost. Why would the Holy Spirit choose a place like this to build his temple?

*****

At home Hutch changed clothes and went down to the bridge underpass. Because of the police barricades you couldn't walk on the grassy slope, but you could go on the other side where there was tall grass, bushes, a path along the river. He broke off a branch from a beech tree and sat on the cement platform. With cars rushing by overhead he whittled a spear with his Scout knife. Beneath the bark there was a layer of green the color of inch worms, then a yellow-white core smooth and hard as bone. He sharpened the tip, testing it against his palm until he drew blood.

If he looked east along the river, he could see the tree where Farrell was hung. The words *sexual assault* fascinated him. He was still trying to figure it out. He knew what rape was: you jumped on a girl and stuck it in. But with a guy, it didn't make sense. *Up the wazoo*, Allie had said. But that seemed weird, way too weird. If it happened to him, Hutch thought, he'd run away. Maybe Farrell tried to and that's why he got beat up. Or maybe he got jumped from behind and couldn't defend himself. That's why Hutch was making the spear. If anybody jumped *him* from behind, he'd poke him hard.

He was almost finished when Allie came scrambling down the embankment pulling Judy Lundgren, a large, big-boned girl with ringlets in her hair. She lived in the next building from Hutch but never said hello or anything when she passed him on the street. Same thing now. Her eyes raked over him like he was transparent. She wore a pink bathrobe with a fluffy collar, and pink slippers—the kind with no backs, that flopped when she walked. She looked as though she'd been moping around the house, sick or something. In the shadow of the underpass she glared at the spear. "What's *that* for?"

"Protection," Hutch said.

"From what?"

"The killer."

"Yeah. Sure."

"Okay," Allie said. "We can do it right here."

She held her hand out, palm up, and gazed indifferently between the cement columns. Allie dug in his pocket and dropped two dimes and a nickel into her palm. She pushed the coins into the pocket of her robe and pinched her nostrils against the river's fishy smell before turning toward the nearest column and bending over. She reached back and pulled up the hem of her robe. When she pushed down her underpants, Allie looked at Hutch and smiled as if he'd just proven something.

Philip Cioffari

Judy spread her legs. She had one arm braced against the column. The bathrobe bunched around her neck so it blocked most of her face. Hutch thought it might have been a nice robe once, but the fur of the collar had turned dark and stringy. On the side of her face there were two pimples, brand-new and bright red. "All right," she said.

Allie took a pop stick from his pocket and stood behind her. Lowering his head, squinting, he stuck the pop stick into her backside.

"Owww!" She shifted the position of her arm on the column and spread her feet wider. Her underpants stretched tight between her legs; a single spot the color of grape juice darkened the white cloth where it folded against the elastic. "Put it in right or I'm going home."

Allie pulled it out, lowered his head until he was looking right into her crack, and stuck it in again.

"That's far enough." The stick was in halfway. The end that stuck out had a raspberry tinge.

Allie motioned to Hutch. "Go ahead."

"What?"

"Touch it."

In permanent shadow dark water flowed between the abutments. The smell of dampness lifted like mist, made it hard for Hutch to breathe.

"Touch it," Allie said. "Wiggle it around."

Spread out like that Judy's cheeks were wide and heavy, two creamy deserts of flesh with a marker between. She wiggled them and looked over her shoulder to watch them move. Hutch's hand shook.

"Go ahead," Allie said.

Judy's blank face had turned sour. "Hurry up, will ya?"

Hutch touched the tip of the stick and tried to move it, just a little. *Up the wazoo.* Something slow and liquid crept inside his fingers, up his arms. This was a mortal sin.

"Owww!" Judy said. "Don't touch it like that."

The wood seemed stuck there, like in quicksand. The vibration of the cars moved down through the column, through Judy, into his hand. It made swirls in his stomach like the river was flowing fast there, cool and dark.

Catholic Boys   145

"That's enough." Judy reached back and pulled the stick, slow, straight out. She straightened up and let the robe fall back into place. When she reached beneath it to draw up her undies, she kept her eyes on the column and acted as if no one was watching. She yanked and tugged them into place. On the way up the embankment her slipper came loose. She had to feel around for it in the weeds.

Hutch felt his knees shaking; he hoped Allie didn't see. His friend was strutting on the platform, shoulders back, chest puffed out as if he'd just won a million bucks, then he was running up the embankment after Judy because maybe, if he gave her another quarter, he could get her to go into the staircase with him.

*****

Hutch walked along the river-path to the grey house fallen to ruin: glass busted-out, roof collapsed and rotting, grass grown high as the first floor windows. This was where he came when he wanted to be alone.

Things were changing fast. Inside him, strange dreams raged at night. Outside, there were *girl* things. He knew it was all connected, but he wasn't sure how. He needed some time to figure it out.

Chunks of stone and plaster, fallen from the caved-in ceiling and the crumbling fireplace, cluttered the floor of the front room. In one corner, stubs of burnt wood lay heaped against a charred wall. Cigarette butts and Knickerbocker beer bottles stuck out from the ashes. Older guys took girls here at night.

As he moved through the rooms, glass crunched under his shoes. Sunlight broke in bold, bright shafts from the windows and fell from holes in the roof.

He was crossing to the stone porch out back when something moved. Upstairs maybe. Or in the next room. A footstep maybe. Something landing on gravel. He froze, listened hard. For a moment he felt relief. See? See? Nothing, just air and space. But fear had turned his insides to ice; he knew he *had* heard something. He heard the sound again. Something brushing or sliding across the floor above him.

Philip Cioffari

A rat, he thought, *maybe a rat;* but even as he was thinking that he knew the sound was too big for a rat.

The kitchen door was closest. If he could edge toward the pantry. If he could not make noise. Each step, though, seemed louder than the last. And there was an echo. *Whatever was above him was moving with him.*

He slipped into the narrow pantry where it was cool and dark. Rotting cabinets clung to the walls, their shelves smelling of dust and mold. Beetles crawled across the wood; bead-like eyes tracked him.

Something moved again in the room above.

He stepped into the kitchen where it was brighter. Rusted metal sinks, more cabinets, an empty space where an icebox might have been. There was a small side door he squeezed through and came out into the yard, running hard through thick and tangled grass. The sky had filled with clouds; he couldn't tell if the drops that hit his face was rain or his own rasping, spit-filled breath blowing back at him.

He was far down the dirt road before he turned around and saw the man.

In the doorway, watching him.

*****

Mid-afternoon. Light rain. Ramsey left the office and drove along the swamp. He still held a vague hope Donald Seward was out here somewhere, alive. On Beach Road, near the old mansion, he came upon Luke Hutchinson, running. He tapped the horn and pulled over. The boy came toward the car, red-faced and breathless.

On the rutted path to the mansion, Hutch stopped and pointed to the doorway. *"He was there, just watching, like he'd been watching me for a long time."*

Ramsey scanned the windows and doors, vacant now, eyeless sockets in a grey and moldy corpse. A few years back the place had been designated a city landmark, but so far the Parks department had made no effort at restoration.

"His face was in shadow," Hutch said. "He was just leaning there, his arms down at his side, holding a cigarette. In his right hand, I think. Yeah, in his right hand. I could see the smoke. And I could see his pants. Grey. Same color as the stone."

Ramsey climbed to the second floor. Swallows flittered in and out the windows. Plaster dust rose through waterfalls of light that fell from the roof.

"His arms," Hutch said when Ramsey came downstairs. "They were weird-looking. Like maybe the guy was in a fire or something, and they got burned."

Something about the man's arms, Dorothy Farrell had said. *Arthur liked to look at his arms.*

*****

Ramsey used a tweezers to lift an unfiltered cigarette butt from the ashes on the mansion floor. "Lucky Strike," he said.

Morales looked at him, dumbfounded. "How the hell you know that?"

"The smell."

"Yeah, sure."

"Smoked 'em for five years."

Morales was unconvinced. "I'll have the boys in the lab check this out."

"Of course. I'm just telling you what they're going to find."

"Smart-ass," Morales said.

Out back they tramped through what had once been the mansion's gardens. Vandalized body parts of lawn statues glowed pale as bones in the heavy grass.

"If he's our man, why the hell show himself off like that?"

"Ask me something difficult, Tommy, why don't you?"

"So now we're looking for a rat collector with burned arms, right? That shouldn't be hard."

At the edge of the garden, through a gap in the trees, they stood looking across the river at Baychester. A banner announcing the availability of rental units hung from one of the buildings facing the parkway. The name MAJORITY LIFE stood in dark blue lettering against a grey background and beneath that the phrase, *Serving The Metropolitan Region With Affordable Housing.*

"The Metropolitan region," Ramsey said, half to himself.

"What about it?"

At the office he told Falcone to go back into the staff personnel records.

"What are we looking for this time?"

"Someone who's worked in all four of the Majority housing developments."

He lit a cigarette and paced before the windows that faced the alley, berating himself for taking so long to see the obvious. The best he could say for himself was that he was tireless. In his own plodding way he eventually stumbled onto solutions. In his own plodding way. He was the tortoise; fate had seen to that. Always one step behind the hare.

He asked Falcone if the maintenance staff uniforms had always been the khaki color they now were.

"About two, two and half years ago, they changed." And then Falcone caught on. "Grey, with blue stitching. They were *grey.*"

*****

On foot Ramsey made the rounds, quadrant by quadrant. Outside the north playground, he came upon Allie alone on a bench.

"Waiting for my brother," the boy said. "Gonna hang out with him."

"Stay close to home tonight, okay?"

The boy stared at him with a cocky, what-for? expression, then he was standing, waving in the direction of the playground. "There's my brother."

Three of the Brando's—Brody, Sparky Donohue and Brian Murphy—lounged against the fence. Brian *Murphy*. He hadn't realized they were brothers.

"Gotta go," Allie said, running off. "See ya."

There was a commotion behind him and Ramsey turned to find a woman shouting from across the ball field. She pointed toward the entrance of building 6 and waved her arms for him to hurry. He ran toward her, too fast at first, his breath heaving out of control before he was a quarter way around the field.

"Hurry," the woman said when he drew near.

Catholic Boys

In the basement he found Deakins, one of his foot patrolmen, talking to a woman in a housedress, hair in curlers, her broad, flat face stamped with shock. With her were two children: one a screaming baby girl that she tried to comfort by rocking her, the other a six or seven year old boy who clung to her waist. "She seen someone," Deakins said.

"We were putting my boy's bike away," the woman explained, pointing to a row of bikes and baby carriages. "Chaining it to the wall right there. When I looked up, there he was, in the shadows, just watching us. I screamed. Next thing I know he's gone."

"Can you describe him?"

Her eyes rolled back in their sockets; she clutched her children tighter. "I don't know . . . white man . . . average height, I'd say . . . I don't know—"

"He's in there somewhere," Deakins said. "I got here fast and no one came up them stairs."

Ramsey drew his gun and moved into the first of the storage rooms. He had been through here before with Morales and Falcone, the day of the blood message: bare concrete walls, dull yellow light, ceiling pipes that threw a web of shadows on the hard floor, and always the drip of water: a sound that seemed at once both close and distant.

Room by room he confronted only shadows and silence. Unlikely, damn near impossible, that anyone but an acrobat might reach the narrow windows high on the basement walls. Which left the door to the sub-basement, directly ahead of him.

He unlocked it and moved onto the landing where he listened to the dead silence before descending the stairs. The tunnel, with its cement floor and rough-edged concrete walls, opened ahead: a lattice-work of shadow and light.

Falcone had given him two helpful tips for navigating the system: first, that each of the four main corridors began with access through the basement of one of the buildings; second, that the main corridors were identifiable both because they had an occasional sign naming them—North, South, East or West—and because they were the only tunnels with small rectangular air vents just below the ceilings. "If you wander off into the shorter halls and get lost, keep moving," Falcone advised. "In most cases, they'll lead you back to a main corridor—except, of course, in the unfinished sections." In other words—Ramsey reminded himself—if you want to find your way out, stay where there's light *and* concrete.

At the first intersection, he took the right-hand tunnel, which brought him quickly to a second intersection. Identical tunnels veered off right and left: dull and vaguely yellowed in the naked light of the overhead bulbs. Each one ended in darkness.

He stood there confused, bracing himself with his free hand against the gritty concrete of the wall. The dead, thin air felt cool and unnatural against his skin. In silence, we feel the curse of eternity. Where had he read that?

He remembered the first time he heard that word, *eternity—* in a story his mother read him. *It's a place you go when you die, she said, where nothing changes.*

It must be a lonely place.

Yes, she said, *I suppose it is, but a beautiful loneliness. I picture tall trees and green meadows and the tears of the dead falling like rain.*

There were no signs on any of these corridors, no air shafts. To travel deeper might mean losing his way. Or maybe he was already lost. Stay cool, he told himself, all you have to do is re-trace your steps: simple as that. His imagination had him wandering for days in this lifeless vault, desperate as the boys in his dream. The terror of that prospect froze him there, as if he had been sentenced to life unending inside his worst nightmare.

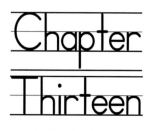

Chapter Thirteen

By dusk the Prefect had worked his way through nearly half the scotch, though he wasn't drunk; he had an enormous capacity for alcohol. Misty light had turned the landscape before him into shades of brown and grey. The shapes across the river—gas tanks, smokestacks, warehouses, tenements—had grown fuzzy as their edges blurred. Everywhere there were distortions of depth and texture. It might have been a landscape from one of his dreams: urban, blighted, haunted by moods of regret and indefinable loss. In these dreams he was always wandering alone through abandoned streets or rooms; now a shadow had slipped into the dream, appearing suddenly on the slope. He squinted and the shadow assumed the shape of a male figure toiling slowly through the heavy grass, bushwhacking his way up from the river.

The priest stood unsteadily. It was not the whiskey that unsettled him but the chilling effect of his visitor's appearance. He left the bottle on the porch and went to his room, leaving the door open behind him. In the arm chair near the window where he read his breviary each day, he closed his eyes. It was a plush and comfortable chair, smelling of perspiration and Old Spice. Briefly he fled inside the familiar world he had constructed these years at St. Jerome's.

Into this world came the sound of footfalls. The screen door wheezed open, then shut. Steps came faint but insistent across the parlor, louder in the hall outside his room. He could feel

Philip Cioffari

a presence watching him. His eyes opened to the figure in the doorway who stood primly on the threshold in a dark suit, complete with clerical shirt and collar. His hands were folded respectfully at his waist as if he had come to lead a prayer service for the deceased.

His evening wear, he had in a previous visit described this outfit. He meant the formal priest's attire, in contrast to the laborer's clothes he wore during the day. *My other self.* This self was clean-shaven, hair parted and neatly brushed. Only the angular face, the slight depression in his cheeks, hinted at leaner times.

With eyes as remarkable for their blankness as they were for their luminous blue color he took in the entire space—bed, dresser, writing table and book shelf—as well as the room's sole inhabitant. The Prefect squirmed at the scrutiny. What did the man see? That his waistline had grown? That his face had become fleshier, his skin more sallow, more liquid? That his eyes had grown heavier too, bulging from their sockets? All this, yes, and more. Those remarkably blue, remarkably blank eyes scoured the parameters of the Prefect's soul and stole something in the process. He could feel the theft as surely as if the man's hand had reached inside his skin and seized an organ.

"Hello, Father." The voice was soft and resonant, precisely nuanced, the voice of an educated man.

"Hello, Deedee." It was the name the visitor insisted upon. *Deedee.* Such a perversity in this context.

Over the years the man's blond hair had turned a dusty shade, creases had appeared on his face, but his eyes had lost none of their startling color. It was the Prefect's eyes that faltered. He was unable to bear the weight of that gaze, its unremitting audacity. He would have preferred punishment of any kind rather than this silence—shouts, rants, even the man's fists.

I am the hell you have made for yourself, the blank eyes said, *I am the hell.*

*****

Once this man *had* accused him openly: more than a decade ago, as a young seminarian. He had come to the priest's room—O'Malley was Assistant Prefect of the seminary then—talking in garbled, incoherent half-sentences about his crisis of faith, his doubts about his vocation, blaming his confusion on the priest and their relationship which had grown so close the young man claimed to have lost all sense of himself. "I don't know who I am anymore, I don't know, I don't know," he kept saying and finally he flung himself at his Superior, pummeling him with his fists and then sinking limply to the floor clinging to the priest's robe, his depthless blue eyes—which that night were wild and troubled and anything but blank—filling with tears. His voice choked with sobs. "Give me back who I was. Give me back my faith. In God. In the Church. In myself."

To this day he remembered the exact words, remembering too his vain efforts to console the boy, calling him what he had called him in their most intimate moments together, *Deedee, my Deedee, my little boy blue* as he touched his face, his neck, his skin as gloriously soft and silken as the fairest of God's angels. He'd always been a troubled boy, prone to wild and erratic outbursts. His impetuous nature the priest had found an endearing complement to his own reserved personality; more than that, though, he thought he could help his Deedee. When he took the boy to bed that day for what would be their final time, undressing him despite the murmured protests, when he spread the thin, finely shaped legs and lowered his head to pay homage to the sacred altar of swollen manhood, it was an act of purest love. He believed that then, believed it still to this day, though the recipient of his love barely spoke to him from that point on, avoided him on the seminary grounds and finally at the end of that semester, having alienated most of the faculty as well as his fellow seminarians with his belligerence and long, vague disquisitions on hypocrisy and moral corruption, left the seminary for good.

It seemed O'Malley would be spared a scandal and in time his affections found their way to another seminarian, Martin

　　　　　　　Philip Cioffari

Shannon, whose passion for theology was as appealing to him as the thick waves of his sun-bleached blond hair and his eyes, not quite as blue as Deedee's, but mesmerizing nonetheless.

It was nearly two years later at St. Jerome's that the visits began: one night like this, the man suddenly appearing out of the darkness, disheveled, unshaven, an old dream turned nightmare. The Prefect had offered him money, gifts, anything to leave him alone. He had begged and pleaded. He had prayed.

I'm your shadow, the man told him. *Whoever heard of making a deal with your shadow? We're joined at the hip, pappy. Now and forever. Till death do us part.*

*****

The Prefect had no idea how long the man had been staring at him. This silence spilled into the silence of other visits: one long silence extending across the fields of his consciousness without beginning, middle or end. Eyes blank and blue. *I am the hell.* What hideous ironies love created. Because it was those same blue eyes, softer and brimming with feeling then, that had first drawn him to this man.

The floorboards creaked upstairs. Father Shannon pacing the length of his room. Back early from his nightly sojourn.

And then his visitor spoke, interrupting the torture of memory's unblinking gaze.

"I'm feeling nostalgic, Father. Old times. Old places."

He pulled the door closed behind him, came into the twilight-grey darkness of the room—tentatively, self-consciously, it seemed—and sat on the priest's bed, spreading his palms flat on the coverlet, his fingers grazing the cotton ruffles and embroidered flowers that lifted from the white surface. A smile played on his lips.

The prefect could only guess at what memories the man was re-living and the relative proportion of pain and pleasure in their recall—the bed in the seminary where they had lain together?—just as he could only guess what fantasies the man had re-lived on previous visits: on one occasion forcing O'Malley to take him into the orphanage where he wandered

Catholic Boys   155

through the second-floor dormitory, room by abandoned room. Another time they had strolled across the grounds, stopping at the garage, the maintenance shed, an isolated clearing above the river. His visitor had volunteered nothing about his reasons and the Prefect didn't ask, was terrified to ask, to know the details. He had always refused to know the details.

Light from the newly risen moon tinged the man's face with a spectral glow. Now, as in the past, the vague and distant complacency of his smile irritated the priest. The irritation flared quickly to rage. How much longer, Lord, must he suffer for the love he had borne this man? How much longer?

"I want to show you the new ones," his visitor said, removing his jacket and slipping off his shirt.

"No! No! I don't want to see—" He was on his feet, pacing in the narrow alley between dresser and bed. "No more. No more—"

"But there's always more, my love. There's been two years' worth of more."

"No—!"

His visitor turned sideways on the bed to catch the full light of the moon. His arms were covered with tattoos—candelabra and crosses, cathedrals and chalices, sacred hearts and crowns of thorn, Lucifer rising from the flames of Hell—but the priest had seen these before. Visit by visit he had seen them increase in number. It was the newest ones his eyes fixed upon: across the man's hairless chest, across the skin he had once loved to touch. Small identical images—Christ's body bowed under the weight of the cross—arranged in the shape of a crucifix, five across, eight down. There were thirteen images in all, one short of completion. The cruel and hideous irony did not escape O'Malley. The Stations of the Cross had always been his favorite form of prayer. How many times at the seminary had he made them with his Deedee?

"For my boys." His visitor flipped the overhead light switch, bathing his disfigured skin in a luminous, unnatural brightness. He flexed his shoulders, gazing in admiration at his chest. "Bless me, Father, for I *will* sin again—"

The priest lunged, clawing at his chest and throat as if to

gouge the life from him once and for all. His visitor made no effort to defend himself or resist, instead holding out his arms and absorbing the weight of the priest as if it were an embrace. In desperation O'Malley grabbed the rosary beads draped over the bedpost and twisted them around the man's neck. The chain snapped in his hands and he held the broken pieces as if it had been his will that shattered. His chest heaved. Sobs burst from his throat. "No more, Deedee. No more."

"One last time, Father."

"But why? *Why?*"

"Death holds me in the palm of its hand."

"I don't understand—"

"Cancer, Father. It's in my blood."

The Prefect searched his face, trying to understand. "But the nearness of death should bring us closer to the Lord, shouldn't it?"

Blue eyes, blank as a cloudless sky, gazed down upon him without mercy. The mouth below the eyes twisted into the simulation of a smile. "You're a New Yawker, Father. You *have* to appreciate the ironies. Stricken, over-the-hill pederast withstands assassination attempt by Roman Catholic prelate of high standing and rallies one final time in bid for earthly satisfaction."

The priest's hands released the broken beads and trailed limply down across the bare chest that bore the images of his Savior. He sank to the floor, clinging to the neatly pressed cloth of his visitor's trousers. "God forgive us, Deedee. Almighty God in Heaven, forgive us."

*****

From his bedroom window, Hutch studied the line of trees where the buildings of the project dead-ended at the swamp. In the dark he couldn't see the tidal pools and the small, raised islands that floated for a mile or more toward the Sound, he couldn't see the river moving black and slow as oil or the tree where Arthur hung; but he smelled the river's damp breath, the smell of wet grass and mud flats, the smell—he imagined—of decomposing flesh.

Catholic Boys   157

He looked for movement: a curl of light through the trees at the swamp's edge or a moving shadow.

Nothing.

He thought maybe the killer was traveling underground through the hundred halls. Nobody he knew had ever seen the halls but he believed they existed and that the killer knew about them, too. In his imagination they were long and curved and dark, crisscrossing like snakes in a pit. You could walk from one end of the project to the other without ever seeing daylight.

For a better look at the trees he pressed his face to the cool glass and cupped his hands around his eyes. From the living room he could hear his parents talking.

"Nothing. Not a clue," his father said.

". . . a threat hanging over us," his mother said. "I just hope . . . ."

Beyond the police barricades, deep in the trees, he saw the killer walking. He was tall and shadowy and he moved with a jerky long-legged stride in the darkness of the trees, traveling in a straight line like he knew just what he wanted to do. Hutch hadn't used his cap pistol since he started at St. Jerome's but he aimed it now and fired just as the killer stepped into view. Again and again he fired: the caps exploded with a popping sound. The killer fell over wounded, then dead.

His mother came running in and snapped on the light. "What's going on in here?" The metallic smell of smoke drifted across the room. "You scared the life out of me."

"I shot the killer."

His mother took the cap gun and set it on the dresser next to the statue of Mary. "He's not still here. He's gone away."

"Where?"

"Away." His father leaned in the doorway. "But just the same we don't want you anywhere near that swamp, you understand? You shouldn't have gone out there today."

"He's probably hiding in the halls," Hutch said.

"What halls?"

"Underneath the building."

"We know you're upset by this, by what happened today," his father said. "But it's best not to let your imagination run

Philip Cioffari

away with you. Sometimes," his head bowed in thought and Hutch could see the thinning hair on his crown, "sometimes our minds make things worse."

"But the halls, they could exist, right? They could reach under the swamp."

"That hardly seems likely."

"Time for bed," his mother said, folding down his sheet. "Say your prayers now."

They watched from the door as he knelt beside his bed. He'd been taught to kneel straight, not slouched or with his arms resting on anything. Jesus gave His life for us so we should be able to suffer a little discomfort for His sake.

He closed his eyes and whispered, "Make us safe. Like you promised in the Bible." When he made the sign of the cross his mother said, "Sweet dreams." They watched him climb into bed. His father winked at him and closed the door. Their footsteps grew fainter down the hall.

All night warm, salty air breathed through the window. Shadows crawled across the statue of Mary. Dreaming, he saw himself deep in the swamp, caught in quicksand. Mud, cool and slippery, seeped around his knees, along the soft skin high on his legs. When he reached for something to hold, the grasses came away in his hand like loose hair. No use trying to squirm free. Mud swelled around his waist. Grease-slick it slipped across his belly, into the hollows under his arms, held him so tight he couldn't fight back, gradually sucking him down toward the hundred halls where the killer was waiting. Before he went under he saw a bird lifting from the clear blue waters of the swamp, gliding higher and higher, its white feathers soft, so soft.

He awoke with his pajamas pushed down below his knees. The mattress felt soft as a hand touching where it was a sin to touch. He tightened his fists and lay still, pretending not to be ticklish. But the tickling had already spread out inside him, like long feathers opening. The Holy Spirit lifted its wings inside his Temple and spit something out.

By midnight there had been more "sightings": an unshaven white male in the staircase of a building at the south end of the project; a second white male, "acting funny" on the roof of building 5; a third standing outside an east end playground, allegedly staring lewdly at the children inside.

By the time Ramsey arrived on the scene the suspects had already moved on, so he had nothing more to rely on than the testimony of witnesses, all of whom believed without doubt that the behavior they were reporting was indeed suspicious. The descriptions of "the killer" varied, and no one mentioned anything unusual about the suspect's arms. What he feared was an outbreak of hysteria: the office phone ringing non-stop with dubious claims, irrational assumptions, neighbors accusing neighbors in an endless free-for-all. He wondered, for the moment, if even the Hutchinson boy's claim had any real merit.

In the Wild Moon parking lot he rested his head against the car seat. Rain drops blurred the windshield. Jukebox music thumped from the back door, something familiar: *say you're gonna miss me, like I miss you, say you're gonna*. . . . He closed his eyes to ease away the pressure inside his head.

He was standing in a courtroom before a faceless judge. When he looked closer he saw the judge was Leo, stern-faced and immovable. *Are you a good man?* Leo asked him. Ramsey struggled for words—what should he say? what *could* he say?—but a voice called to him for help and he stopped trying to defend himself. He went, instead, in search of the voice—someone in need, a victim of some crime—though he saw no one. Then he heard Krissie's voice. A door opened and suddenly he was wide awake. Krissie slid into the front seat beside him, her short black skirt riding high on her legs. She was flushed and out of breath. "I was hoping you'd come by."

He started the engine and guided the car along the narrow driveway.

"Guess what?"

"No more mysteries tonight."

"Take a guess. *One* guess."

He pretended he was thinking it over.

"Give up?"

"Yeah."

"I've decided to go back to school." She sat sideways, facing him, her smile so all-embracing it sent a shiver through him. "Next month. Right here at Hunter."

"Good for you."

"It was like living inside a circle," she said.

"What was?"

"Being with Mike."

Her street was a left-hand turn off Gun Hill. Mid-block he pulled to the curb in front of a frame house with an enclosed porch on the second floor. "Couldn't stand myself after the accident," she was saying. "Couldn't stand *being* with myself." She stared at the windshield with its rain-blurred images. "There was this parade of guys. Then along came Mike. All revved up with his crazy energy."

She pushed her hands into her pockets and bowed her face between the raised lapels of her windbreaker. "It was like I was living some kind of lie he had to catch me at. He wanted to know why I cut my hair, was I trying to look like a boy? When I changed jobs he thought it was because I was sleeping with Leo, then he had me involved in some lesbo thing with one of the dancers. He was always pushing me around, telling me who I could see, who I couldn't." She shrugged her shoulders and looked across at him with a sheepish smile. "My deep, dark secrets."

Maybe it was the I'm-no-angel tale she was spinning or the way her bare legs caught the spectral light of a street lamp. The thought of her body caught in the throes of what he figured had to have been rough and violent sex with Brody aroused him in a way he found disturbing.

"Funny, isn't it?" she said more to herself than Ramsey. "Inside that circle there's no room to dance. But outside I can boogie to the moon, if I want."

She watched him with eyes that were steady and serene. He felt himself falling to a place he was afraid to go. "I'm taking advantage of your kindness," she said.

"How's that?"

"Going on like this."

"I don't mind."

"You want to come up? I can make you coffee."

"It's late."

She gave him a bittersweet smile. "Your wife, I know—"

"She's left."

"Oh—"

We've—" *Separated.* He couldn't say the word out loud. "It's just that . . . she's gone for a while."

"I'm sorry. I—" She sat crossways on the seat, an urgency in the way she leaned toward him. "I know you can never forgive me—I wouldn't even dream of asking you to—but just seeing you like this and talking to you means so much. I know how crazy that sounds. But I feel you understand me. Even though we're really strangers, even though death's the only thing between us."

He rolled down the window for air. Something caught his eye, some movement in the shadows farther up the street: a cat jumped from a wall. "I'll walk you in."

While she unlocked the door he stood in the rain, then climbed the stairs behind her and waited again while she unlocked her apartment door. The room depressed him: four or five unopened cartons, a mattress, a wooden stool: the bare essentials of a life.

"Your sister—?"

"Back with my mother. We couldn't work it out."

"Brody comes anywhere near here, you call me."

A lock of hair fell across her forehead; he reached to brush it back. She raised her mouth and they kissed—a brushing of lips—her arms around his neck, her eyes with waiting in them. He caressed the soft skin of her neck, thinking how easily it would be to break her—a life for a life—then he was kissing her again, harder this time, open-mouthed and deep-tongued. She pressed against him: he shoved his fingers between her legs and she cried out. His body froze: he didn't know if he wanted to fuck the breath out of her or simply comfort her.

She tried to hold onto him as he lurched away, grabbing at the wall for balance and making his way unsteadily down the stairs.

Philip Cioffari

Chapter Fourteen

FRIDAY

Shortly past eight in the morning a Parks Department clean-up crew working a section of the riverbank found Arthur Farrell's undershorts and socks stuffed in a shoebox which in turn had been hidden on the bottom shelf of an old refrigerator.

Ramsey waded through the usual collection of riverbank detritus—tires, automobile carcasses, broken TVs—scuffing his shoes and tearing his pants on the jagged edge of a fender before ending up muddied and empty-handed for all his poking around. He was making his way back up the riverbank when the call came in over the police radio.

Morales shouted from the cruiser on the service road. "Your boy, Falcone. Thinks he's got something."

*****

"Daniel David Cafferty. Born January 29, 1928—Jacksonville, Florida. 5'11"/160 lbs. Between '54 and '58, he worked in all four Majority housing projects," Falcone said. "Right place, right time."

He handed Ramsey the personnel folder. "Guy was within

a few miles of each of those kids when they disappeared. Right here June of '58 for Oster. Hempstead—August of '56—for Lionel Hayes. Pearl River—July of '55—for Rizzo. East Paterson—June '52—for the Nordstrom kid. And he was here three summers ago when Farrell was playing games with someone in the hallways."

"Cafferty's the only one?"

"Few other guys bounced around. Nobody else was in all four places at the right time. Check out the mug shot."

A small I.D. photo clipped to the back of the folder showed a light-haired man with a vacant-eyed stare and sunken cheeks, a narrow angular face.

"You remember him?"

"Vaguely. Only time I had anything to do with the maintenance staff was letting them into the tunnels for the semi-annual inspections. And I sure as hell don't remember a mess of tattoos."

"You talk to Bernie over at Maintenance?"

"Yeah—the usual story. Cafferty was a quiet guy, kept to himself. A smoker, but Bernie couldn't remember the brand. Didn't recall an armful of tattoos, either. "

"Long-sleeve shirts would have covered them."

By mid-afternoon Morales had filled in some of the gaps. In between his maintenance work at Majority, Cafferty would drop out of sight for a while. Twice he re-surfaced in Florida, which might possibly, Morales conjectured, account for several missing children cases in the Panhandle. He worked odd jobs, mostly as a handyman. Couple of gigs as a clerk: once for a supermarket chain in Tallahassee; once for an insurance company in Jacksonville. "Weird fucking job resumé, you ask me," Morales said. "Here's the good stuff, though. Guy owns a '54 Merc, maroon, Florida plates. Most recent address: 1285 Jerome."

*****

The building on Jerome was a sorrowful-looking, grey brick six-story with fire escapes that faced onto the EL. When Ramsey arrived, Morales had already located the super, a hump-backed Puerto Rican named Espee who let them into the apartment, 4F. Cafferty had moved out exactly a week ago.

Two narrow rooms and a tiny Pullman kitchen. Though the walls had been painted and the floors buffed, the place seemed dingy, what little light the windows offered dulled by the imposing steel facade of the elevated tracks. Ramsey paced the rooms as if he had been caged there for weeks, while Morales talked to the super: Meestah Cafferty had no visitors that he could recall . . . he went out mostly in the evenings . . . sometimes he entertained the neighborhood children by doing tricks with his muscles . . . them tattoos, man, he could make those suckers wiggle and dance.

From the window Ramsey stared at the head-on view of the EL, the smell of summer heat lifting like a slow, fevered draft from the pavement below. Despite the street traffic there was a humdrum stillness, a monotony he knew too well on hot afternoons like this: it gathered thick as the summer air, suggesting that time—even the memory of it—had ceased, that what remained was only the changeless purgatory of the present, without hope or promise.

He drove to the mansion and walked a makeshift trail through the woods, on the remote chance Cafferty was camping out.

A rage was rising within him like a lashing tide—a very specific rage now, directed at the face in the I.D. photo. Fighting his way through brambles he imagined what he might do if he came upon the man, what powers of vengeance would be unleashed within him. Like the time Evan was eight and one of the neighborhood's tough guys jumped the fence, pushing Evan to the ground and punching his face mercilessly, swinging as if to make the face unrecognizable, as if Evan's affliction might be contagious and so had to be obliterated once and for all. Ramsey, hearing his son's cries, had come running from the house. He dragged the bully by the shoulders and lifted him with a fury all-consuming, swinging him high in the air and running in a blind charge toward the fence with every intention of heaving him into the street, into the crowd of boys gathered to watch Evan suffer. It was only Helen's cries

Catholic Boys   165

from the porch, "Alex, you'll kill him, you'll kill him!" that stopped him long enough to get his bearings, to see where he was, in his yard, his neighborhood, to see that the wriggling boy in his grip was now as terrified as Evan had been, so that instead of heaving him he simply dropped him over the fence and warned him if he ever so much as passed by the yard again he would have him shipped upstate to juvenile prison, *Do you understand that, do you?*

Deliberate cruelty to children. There was no more unforgivable sin.

*****

To calm himself he visited the Church of the Precious Blood where he took a few moments' comfort in the colorful murals and flamboyant statues, the high dark shadows, the stained glass that softened sunlight late in the day, thinned it to bands of golden brown, a murky and mysterious color that suggested timeless depth and distance, the quality of light seen from beneath the surface of the sea. These were the moments a church meant most to him, when it was empty, still, unsullied by ritual. If there was such a thing as grace, this was the time it would enter a person's soul.

When he returned to the office, Morales called to say that Cafferty's handwriting sample—his signature on the job application form—didn't match the handwriting in the hallway *or* the playground.

"It's what we figured, Tommy. Somebody's idea of a sick joke. It doesn't mean Cafferty's not our man."

"I hope you're right, Ram. I hope we're not chasing phantoms here."

And Ramsey hoped so, too. Because where else would he focus the fury inside him?

*****

The Prefect had not left his room in twenty-four hours. Once his visitor departed he locked the door—a futile gesture—and retired to bed. The man's presence, despite all efforts to expunge it, would linger in the room indefinitely like the damp smell of the river. He finished the whiskey and lay awake through the night: not nearly numb enough to find peace. The point had come, and he had always known one night it would, when he had fallen too far from grace for hope to save him.

Except to urinate he hadn't been able to overcome the heaviness that pinned him to the mattress. He ignored the morning bells' call to prayer. He didn't dress in his robes to watch, as he did every day, the boys of St. Jerome's line up in the yard. Nor did he join the faculty for lunch.

As the day wore on he felt feverish and achy beneath the grimy clothes he'd slept in. Time and again he ignored Father Benedict's petitions that he eat something. Now, with the sky greying beyond the window, Shannon was knocking insistently on the door. "Tobias, I've brought you tea and toast. You've got to keep up your strength."

"Not now, Martin. Not now," he said hoarsely from the bed.

"Yes, now, Tobias. Open the door."

The Prefect hoisted himself to a sitting position. It was Shannon's repeated knocking that brought him to the door. He stumbled back to the bed while the young priest swept into the room bearing a tray. "You wouldn't want to deprive me of the opportunity to perform a corporal work of mercy now, would you, Father?" Shannon set the tray at the foot of the bed and flipped on the light.

"Leave me be, Martin."

"Hung-over, are we?"

The older priest, his belly thick beneath the folds of the sweat-stained T-shirt, slumped on the edge of the bed and laughed bitterly. "You don't know the half of it."

"You look terrible, for damn sure. Visit from an old flame?"

"You shouldn't joke about matters you know nothing about."

Shannon stood in the center of the room, grinning. "Back at the sem, everyone knew you were sweet on Caffee."

His eyes flashed darkly at Shannon. "Did *everyone know* why he left?"

"Broken heart?" Shannon shrugged. "We figured you

dumped him."

"Hogwash."

"What then? What's the real story?"

The Prefect shook his head. "No," he said. "No."

"I bared my dirty secrets. It's your turn." Never had he seen his mentor so beaten. It wasn't only the grubby shirt and wrinkled pants. It was the posture of defeat his body had assumed, drooping eyes and shoulders and gut, as if the frame of bones could no longer sustain the weight of his being. This uncharacteristic lack of spirit stripped the fun from their ongoing hostilities. No pleasure in hurting if you won't be hurt back. He settled on the bed near the aging priest. "Come on, Toby, 'fess up."

The Prefect sat with his large hands on either side of him, gripping the bed cover. His head tilted forward as if about to roll free and he began to cough, softly at first, then with increasing vehemence, a deep and phlegm-y cough that would not quit. Shannon felt a moment's panic. The possibility that his mentor might be seriously ill unnerved him. The man was indestructible, wasn't he? No matter what Shannon dished out he'd be able to absorb it and come back at him feet planted squarely on the ground, wouldn't he?

"Here," Shannon said, offering the tea. "This will help."

The Prefect's hand shook as he held the cup. He endured the silence and the tea's bitter taste. Then he was standing at the window with his head against the frame, his bulging eyes adding to the haunted look of his reflection's face as he stared blankly at the fat round moon above the river. The realization that he might never again find comfort in God or nature terrified him. He began talking in a deep, plodding voice about his suspicions: the higher than normal runaway rate at the orphanage during the time Cafferty worked on the grounds, the timing of his visits in subsequent years immediately before or after a child's disappearance, the eerily detached blankness of his stare. "I tried to kill him last night," he said. "I've become as deranged as he is." He turned to face his erstwhile protégé for the ridicule he knew he had earned. "Now you have as much on me as I have on you. We're at each other's mercy."

The younger priest was stunned into silence. Within a

matter of days his world had been turned on its side. God's punishment, delivered without warning or mercy. He loved it here at St. Jerry's—his differences with his Superior notwithstanding—he loved the school, the boys and yes, in a perverse way, even the Prefect's leadership. At the foot of the bed his tall athletic body bent forward with purpose, his hands clasping and unclasping as he rushed to defend his Prefect as if it were his own case he was pleading. "He's taunting you, that's all," he declared. "Trying to make you suffer. Don't you see? It's his strategy. Make you feel guilty. Make you pay. He can't face his own failure, so he's blaming you. Don't be taken in. Don't be fooled—"

O'Malley turned back to the window. Superimposed above his own image he saw again the blank eyes, the thin emotionless smile. "It wasn't so much what he said—"

"If you were certain he was guilty you would go to the police."

"Would I?"

"Of course, you would. Why wouldn't—?"

"For the same reason you didn't." In the window's reflection the Prefect watched, with an uncharacteristic self-loathing, a grim smile spread like a stain across his lips. "Who of us would not disown the consequences of his actions, given the chance?" He was thinking: how much God must hate me to send him back here now.

"You don't know anything for certain, remember that. And as long as you don't know, how can you be held responsible?"

"Before God or before the law?"

"Before God *and* the law. The ambiguity of responsibility. Your theory, remember? *In matters of moral complexity we should always be given the benefit of the doubt.* Your words, Tobias. Your exact words."

The older priest's voice, directed at the window, came back muted and resigned. "Why do they mean so little to me now?"

Shannon tried to quell his sense of helplessness. In a matter of hours their positions had been reversed. If the Prefect had lost his determination, he would help him regain it. He stood directly behind his Superior, speaking not to his back but to

Catholic Boys   169

the solemn outline of his face in the window glass. "It's all supposition. Everything you've told me. Besides, there's no way the police can prove anything. No way. Remember that. You're safe. We're both safe. As long as we keep our mouths shut." What he didn't say was: Come back. We need you, Father. *I* need you.

The Prefect stared at the streams of moonlight igniting the dark river. He might have been thinking, this is the river of the dead across which the bodies of the young and innocent are transported. Or he might have been looking for something on the dark slope to suddenly take the shape of a man. "For years I've taken comfort in the fact that I might be wrong about him. But I feel no comfort now. No comfort at all."

*****

"Lab report's come in," the desk sergeant at the precinct called to tell Ramsey. "The shoebox had that fisherman's prints all over it. Morales went to bring him in."

*****

"It's not exactly by the numbers," Morales said outside the booking room, "but the Captain's not around, so what the hell, Ram. You want to go in and give it a try? I've been knocking my head against a wall."

The old man sat with his head bowed so low it nearly touched his chest, hands loose in his lap, thin legs turned in at the knees. He looked more like a marionette than any living thing, something abandoned in a carnival museum's basement.

"You realize how much trouble you're in, Mr. Elmore?" Ramsey said.

The old man's eyes narrowed beneath his cap. His face had small, dark cut-marks from shaving.

"Why did you take the boy's underwear?" He leaned forward as the fisherman squirmed against the back of his seat. "Why did you hide it in that refrigerator?"

"I didn't."

"You didn't?"

"I mean, *I had to.* They made me."

"Who made you?"

"Them."

"Who's them?'

"Them voices. In the swamp." Bent forward the old man crossed his arms and rocked himself. A squeal like the sound of a hurt animal came from deep in his throat. "They come after me. Whispering at me, *telling* me. Go up there, hide them clothes where they'd be safe. From the evil ones."

"The evil ones?"

"Them that killed him. Them fiends."

Ramsey watched a line of yellow drool form along the old man's lower lip. "So you walked along the edge of the river until you reached the dead boy?"

The old man nodded, arms folded, shoulders trembling.

"Did you walk up as far as the fire?"

"Nope."

"You didn't walk into the grove of trees for any reason?"

"Nope."

"You stopped at the tree where the boy was hanging?"

"Yup."

"Did you touch him?"

The old man jerked his head back at the suggestion. "Holy Jesus, no!"

"You're sure?"

"Ain't no pervert."

"You didn't touch him, just a little bit?"

"Jesus, no. I told you."

"You weren't curious? What a dead body might feel like? You didn't want to stick your bad-boy up his ass?"

The old man had his eyes lowered and he chewed hard on his lips. Ramsey waited. "Then what?"

"Took the underwear. Went back up the slope."

"Which way?"

"Same way."

"You mean you walked back from the dead tree to the path along the river until you reached the bridge?" The old man nodded yes.

"Then?"

"Brought them where they told me."

"The refrigerator?"

"Home."

"You brought them home?"

"They told me to. Then they changed their mind. Said it wasn't safe. Told me wait till dark, take them the other side of the river."

"When did you call the police? *After* you brought the underwear home?"

"Yup." The line of drool had oozed onto the man's chin. Ramsey handed him a handkerchief. "You shouldn't have lied to us, Mr. Elmore. You should have told us this right away."

"They would have got me," he said, his voice shaking.

In the hallway Morales said, "The guy's a hundred and ten percent bonkers. Plus he can't shave without making a bloody mess of his face. No way he'd be strong enough or even steady enough to string the kid up."

"Have somebody tail him," Ramsey said.

"What the hell for?"

"In case."

"In case what?"

"I don't know *in case what*. In case there's something he's not telling us. In case . . . *anything*."

They watched him through the glass. The old man rocked himself with his eyes closed, arms folded as if something hurt him bad. Morales snapped his gum and clamped his hand on Ramsey's shoulder. "You were on a roll in there, old buddy."

"Yeah, but what'd I get?"

"Late breaking news," Morales said before Ramsey left. "Cafferty's a failed priest. He was up at that seminary, Holy Cross-on-the-Hudson, with our friends O'Malley and Shannon. Guess who else was up there same time?" Morales grinned triumphantly. He'd gotten sun in the past few days; his brown face intensified his already strong, good looks. "Your boy, Falcone."

"So what are you saying, Tommy? We've got some kind of conspiracy here?"

Morales shrugged. "I'm saying Eddie boy gives me the creeps.

Never trusted him." He bit off a link of Double Bubble and chewed thoughtfully. "Figured I'd better look into St. Jerry's while I was at it. The Diocesan office wouldn't talk to me. But I did find out a few things from Child Welfare. Like, for example, the orphanage was cited forty-nine times between '41 and '54 when it closed. Overcrowding, lax supervision, unsanitary kitchen facilities, assorted health and safety violations, high runaway rate. We got a sewer here, Ram. Who knows what's gonna crawl out?"

*****

Ramsey went looking for the Brando's. No sign of Brody's Fairlane along the service road, but he did find Nina Varick crying on a bench near the flag pole. Pink tank top, tight pants, wild hair.

"Boy trouble?" he asked.

She choked back her tears, stiffened her shoulders and stared at the flag hanging limp in the heavy air. A falling angel, Ramsey thought. Grown-up clothes, a little girl's heart. "Y'know, a guy forces you like that, he doesn't really care about you."

"How would you know?" Her words were hard but he was encouraged by the flick of her eyes in his direction. Brody's anal fixations may have wised her up: his violence could turn on *her*, too. He offered her a cigarette. She ignored him. "Smart girl." He held out his right hand to show her the yellowed skin between his forefinger and middle finger. "Twenty years' worth of nicotine. Imagine my lungs."

"Why don't you quit?"

"Some habits you can't kick."

She opened her purse and took out a cigarette. "I know that song."

He held out the Zippo thinking she would refuse that, too, but she raised her hand to cup the flame. "I know what you're gonna ask me. No, I wasn't with Mike Wednesday night, but he knows the police are watching him. He wouldn't do anything to Seward right now. I mean, he's an asshole but he's not *that* much of an asshole."

Catholic Boys   173

"Sunday night. You guys went *looking* for Farrell, didn't you?"

She shrugged indifferently. "Mike had this thing about teaching him a lesson." Ramsey thought he'd have to pry the rest out of her but the tightness around her eyes and mouth seemed to ease. "We knew he went up to St. Jerry's at night so we waited by the gate. When he came out we followed him in the car. The guys were yelling things and Mike would drive up real close trying to force him off the road but the kid didn't even care. He kept walking straight ahead, looking funny, funny-weird, like he'd been crying."

She took another drag and spit out the smoke, her voice oddly distant and faraway, a story she was telling that might have happened to someone else. "When we got to the swamp Brody said he wanted to talk, would he mind coming down to the river with him. And the kid came, the stupid kid came. He had to know what was gonna happen and he didn't even *try* to run away."

"They beat him up."

"Real good." When she ground out her cigarette her eyes seemed uncertain. "Stupid kid. Even after they beat the shit out of him, he still wouldn't go. He went down to the river and sat there."

"They left him like that?"

"We went cruisin.' "

"Could Brody have gone back later?"

"I was with him pretty late. And the other guys had gone home. Mike never does anything alone."

"That was the last you saw of him?"

"The kid? Yeah."

Ramsey thought he heard a moment's sadness pass through her voice; but he couldn't be sure.

*****

Behind the power plant he found the Brando's drinking beer with two girls in black jeans and stiletto heels. He went directly for Brian Murphy, yanking him by the arm so roughly the kid came off the bench sideways, his free arm flailing at the air. "Hey, what the hell—"

Brody said, "What the fuck, man?"

"It's Murphy I want. Rest of you get lost, or I'll run you in. Public nuisance."

"We didn't cause no public nuisance."

"No alcoholic beverages allowed. But I guess you boys have trouble reading that big sign on the fence there."

"That's bullshit, man."

"You want to take it up with a judge?"

"Why me?" Brian Murphy said. "What did *I* do?"

Ramsey tightened his grip. Brody glanced down the walkway, unhurried, considering his options.

"Move," Ramsey yelled and Brody ambled away, the two girls in tow.

"Who the fuck is that asshole?" one of the girls said glancing back, her heels dragging on the pavement.

"Why *me*?" Brian Murphy whined. For an answer Ramsey slammed him against the chain-link fence. The kid's eyes peeled back in fear. "The matter with you, man?"

"What's the matter with *me*?"

"Wasn't doin' nothin'."

"You want to do some work-farm time?"

"No."

"Those messages. In the hallway, in the playground. Who wrote them?"

He had a blank moon face, a freckled nose, eyes too dulled for someone his age. "How should I know?"

"I think you know."

"I don't. I swear."

"One of the Brando's?"

"No."

"One more time. Was it one of the Brando's?"

The kid glanced in the direction of Brody who watched from farther down the walkway. "No," closer to a whisper this time.

"You're lying."

"No."

He lifted him against the fence, pinning him there. "You're a lying son-of-a-bitch."

"You're hurting me."

"I haven't *begun* to hurt you." Ramsey pushed him deeper into the fence. "Give me something or I have you booked right now for withholding."

Murphy glanced toward Brody again. His voice broke: a pathetic quaver. "Don't make me."

Ramsey flung him so hard the kid came bouncing off the wire netting like a ball. Murphy gasped for breath, began to cry. "Please."

"Give me something!"

Before he could hurl him again, the kid went limp in his arms. Ramsey had expected him to break, though not this soon. He was sniveling, wiping his nose. "Rat-boy."

"Who's rat-boy?"

"Albino kid. Over on Tremont."

"Who is he?"

"Lace Marcom. Weird fucker. Hangs out at the dump. Hunts rats with a bow and arrow. Hundreds of them, man. He's killed hundreds. Then he like, you know, mutilates them."

"What's he doing over here?"

"I don't know."

"You mean to tell me this kid collects all that blood, brings it the hell over here and decides to paint that stairwell, on his own?"

Murphy glanced down the walkway and lowered his voice again. "Brody got him to do it."

"And the playground?"

"Harry Walsh."

"Who's he?"

"Just moved here. Wants to be a Brando."

Ramsey shoved him again, out of disgust this time. "It was funny, right? You stood around and had a good laugh about it, right? You beat the shit out of Farrell. Then you make a joke out of that, too." Murphy collapsed against the base of the fence, curled into himself. "Some tough guy."

But Ramsey felt just as disgusted with himself. The wolf-pack approach to investigation. Choose the weakest prey. Go after it with all you've got.

The moon hung suspended above the swamp, its light allowing Ramsey safe passage over uneven ground. Under the bridge the river made a gurgling sound; car tires hummed overhead. On the cement ledge, shadows enveloped him, the air thick with the sour smell of heat and rotting fish and dampness. He stepped cautiously, looking ahead for guidance to the greyer light beyond the overhang.

Halfway across the ledge he stopped to get his bearings. From here he could observe, unnoticed, anyone coming down the path, anyone who happened to be sitting on the rocks along the river. *Hidden from the eyes of the world, a lonely man watches the boy he's been waiting for, hoping for. A shadow separates itself from the wall of shadows; it stalks the boy along the narrow ledge. To love, to kill. To love and kill. The line is easy enough to cross, easy enough. He's crossed it before. . . .*

That had been the official thinking all along but if the sodomy had occurred *before* the boy came down to the swamp. . . . If the hanging had been an act of despair rather than murder. . . . According to Seward, Arthur felt unloved. Nina Varick claimed he willingly gave himself up to his tormentors. If the kid had climbed the tree and strung himself up that would explain the traces of his blood and the mud caked along the limb. It would also explain why his neck wasn't broken. Because if he'd been hoisted to the limb pulley-style and dropped forcefully, death would more likely have occurred from a crushed spinal cord than strangulation.

*****

Ramsey drove to St. Jerome's and parked outside the gate. Climbing the hill he kept to the shadows—trees, bushes, an occasional outcropping of rock. From this angle the hulking mass of the former orphanage appeared to rise taller than its five stories; it leaned aggressively outward from the crest. If by day the building had a vaguely menacing look, in darkness it was the stuff of nightmares with its vacant arched windows, its turrets and jagged-edged roof line.

He wasn't sure exactly what he was looking for, but the Prefect had suggested the interior had been left intact from its operational days, pre 1954. What was it Morales had said about St. Jerome's? *It's a sewer, Ram. Who knows what's gonna crawl out?*

He used his flashlight to break the glass of a basement window, lowering himself into a chapel with rows of oak pews. A crucifix was the lone adornment on the altar's marble slab. On the side aisles statues stared vacantly into the musty air. A room even God had abandoned.

Upstairs a dull, vaguely unsettled sensation pulled at his gut as he moved down a long hall, turning his light into rooms where beds were arranged barracks-style, each with the same type of grey-and-black striped mattress. He swore he could smell the stench of hurt and abandonment in the dust-choked air.

A broad central staircase led to the top floor. There, in a turret room with long narrow windows, he found a double row of file cabinets that had apparently been moved from elsewhere.

The first drawers held files of the wards themselves, dating back to the early 40s: boys with Irish, German and Italian names, the sheets inside their folders yellowed and flaking at the edges. Except for the letter *M* and a date handwritten next to some of the names, there was little variation in the files— classic cases of abandonment via death or neglect. In the second row of cabinets, among the personnel files, he came across two things that stopped him cold, made him think that Morales' conspiracy theory might have some merit after all.

The first was a file for Daniel Cafferty, originally employed by the orphanage as a maintenance assistant, March 8, 1951. According to the file he worked for St. Jerry's sporadically, months at a stretch, over the following three years. The second piece of information came as even more of a shock: a file for Edward A. Falcone. Between '52 and '54 he'd served as a part-time volunteer counselor, assigned to assisting the permanent staff on day trips and outings.

Failed priest seeks alternative spiritual outlet? The guy

Philip Cioffari

was just a Good Samaritan? There were any number of justifications, Ramsey figured. But why wouldn't Falcone have said something? And didn't this make it even more likely he'd known Cafferty?

He went back to the children's folders and pulled out the first ten he came across with the *M* designation. A random sample, to be sure, but he looked for a pattern. Was it *M* for Missing? Of the ten, seven were dated after March of '51 when Cafferty first came on the scene here. Six of those seven were dated 1952 or later, when Falcone served as a volunteer.

Ramsey stood at the north window mulling this over when he noticed a figure silhouetted in a window of the priests' residence. The room was dimly lit, a night-light most likely, and it took a moment to be certain. Father Shannon. The priest, bare-chested and standing stiffly as a Greek god, seemed to be staring directly across at him. No matter that his rational mind told him he couldn't be seen at this distance in the dark, he instinctively backed away. The priest's immovable presence in the window unnerved him.

Chapter Fifteen

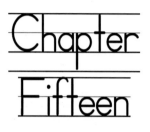

"Check this out." Falcone pulled out a sheaf of loose-leaf pages filled with his cramped, back-slanted scrawl. "Notes on tunnel maintenance, back to '53. Cafferty was on the crew six of the fourteen times we went down."

"We already figured he knew his way around the tunnels," Ramsey said. "Give me something I don't know."

A hangdog look crept into Falcone's eyes. "I thought you might like some confirmation, that's all."

"Sorry, Eddie. I'm just beat tonight. You, too, from the look of things." Falcone's face had the washed-out color fever leaves in its wake: the result of five straight days and nights on the job. Or was it something else? "Why didn't you tell me you knew Cafferty in the seminary?"

Falcone stared at him across the desk, without blinking. Ramsey could see the processing going on behind his eyes: assessment first—that Ramsey *knew*, that he'd been checking on him; then adjustment—how to deal with it. "I didn't. Not really. I was leaving as he was coming in. Couple weeks overlap, maybe."

"Yeah but, Eddie, you didn't say anything about knowing O'Malley and Shannon either."

"Don't like to talk about that stuff."

"What stuff?"

"My seminary days. Sensitive about it, I guess." Embarrassed by the scrutiny, he picked up a pencil and began tapping the point into the blotter, keeping his head lowered. There was a suggestion of apology in his eyes but something hard and defensive, too, that made Ramsey feel like a trespasser.

"You could have at least told me you worked as a volunteer at St. Jerry's."

"I know," Falcone said, without raising his eyes.

That's *it*? Ramsey thought. That's all you're going to say? "What about this guy, Shannon?"

"What about him?"

"Could he be the one who sodomized Farrell?"

"He's a priest, for God's sake," Falcone said with such vehemence that Ramsey was taken aback.

"Eddie, you know the old joke about how psychiatrists are crazier than their patients?"

"Yeah, so?"

"You ever figure that same principle might apply to priests, too? They've got a greater capacity for sin than the rest of us so that's why they enter the priesthood, to try to heal themselves?"

"No," Falcone said flatly.

"You go to church regularly, Eddie?"

"Course I do. Don't you?"

Ramsey sighed heavily and pulled out a cigarette. "Go home. Get some rest. That's an order."

He drew on his Viceroy while Falcone stared back at him as if he'd been slapped, the hangdog look even more pronounced as he stood up reluctantly. Muttering to himself, he shuffled toward the door, slack-shouldered and listing slightly to the left, in no hurry to reach the empty rooms awaiting him.

*****

He should have gone home then, called it a night. That's what he would tell himself later. Instead he stopped at the Moon for a beer, just one, surprised at the jealousy he felt when the waitress told him Krissie had the night off. He imagined her with Brody or some other old boyfriend, or maybe she had found someone new—he wasn't sure what she might be doing or which fantasy was more hurtful, but he

Catholic Boys   181

was sure he hadn't had feelings like this in years. He tried to stifle them with the music's mindless rhythms, the simple longings of the lyrics: *please say . . . darling won't you please . . . please say that you . . .* As soon as he had drained his glass Leo stood beside him, bowing, reaching to set another bottle of Rheingold on the table.

"This is it for me, Leo. I can't stay long."

"Would you mind if I joined you for a moment? The night is slow and I have time on my hands."

He doubted Leo's motivation was quite that simple, but he reached across the table to pull out a chair.

"I consider this an honor, as always, to share the pleasure of your company, Detective."

He waited for whatever was on Leo's mind, but the club owner seemed in no hurry, sitting statuesquely as he was, legs crossed, fingers lifting an errant thread from the sleeve of his evening jacket. "This man, John Francis Kennedy, will he make things better for the people?"

"The Catholics seem to think so."

"These Catholics," Leo said earnestly, "they are bound together, are they not?"

He laughed at the man's choice of word. "Yes, they are *bound* together. By their love affair with guilt, by their obsession with repressed sex, by—" He stopped when he saw that Leo was taking him too seriously. "I was joking with you, Leo."

"I do not like these people who see sin everywhere. They destroy so much that is good. "

"You may have more to fear from Nixon."

"But Mr. Nixon has hard values, does he not?"

"*Hard?*"

"Perhaps the word is 'solid.' *Solid* values. He is tough with the Communists. He wants to keep America strong."

"We're already strong."

"Perhaps not so much with this U-2 situation. Or with Mr. Castro in Cuba. And now there is this new device for preventing babies. The pill, they call it. What will happen when women have so much freedom?"

"Maybe they'll be happier."

"But they have husbands and children. What will become of

the family?"

"I'm not sure I see your point."

"Unless there is a strong hand—" His used his fingers delicately to pat his oiled hair. "I came to America because of the way it is. I do not want it to change." He folded his hands on his knees and raised his head smugly as if something had been settled. On the platform, a dancer in a diaphanous mock-wedding gown swirled into blue light. "You like her?"

The woman was someone Ramsey hadn't seen before: blonde, short-haired, a body like Krissie's, thin and athletic. "Why wouldn't I like her? She's young and pretty and she moves like wind." He gave Leo a blank smile, offering nothing.

"I know how *complicated* Krissie can be," Leo said in a measured voice.

So he knew the situation, Ramsey thought, probably had known all along.

"But Lisa is not so complicated. And her face is prettier, is it not?"

"Is there a point you're getting at, Leo?"

"Sometimes a man does not know what's best for him. He becomes so caught up in details he loses sight of his objective."

"What have I lost sight of?"

"That you want to give meaning to your life."

"I have a child to find and a death to solve. That's all the meaning I need."

"If that were only true—"

Ramsey pushed the table back to give himself room to stand; Leo leaned forward and touched his arm. "One minute, Detective. Lisa is dancing for *your* pleasure."

The music had grown louder, more upbeat, a man's voice wailing above the drumbeat. Lisa ran her hands along her arms in a lingering way, smiling at Ramsey, singling him out. If it weren't so transparent that his table companion was up to something, he might have allowed himself the illusion of a moment's flattery.

Leo watched her with unblinking eyes: a dark stare that might have been the closest he ever came to revealing pleasure. "Do you follow popular music, Detective?"

"Not anymore."

"Jackie Wilson." He cocked his head as if concentrating on the music. "He's very good, isn't he?"

"He has a strong voice, yes. But I'm afraid I'm not much of a music critic."

"If he were a white man, he might have been an opera singer. It's not so simple in America for those of us who—"

"You seem to be doing all right for yourself."

Leo stroked his beard slowly. "Believe me, it is with great ardor to run a club like this outside of Manhattan. I have no friends in high places. I am alone in the work which is sacred to me: to create a room like this, where only a man's fantasies must be allowed to flower." His lips parted in the beginnings of a smile. "And that is why it would be an honor to extend you any courtesy"—he waved toward the platform where Lisa had let the gown fall from her shoulders, the bridal virgin becoming undone, her skin strikingly white and glistening in the sudden exposure to light—"if Krissie is unsatisfactory in any way."

Ramsey got slowly to his feet. "You don't owe me anything, Leo."

"I consider you my friend, Detective Ramsey. Among friends it is not a matter of debt but gratitude. And I will be even more grateful if you can put in a good word for me with the Baychester Community Board. They meet next week. One of the items on the agenda is whether to declare this establishment a public nuisance. Some of our citizens, *especially* the Catholics, have the misguided notion we breed degenerates here. Some have even suggested we are to blame for that poor child's death." He stood across the table from Ramsey and shook his head with grave disappointment. "It is a dangerous thing, is it not, when reason falls prey to emotion?"

"I can't promise you anything."

"I do not expect promises. I ask only for your consideration. Surely, Detective, you, of all people. . . ." Leo regarded him with a look of such deep sympathy that Ramsey felt degraded. "Surely *you* understand the necessity of a place like this, where a man can find refuge."

"Good-bye, Leo." He turned away, avoiding Leo's hand and Lisa's sweet, baby-doll smile. On the back steps he stood uncertainly, fishing in his pocket for his car keys, reeling from the humiliation he felt. He had been shown how pitiable he was: a man with all his secrets exposed and nowhere left to hide.

*****

Shame ate away at him. How foolish he must appear: a father grieving for his son in a cheesy strip joint. *For surely you, of all people, understand the necessity of a place like this, where a man can find refuge.*

There was only one way he knew to survive the pitiable self. The way he had been taught by his faith in the days when he *had* faith: to sacrifice his happiness for the happiness of another. That was the ideal he'd fallen from. That was the promise to Helen he'd forsaken.

His intention was to say good-bye to Krissie once and for all. He had fulfilled his obligation to her—hadn't he?—he had made her world safer. He would stay with her only briefly. Make sure she was all right, tell her to call if Brody threatened her again. He would tell her, finally, that he had to try one more time to make things work with his wife.

That was the plan. But he watched it unravel from the moment she answered his knock and he saw her standing in the bright yellow light of the hallway, eyes wide with the joy of seeing him, her smile shy and yet knowing, then the spontaneous kiss she gave him—not quite innocent and not quite seductive. The spontaneity was what transformed him: the eagerness as she leaned toward him, the way she hesitated when their lips touched as if she had reached some dangerous crossing.

"I can only stay a minute," he said.

Inside the room he was transformed again: by its spareness, its unsettled condition. There was a small table with two wooden chairs, and near the porch an armchair he had not seen his last visit, its arms lumpy and threadbare. On the floor, pushed into the room's far corner, was her mattress, sheets rumpled and messy, a reminder of the empty bed that awaited him at home. So that when she asked him if he'd like a beer he said he would, and when she offered him the armchair he settled into it. *She* needed him too. How could he just walk out?

"Sorry it's not a cheerier place," she said.

It's fine, he told her, but she shook her head. "I've always had this idea what a home should be like. But every guy I've gone out with"—she hesitated—"let's just say his idea was different than mine. And my mother, she had so many problems, making a home wasn't something she gave much thought to, you know? So now it's just me, no one in the way, and I'm trying to figure it out."

She showed him some blue-and-white patterned material. "I've even gone domestic with this curtain thing, if you can believe that." She held the cloth against the window. "What do you think?"

"I like it."

"The pattern, the colors—they're comforting, don't you think? A home's got to be warm and comfortable but it's got to have something else, too. Room to grow. It's got to be a place that allows you to become more of who you are."

She set the material on an unopened box in the corner. "You think you know, you say this is who I am, and then a tragedy strikes you and you find some other part of yourself, something you hadn't known was there, and you realize who you thought you were doesn't exist anymore. Or maybe it just gets pushed aside. What do you think?"

"When I figure it out, I'll let you know." He tapped a cigarette against his Zippo. "I'm curious how you got mixed up with Leo."

"Fate, I guess."

"Fate?"

"After . . . after the accident, I couldn't go back to work at the Manor. Bad associations. And—I'd stopped driving, so I couldn't get there anyway. A girl I went to school with worked at the Shimmy. She brought me in. Then you get hooked. Easy money, and the dancers fascinate me. Most of them don't know who they are. They take off their clothes, hoping they'll find out on stage. Which is a hell of a lot like my dating career. Every guy's had some show going on inside his head. And me? I'm just a dancer in his show. So then I started looking for someone to see the real me. At first, Leo was really kind, you know? Telling me I had personality and character, that I'd help him build the kind of classy establishment he wanted. I was flattered. Till I figured out he wanted me to be a dancer. That serious face doesn't fool me anymore. He just wants to see me without my clothes. But waiting on tables is one thing, dancing's another." Her eyes brightened and she laughed at herself. "Which makes me a hypocrite, right?"

"Not necessarily."

"I think it does."

"I had an ethics teacher, a priest at Fordham, who used to say all the choices we made were choices between evils of one kind or another. His definition of a moral being was the man who consistently chose the lesser evil. Pretty cynical, I used to think. But now—" He shifted in the chair and forced his eyes to meet hers. "You're probably wondering about *me*, right?"

"Truthfully, yeah. I mean, you're not like most of the guys that come in, the droolers and gawkers. I figured maybe you just needed some place to rest, you know? And then I started hoping it was me you came to see."

It seemed he should say something, but no words came.

"I'm gonna make you something to eat. You're probably starving."

He protested, saying it was late, but she insisted and while she moved about the kitchen he sat on her mattress and used the phone. He left her number with both the desk sergeant at the 47th, and the night officer at Security.

At the table by the window she served him a simple meal: steak and vegetables, a lettuce and tomato salad with Italian dressing. He was embarrassed at how sentimental it made him feel. Halfway through he stopped eating.

"You don't like it?"

"I do."

He was just tired, he told himself. He was tired and subject to all sorts of illusions: the long ago past with Helen reincarnating itself in the present, the present moment holding out more promises than it could keep. He excused himself and went onto the porch.

Catholic Boys   187

The moon transformed the dull street with a silvery gloss. From the kitchen came an old Bunny Berrigan song heavy with nostalgic horns and violins. Then he was watching her cross the porch, her long legs moving lightly, the way she moved in the dim light of the bar.

"You blame yourself, but it's me you should be blaming." She stood at the railing and stared across at the dark houses. "When Evan was in the hospital, I used to stand outside in the parking lot. I'd watch you and your wife coming in and leaving, always with the same sad expressions. I wanted so much to pray to God to take my life and spare Evan's. But as terrible as I felt, I couldn't ask God to take my life. I couldn't."

She leaned forward with both hands on the railing. Instinctively he reached for her. "It's solid," she said. "It will hold me."

He followed her gaze down Gun Hill to the lights of Freedomland visible against the dark line of the Sound. "You know I can't keep seeing you."

She nodded, without turning her face to him.

"It's that—"

"I *know* all the reasons. I've been expecting you to vanish, not show up one day, but then you do and I start to feel all these things I don't know what to do with. Hope can be a terrible thing when there's really no hope at all." She was shaking and he reached out to comfort her and then she was in his arms crying against the damp cloth of his shirt saying she never understood why he had been so nice to her when all she deserved was his hatred and scorn. He assured her he felt nothing even remotely like that, only a blind futility sometimes and something else, too: something he would never have expected, didn't have the words for.

"Pity," she said through her tears. "You pity me."

"No," he said, "it's not pity," although pity may in fact have been part of it. She was his partner-in-crime. Separately at first and now side by side they were serving out their life sentences.

She asked him if he would take her to Evan's grave. She'd been there on her own. But she wanted to go with him. Just once.

Philip Cioffari

He said that yes, he would take her, and she lifted her head from his chest. "Look at the mess I'm making on your shirt. It's soaking wet." She broke away and went inside and he followed her, watched her open and close kitchen cabinets in search of tissues. Finally she pushed past him in the archway, went into the bathroom and came out dabbing her eyes with a towel. She sat on the mattress and he sat beside her with his arm around her and she was whispering something he had to strain to hear. "All this time you've been looking for a killer and she's right here in your arms."

No, he said, *no* and he was telling her in time she would find a way to forgive herself, then he was kissing her: hard lips against her soft, wet mouth, his hands pushing up her T-shirt so that his palms could graze across her nipples and she was laughing through her tears, saying, "See, see, I've got tits the size of Spaldings, I couldn't be a dancer if I wanted to." They felt so good to him he was beyond speech and he put his mouth there, drawing out her nipples with tongue and lips, his hands grazing across the flat of her belly, tugging at her shorts. When she was naked beneath him, turning in his arms, he jammed himself inside her with such force she cried out.

One hand wrapped around the nape of her neck; the other pressed into the small of her back so that he could feel her spine. *How easy*, he thought, *to break her.* It was her softness, the skin on her neck, the boyish short hair, the curve of her scalp in his palm that drove him into her harder and deeper, without mercy or tenderness. She clung to him, saying "Yes, hurt me, hurt me" and he *wanted* to hurt her, make her feel his pain: *he saw himself raising his arm and releasing the ball, overhand, not a hard throw but harder than he intended, seeing his mistake immediately in the disappointed look on Evan's face, his hands moving too slowly, the ball slipping through, bouncing across the grass and rolling down the incline, Buckey racing after it, Evan following, running hard to try to catch up—Evan! Wait! Wait!—his boy tilting left and then right, his head down, his arms like the wings of a plane he was flying as he runs between the trees, Buckey lunging for the ball and just missing it, knocking it with its snout so that it bounces into the street, the blue car out of nowhere—it seems—appearing first*

Catholic Boys   189

*as blurred and silent motion, until the cry of brakes makes it
real. Swerving to avoid the dog. Striking Evan head-on.*

He would fuck death out of their lives once and for all—if
only he could, if only he could—and then he was swinging the
flat of his hand against her head, her face turning this way and
that in response to his beating until he was able finally, *finally,*
to stop his hands by burying them as clenched fists deep in the
folds of the pillow.

Overwhelmed by her loud sobbing, he closed his eyes and
thought he might rest a while: no more than a moment, maybe
two: then there was Evan with his arms raised running free
and mindless again across the grass, the blue car, *her* blue car
appearing out of nowhere, Evan rising against it and falling, a
small broken figure on the roadway: then she was lifting him
from the hard ground, cradling him as a mother would as she
rocked him gently back to life.

Ramsey felt something break inside himself and he was
crying too, his tears indistinguishable from hers, her words
or his—he couldn't be sure—saying everything would be all
right, *everything everything;* and to make her feel loved in this
world he kissed her forehead first and then her eyes and her
lips and in turn he was calmed by her tear-stained face that
quivered when she came, and the way her brown eyes with
their flecks of green and gold sought his in that long moment
after; and he was saying *love, love*—or she was, he couldn't be
sure—and then it was her voice alone, whispering, "Tell me
your secrets, tell me your fears."

Or maybe it wasn't Krissie speaking at all. Only the voice of
his weariness, his illusions, offering the comfort he'd given up
for lost.

*****

The nightmare vanished while his eyes adjusted to the
darkness of an unfamiliar room—her body was curled into
him, her breath warm and moist on his chest—then the
dream's image came back like a fist shoved into his gut: Evan
calling to him from the grave, a place with steep walls, long
and narrow as a hall.

Philip Cioffari

He rolled over and groaned. The stillness of the street told him it was late. He slid his arm from under Krissie and read his watch: 2:25. Had he slept that long?

He tried to disengage himself without waking her but she stirred and opened her eyes, her voice liquid with dreams. "Are you okay?"

"It's late. The phone—"

"Over there." She raised the sheet to cover her nakedness and pointed behind him.

"O, Jesus!" A pillow had been shoved against the phone, raising the receiver from its cradle. He pressed for a dial tone and called the precinct.

The desk sergeant's voice came at him too fast, too hard. "Where the hell you been? We've been calling all over the goddamn place?" There was a dead space, two or three seconds. "That Hutchinson kid. Went to some dance at the church. Never came home."

Chapter
Sixteen

SATURDAY

Shadows moving.
A sickeningly sweet smell.
Voices far off like they're under water.
Then one voice, a man's, close by, calling him.
A wax face stretches wide and dripping. Then shrinks.
Slipping inward at the edges: a nose and mouth take shape,
two eyes.
The wax melts into nothing. No thing.

Something hit his cheek hard and steady, one cheek then the other, his face burning, the voice from under water saying, "Open your eyes, son." Hutch felt his shoulders shake. Someone's hands shaking them, rough and fast. The shadows stopped moving. "Time for the Sacrament," the voice said.

"Sacrament?"

"What we came here for. The Holy of Holies. The sacrifice."

Hutch blinked his eyes and shook his head to clear away the fog. He had no idea what the voice was talking about.

"The way Christ showed us," the voice said. "Suffering precedes redemption."

Hutch blinked again. Shadows stretched then shrunk.

Yellow light seeped along the walls, the floor, down one side of the man's face.

The voice said, "You're the lamb of God."

Hutch pushed against the prickly wall behind him. He crawled to his knees and, bracing himself against the wall, managed to stand. The room tilted, then steadied, like water settling in a glass. He blinked but everything was still blurry. A long room, he thought. Patches of yellow light broke the shadows. Then he *knew*. The light and shadows, the prickly walls, the dry and dusty smell of concrete. *The Hundred Halls*.

He was feeling too dizzy to move ahead, so he lowered himself to a crouch and dropped to the floor. "What day is it?"

The voice laughed. "Day, night, winter, spring. No such thing. Not here."

He had been at a dance. That, too, was like a dream: a different dream than the one he was now in. Kids were slow-dancing all around him. Guys holding girls tight, nobody moving very much. From the far side of the basement Allie waved to him. *Come on*—his lips shaped the words—*come on!* In the dream Hutch saw himself with his friend, Allie bending his head to whisper, "Girls. They want to be kissed. Come on." Hutch followed him outside into the churchyard through a series of ivy-walled gardens, each with its individual shrine: the garden of St. Francis, the garden of St. Anthony, the garden of St. Theresa the Little Flower.

Behind the gardens the catacomb entrance, guarded by St. Michael the Archangel, opened black and deep as a cave. "Inside," Allie said, "That's where they wait."

"Who?"

"The girls, dummy."

Hutch asked how he knew that and Allie said from his brother. All the older guys knew about it. They came here to make out so Monsignor wouldn't see.

The passage smelled of stone and melting wax. No windows. Rock walls with candles stuck in the cracks, dim alcoves with statues lurking. Mary Magdalene washing the feet of Jesus, St. Sebastian with a bright-red bull's eye heart pricked with arrows, St. Lucy reclining on a slab of stone, her eye sockets two holes gaping at the ceiling. He stopped, as he always did, to stare at her eyeballs displayed like two eggs frying on the plate she held. Allie went on ahead while Hutch stayed behind to whisper his usual prayer, *Lucy, please don't let anything like this happen to me.* Quickly, he made the sign of the cross three times for good luck.

The passage took dark turns past the vault where dead priests were buried, past narrow side passages that snaked away toward hidden shrines. He heard voices, but there was no sign of Allie and he was afraid to leave the main passage to look for him. When the catacomb opened into a courtyard he stood uncertainly before the grotto of the Madonna, which was separated from the alley by a stone wall. Both the alley and the courtyard were heavily shadowed and for the first time he regretted having left the safety of the dance floor.

It was strangely quiet yet he knew he was not alone.

Water from an underground spring dripped down the grotto walls, striking the Madonna's head and exploding in tiny bursts of spray. Somewhere farther down the alley a gate banged shut. One moment he was sweating profusely; the next, his skin felt cold as ice.

Someone was watching him, he could feel it, like at the mansion.

Shadows moved inside the grotto. It was like someone had ripped the air from his lungs. He looked around the courtyard to see which way to run, toward the alley or back inside the catacombs. A man stepped toward him; Hutch breathed easier because he could see it was a priest and no one to be afraid of.

"Son?" the priest said to him now in his new dream, the Hundred Halls' dream. "Son?"

He tried to focus on the priest's face—the long, narrow cheeks and chin, the vacant blue eyes. The priest's lips twisted in a funny way and then he was holding something—a knife, Hutch thought at first—but it was gold and in the shape of a cross with thin, sharp edges. The priest was forcing it against his mouth. "Kiss it, son. Kiss sweet Jesus before we begin."

Hutch moved his lips and tasted the cool, shiny metal. It

was for a grave, he thought, something to mark a grave. Why was he kissing it? Then the cross was gone replaced by the priest's face close up, looking at him funny.

"Am I dead?" Hutch asked.

The priest opened his mouth wide and laughed. The gold cross appeared again, flashing in the dim light and Hutch heard the tear of cloth, felt a stinging pain. He lowered his eyes to see his good white shirt ripped open; a thin line of blood darkened the center of his chest. In disbelief he stared at the man crouching there.

The priest placed both hands on Hutch's shoulders and leaned to kiss the wound. "This is my Body. This is my Blood." Hutch squirmed to free himself. The priest, his lips wet with blood, held onto his shoulders a moment before letting go.

The burning on his chest, the shock of it, had awakened Hutch. His vision cleared: the walls stood still, the man's face stopped expanding and contracting. At this distance, too close, he could see a dark stain on the clerical collar and the bruised smudge of a tattoo creeping out where the man's coat sleeve had risen. "You're not real," he murmured, inching back along the wall. "You're not real at all."

"I'm the realest thing you'll ever know."

"Why?" Hutch said. "*Why?*"

"You think because there's a question, there's got to be an answer? Do you?" He leaned toward Hutch, his breath warm and sour in the close air. "I want you to spread your legs now. Can you do that for me?" He shifted out of his crouch and dropped to his knees.

In that moment Hutch pushed away the hand that reached for him, catching the man off-balance and knocking him backward. Hutch felt dizzy again. Shadows began to swim around him and he thought he might pitch forward but his feet were already in motion and he was running down the hall.

"You'll get lost in there, son," the man called. "It's dark and lonely. You're going to need me."

One of his Security officers on overnight patrol had located Cafferty's car, the maroon '54 Merc, in the North parking area several hundred feet from the swamp. When Ramsey arrived squad cars barricaded both ends of the Boulevard and a foot patrolman stood at the entrance to each walkway. Above the swamp a police chopper hovered, its searchlight sweeping the dark grass. From somewhere, beneath the overpass or along the far bank of the river, came the relentless yelping of dogs.

The PD had set up temporary headquarters at Housing Security where, amid the crowd of police brass and reporters in the outer office, he found Morales leaning against the back wall, chomping on bubblegum and sulking like a child whose favorite toy had been taken away. "The kid was last seen in the church catacombs about 10:30," Morales explained. "They're goin' through Cafferty's car right now. What they've got so far is a bunch of maps—city parks. That's it."

Eddie Falcone joined them and Morales gave him a wary, less-than-welcoming look. If Falcone noticed, he didn't let on. Ramsey asked him what they were waiting for.

"Moriarity," Falcone said. "He's on the phone with the Commissioner. In *your* office." He shrugged apologetically. "They were already set up in there by the time I got here."

Morales snapped his bubblegum in disgust. "Dogs, choppers, TPF units. It's a friggin' circus out there."

Ramsey managed a half-smile. "Subtlety was never Moriarity's strong point."

The door to his office opened and they were waved in. The reporters were told to wait. There would be a news conference immediately following the meeting.

It took a disciplined effort for Ramsey to squelch his resentment at his old boss who stood behind *his* desk, looking as if he owned the place. Beside the Captain was E. Murray Albright, a thin silver-haired man in a dark blue suit, conveniently back from Nantucket in time for the showdown.

Moriarity yelled for quiet in the crowded room. Red-faced, thick-jowled, he stood before a display stand with a map of the swamp. He always wore a shirt too tight in the neck, it seemed to Ramsey, causing a fleshy bulge over his collar and making it appear the guy was choking half to death. He cradled a clipboard in his left arm and cleared his throat. "We've just received word that Alan Murphy of building 6 has been reported missing. He was last seen at"—he checked the clipboard—"12:30 p.m., walking east on the service road."

"Who reported him missing?" Ramsey asked.

"The kid's father, why?"

"Allie's got an older brother in one of the gangs. Perhaps he's with him. Is the older brother missing, too?"

"I don't know a damn thing about any brother. What I *do* know is this kid's a good friend of Hutchinson, who had a previous run-in with the suspect, as you should damn well know. I have to believe their disappearance on the same night is more than coincidence." He recovered from his annoyance at Ramsey's interference by turning his attention to the room-at-large. "I also have to believe—given where Farrell was murdered, given the location of Murphy when he disappeared, given the maps we found in Cafferty's car—the suspect and the two abductees are presently somewhere in that swamp between here and the beach."

With his finger he drew a large circle in the center of the display map. "We're moving through the marshes now. By daybreak we'll have this cocksucker flushed out." His blue eyes glowed, his cheeks rosy with satisfaction.

Ramsey knew what that expression meant. Finally the Captain had gotten this investigation in his own hands. No more shilly-shallying. *Apply the law, and apply it vigorously.* He didn't so much want to *apprehend* the killer as *crush* him. Pure heavyweight force applied non-stop. As usual, though, flaws glared neon-bright in the good Captain's reasoning. Too many dubious assumptions, for one thing: like linking Farrell's death and the two disappearances to the same perp.

"What about the sub-basement tunnel system?" Ramsey asked. "You forget about that?"

"What tunnels?" Moriarity looked from Ramsey to Morales, then to Albright. "What the hell's he talking about?"

Ramsey knew why Morales might not have mentioned

them to his boss. It was the kind of thing Moriarity would scoff at—a mysterious underground labyrinth? a grown man using secret passageways?—and no one wanted to be the butt of the Captain's ridicule, especially in a situation of this magnitude. Or maybe he *had* mentioned them and Moriarity simply ignored him. But it was Albright who puzzled Ramsey now. The man's face had blanched and he looked clearly uncomfortable, as if a shameful family secret had been exposed.

"They've been sealed off for years," he explained, forcing a cough to help him regain his composure. "I highly doubt—"

"Right here." Ramsey moved to the blueprint taped to the wall. "Cafferty could have gained access from the basement of building 5 or 7 or 9, all of which are easily accessible from the North parking lot."

The Captain came from behind the desk and scrutinized the interlocking grid of passageways. His face grew an even deeper shade of red. His jowls expanded, it seemed, to a point of near-explosion.

"I'd like to handle this," Ramsey told him. "With Morales and Falcone."

Moriarity glared at him, and in his look Ramsey could see the scorn—or was it pity?—that had made his last days on the force unbearable. "Out of the question."

He appealed directly to Albright. "This is on company property, sir. I'm responsible—"

"But it's *my* jurisdiction," Moriarity shouted. "Besides, we have no reason to believe he's down there, for god's sake."

"It's highly unlikely, highly unlikely," Albright kept insisting, "that even a murderer would choose such a place."

"With all due respect, sir. He wants to be alone with those boys, right? Other than the swamp, or an apartment if he has access to one, where's he going to be more alone?"

Moriarity stepped back from the blueprint and swung around to face the room. "We'll send the dogs in. He's there, we'll sniff out the cocksucker."

"What about the boys?" Ramsey argued. "If they're still alive. You come on like gangbusters you don't think Cafferty's going to use them as hostages?"

"We don't even know he's down there, for god's sake," the

Captain whined. He gave the grid of passageways another look and pulled at his collar. "Who says Cafferty even knows about the tunnels?"

"We have maintenance reports to show he's very familiar with the tunnels, Captain," Falcone said.

Moriarity pulled at his collar again and twisted his neck side to side. He might have loosened his tie, except there were too many reporters outside waiting to take his picture.

"Look at it this way," Ramsey said. "No way you can lose. If Cafferty's in the swamp, the dogs run him down. If he's in the tunnels, you'll have that covered, too. And if we can take him quietly, by surprise, the boys might have a chance."

Moriarity turned his attention to the blueprint again. "How much of a tunnel you got down there?" he growled at Falcone.

"Two, three miles maybe. The finished part, that is. Another mile or two we got dirt passageways—no lights."

"Jesus!" Moriarity stared at Ramsey as if this were somehow his fault. Then he was talking to the Commissioner on the phone. He kept nodding his head. "Yes," he said. "Yes, yes. Yes, sir. Yes, sir."

When he hung up he looked as though he might spit in Ramsey's face. "Two hours. You don't come out with that dickhead son-of-a-bitch, we send in the fucking dogs."

*****

Hutch was running. Turning left then right then left again. One tunnel led into another into another. Each one too long, too deep, too dark. So quiet nothing could live here, not even rats. The walls were sand-colored and dripped with shadows. A maze like the mazes in his puzzle books. You thread a line through the maze. If you find the way to the center, you win. But what if there is no center here? What then?

Allie's brother said there were lots of doors down here. You just had to find the right ones. But where?

In the wall's shadow he stopped to catch his breath. He listened for footsteps, heard them, *thought* he did, but couldn't tell which direction. He ran until another hall opened, a shorter one, dark except for a light at the end. *A door beyond the light.* A green, thick door like for the incinerator rooms upstairs. When he reached it there was no humming sound from the incinerator, no heat coming through. What was on the other side? Another hall? A staircase to the swamp? He turned the handle. Locked. *Locked.*

Something moved behind the door—a step, then the knob turning. He backed away, turned and broke into a run. At the end of the hall he glanced back. The man in the priest's suit came through the door, noticing him there and not surprised one bit: walking down the hall in an ordinary way as if he had all the time in the world. Hutch opened his mouth to scream, but no sound came out. He was a sinner and sinners had their voices taken away so they couldn't call for help. That's why he'd been taken here. Because he'd committed sins of the flesh. Because he liked the way sin made you feel.

This was how Satan got you. *Without mercy.*

*****

They were making their way along the main North corridor when Ramsey, in the lead, heard something ahead. Or *thought* he did.

He raised his hand in warning.

The sound came again: blunt, dull, far-off.

He was more certain this time—or was he? These halls leant themselves to wild imaginings, tricks of the eye and ear. The bare concrete, the interminable silence and the ceiling's long procession of naked bulbs played havoc with your sense of reality. You squinted into the tunnel's narrowing patches of shadow and light but the eye quickly lost its way. Even with the help of field glasses, he could discern no movement ahead.

Each main corridor ran for nearly 500 yards. Ramsey's guess was that the sounds, if he had not invented them, must have come from one of the secondary halls that branched off to the left and right. With his pistol raised he moved ahead, Falcone falling in behind him and Morales bringing up the rear.

This was no time for regrets but he still wasn't sure about bringing Eddie with them. Morales insisted he couldn't be trusted. You sent him home at ten o'clock, he'd argued privately with Ramsey, plenty of time to be part of the abduction. True enough, Ramsey conceded, but the plain fact of the matter was he had to take the chance: Falcone knew the grid system better than anyone: he was needed. It had taken Ramsey no more than these few minutes for panic to threaten again. The unfathomable maze. The tomb of death from which there was no escape.

In the office upstairs Falcone had briefed them on what they were up against. There was one main corridor like the one they were now traveling through in each of the grid's four quadrants, each corridor aimed toward a central point: a square locked room that had been intended—in the event of a crisis—as an emergency headquarters of some sort. The transverse or intersecting halls served as connections between the four longer ones; and a series of shorter halls made perpendicular links between the transverse halls—a spider-web design, with an occasional door separating the halls. The original idea was that during an atomic attack the residents would be marshaled by quadrant into their own set of halls. An underground web for the dispossessed, Falcone called it.

When Morales asked why the tunnel complex was so goddamned elaborate, Falcone reminded him that the idea had been to provide room enough for all 40,000 of the project's residents. It had to be big, he explained, if that many people were going to live there for an indefinite period of time.

But that didn't explain the freaky shape of the place, did it? Morales had insisted. What kind of warped mind would design a shelter in the shape of a spider web?

To answer, Falcone had to rely on hearsay and rumor. The architect, a renowned German Jew who had come to the States to escape the Nazis, had apparently fancied himself an artist. He wanted the shelter to be more than simply functional. If it was to be a habitat for human beings, however temporary, he believed it should reflect the intricacies of the natural world. It should possess a beauty of its own.

And Morales had laughed. *Whose idea of beauty is a fucking spider web?*

Now Falcone's eyes were wide with fevered intensity. He

Catholic Boys   201

had drawn his gun, a sub-nosed .38 he claimed he'd never fired except on his weekly trips to the range, and Ramsey remembered something Morales had whispered to him before they set out: *if we get split up for some reason down here, don't turn your back on the guy.*

The sounds were unmistakable now. Fifty or sixty feet ahead and off to the right, Ramsey estimated: a voice, several voices, a laugh, more laughter: the clink of something metallic followed by a second clink, a third, more laughter.

He motioned for Morales to watch his back and he swung around the corner into the first transverse hall with his pistol at arm's length, stunned by the sight before him: a girl, naked except for her panties and stiletto heels, kneeling on a floor littered with crushed beer cans. Along the wall, sitting with their backs against it, a half dozen teenage boys gawked at her.

In a split-second the scene was in motion. The girl, and the gang of boys startled by the intrusion, turned it seemed as one, the laughter frozen on their faces, becoming fear first then in varying degrees embarrassment and shame, the girl grabbing quickly for her halter top and pulling it on, the guys—Brody and the Brando's—struggling to their feet, tipsy. The smell of beer infiltrated the stale odor of concrete and dust.

Ramsey holstered his gun and came toward them. "What in hell you think you're doing?"

"Nothing," Brody said. "We ain't bothering nobody."

"The hell you aren't," Morales said. "How the hell you get in here?"

"How the hell you think?"

"I asked you a question."

Brody's upper lip peeled back in his familiar sneer. "Never met a lock that couldn't be jimmied."

"Don't get wise-ass with me, you fucking punk." Morales started toward him but Ramsey stepped between them. He said, "This isn't a playground," but Brody's blue eyes, dulled by the beer, offered no concession. The girl huddled against the wall as if she were cold. She was the young woman by the power plant who had called him an asshole. "You don't have to put on a show for these clowns, you know."

"It's not like that—"

It was then that he noticed Allie Murphy hiding behind his brother, Brian, at the back of the gang of boys. *At least one of them is safe*, he thought.

"Come here, son."

The boy took several steps in Ramsey's direction and stopped, his face red, eyes lowered. It was obvious from the way his head lolled forward that he'd been drinking with the others.

"You know, your father's very worried about you right now. You know that, don't you?" He looked over at Brian Murphy. "And you, too, son."

"I guess," the older boy said without conviction.

"Is this the way you take care of your younger brother?"

The older Murphy jammed his hands into his pockets and stared down at his feet. What he had at first thought was dirt on the boy's face he now saw were bruises. Payback for talking to a cop? At another time he would have held Brody accountable. He turned, though, to Allie, who seemed to be regarding his brother with disdain.

"Your friend, Hutch."

"What about him?"

"You haven't seen him, have you?"

"He went home." Allie had his hands on his hips, puffing out his chest. "I get us some girls and he splits. Sometimes he can be a real faggot that way, you know?"

"He didn't go home, son. We're looking for him now."

Before he sent them back to the nearest exit where there was a police guard, Ramsey asked if anyone had seen or heard anything.

"It's a goddamn tomb in here," Brody said. "What do you think we heard?" And then he added, a moment later: "Oh, yeah, we did hear somethin'. The tears of the fucking dead."

*****

"Goddamn kids," Morales mumbled, glancing back at the beer can-strewn hallway. He leaned aggressively as he walked, ready to take the fight up with the shadows. Ramsey raised a hand to steady him. *Cool it, Tommy. You're a halfway-decent cop when you keep your mind on things. Keep it cool.*

They followed the main corridor until it formed a T with one wall of the central room, the heart of the web. There were doors along the wall, but the plan was to ignore them for the time being. Opening them would be noisy, might give away their position. Instead they would move around the central square, search each main corridor first, working their way quadrant by quadrant—North, East, South and West in that order—then through each of the transverse halls, before returning to the center. That way they minimized the risk of getting lost. The system had a design and if they paid attention to that design, Ramsey reasoned, they would always know where they were. The central room would serve as their anchor.

And they would *need* an anchor, he knew, especially in light of what Falcone had said about the condition of the tunnels. During the initial stages of the system's construction, the North and South networks had been completed end to end. Apparently it was in the second stage of construction, with the grid system already far over budget and the entire enterprise so far behind schedule, that the company decided to avoid what was becoming a huge liability and abort, or at least postpone, the completion of the grid. That left the East quadrant three-quarters finished and the West quadrant three-quarters *un*finished. The Badlands, Falcone called them. Uncharted territory. Dirt passageways of random length: mostly dead-ends, no lights, no spider-web design to rely on.

"We've got to hope to hell Cafferty doesn't have the kid holed up in there," he had warned them while they were still back in the office. "Or maybe we should *pray* instead of *hoping*," he'd added. "Because we end up in there we're gonna need divine intervention."

As they moved around the perimeter of the central room that was exactly what Ramsey found himself doing, *praying*, his version of it at least, bargaining with an ambiguous God— or was it the God of Ambiguity? *Please, in your mercy . . . take my life if you have to but let the boy. . . .* Wasn't this, after all, the essence of a life, what we call purpose? Not to undo the harm we've caused—that was not possible—but to make amends in kind.

In the main East corridor they traveled far enough to see to the end, to verify that nothing shifted in the shadows, that no body lay slumped or abandoned on the hard stone floor, and Ramsey took what little consolation he could find, the hope of all the parents of the world whose children vanish unexpectedly: *As long as he's still missing, there's a chance.*

Keeping to the shadows at the wall's edge he led them into the South corridor where again they saw nothing but the static interplay of shadow and light, a hall-of-mirrors effect with the corridor appearing to narrow as it found its way into the black hole of infinity. He blinked to clear away the illusion. Again they walked far enough to establish that there were no visible signs of human activity, before making their way back to the center of the web.

"Here we go," Falcone whispered at the head of the West corridor. The excitement in his eyes had been replaced by dread, the dark inward look of the terminally ill. Ramsey was reminded of the look in Helen's eyes, though her eyes had more of a flat, anesthetized stare as if she'd traveled beyond mortal pain and terror. In Falcone's eyes fear, like a stalker, lurked at the edges.

"You want to go back, Eddie?"

Falcone squared his shoulders. "Not a chance."

"You're sure?"

"Dead sure."

"We'll take it from here," Morales said.

"I'm okay. Really," Falcone said, ignoring Morales' proprietary tone. "I'm fine."

Morales gave him a dirty look and lunged ahead into the corridor, head and shoulders pitched forward for combat.

"Easy, Tommy. If he's here, we don't want to spook him."

Morales breathed deeply to ease the pressure and slowed his pace to let Ramsey assume the lead again.

The corridor's first section had been finished like the others: the same drab cement walls, lights hanging from the ceiling every fifty feet or so. Soon this would end, Ramsey knew. The main passage and all the secondary passages would turn to dirt. The blueprint upstairs failed to reflect the exact condition of the tunnels beyond that point. They'd be on their own.

Catholic Boys

At the entrance to the first transverse hall he spotted traces of dirt on the floor. He knelt to rub a sample between his fingers. Dry and thin. *The unfinished tunnels. Somebody had recently tracked this out.*

A short distance ahead the lights quit; a black section of tunnel reached into the void. It seemed to him that they had traveled deep into the heart of the web, though that was merely another illusion; if anything, they had moved in a circular direction. He had to remind himself that the center of the web was behind them, that it was an easy walk back—a straight line—no way they would get lost. At the edge of the darkness ahead he saw a small body curled at the foot of the wall and his heart stopped. *O Jesus, no—*

Before he could reach for his own light, Falcone's flashlight found it: not a body but an army-issue duffel bag. Nothing inside. No traces of blood. He sniffed the canvas. Possibly Cafferty had drugged the boy and transported him in the bag.

"Got something," Morales said a few feet farther down the hall. He held up a small white, opalescent button. "The kid was wearing a dress shirt, right?"

*****

Dead air, dead silence.

The hallway held its breath.

Hutch might have been down this hall before. He couldn't be sure. A shape like his head floated partway up the wall and moved with him down the hall. Abruptly it leapt up and scared him. The shadow wavered, settled down, moved side by side along with him.

Ahead there were burnt-out lights then no lights at all. It was darker than the catacombs. *Please God please, don't make me go in there.* Footsteps came behind him: he had no choice.

The cement walls of the tunnel ended; the floors turned to dirt. Not even shadows now, only blackness darker than night. And a bad smell. He wanted to hide here, but *the smell*. A hundred times worse than the sewers where he'd gone hunting for balls. A thousand times worse than a dead rat rotting in swamp grass.

Hand clamped to his nose, he walked deeper into the tunnel so the priest wouldn't find him. The smell slipped through his fingers. His stomach turned over hard like in an elevator dropping fast. He gagged, swallowed to hold back what was rising inside him. His foot kicked something hard as bone. He lost his balance, stumbled forward and then he did get sick. He was running and throwing up at the same time. Back toward the light.

*****

Ramsey moved alone into the unfinished section of the main corridor. He had sent Morales back through the transverse hall to find another point of entry into these unfinished passages. The pincer effect—*if* they could trap Cafferty between them—Ramsey coming in from one side, Morales from the other.

He left Falcone at the point where the main corridor turned to dirt, in case Cafferty got past them. As he walked away, Morales' warning screamed at him *don't turn your back on the guy*, but there were times you just had to put your trust in somebody, you had to take the chance.

"You're our reference point, Eddie," he'd said before leaving. "You're the compass."

In the office upstairs they had argued about what equipment to bring. They figured walkie-talkies would be useless, given the concrete walls. Besides, if stealth was their objective, the noise of the things would give them away, even *if* some kind of limited transmission were possible. If they got separated, as was the case now, they would just have to take their chances.

In the darkness the air seemed even thinner. His flashlight revealed the rough edges of the tunnel, more cave-like now: raw, hollowed-out earth supported by steel pilings and overhead beams. He looked back to get his bearings. The lights of the main corridor illuminated Falcone's small figure crouched against the wall.

Before moving on he pressed the flat of his hand against the ceiling beams. They were solid—what did he expect? These tunnels had held up for years, why would they fail now?

Catholic Boys

He forced away the image of being buried alive and moved ahead. Deeper in the tunnel his light picked up an opening: one on the left, one on the right—the rudimentary shafts of a transverse hall.

At the intersection he flashed his light into each of the shafts. Half as narrow as the main shaft, they were swallowed in darkness beyond the feeble reach of his beam. The possibility of having to enter these secondary tunnels terrified him and for the moment he stood frozen in the main shaft.

He heard something behind him, or thought he did. A footfall? A rat? But what would rodents live on down here?

He listened to the deadening silence. Nothing but the beating of his own heart. Nothing but the whisper of his fear. *Or was there something else*?

He thought maybe it was Eddie, following him as back-up; but Eddie would have flashed his light, would have communicated *something*. Wouldn't he?

From the darkness to his left, unmistakable now, came the sound of footsteps. He swung his light into the shaft. Something flashed across the outer reaches of the beam. Or was it only the light itself reflected off the piling? He moved several yards into the shaft and stopped. Nothing at first: then he heard it again. Footsteps, *running*. Too light a step to be Morales coming in from the North corridor. Too *quick* a step.

Moving as swiftly as he dared he followed the shaft. Was it his imagination or was the shaft narrowing? Was the air thinning even more? Sweat broke across his face and neck with the fury of a fever. You can still breathe, he reminded himself. There's enough air to make it through, as long as you don't panic. When he stopped to get his bearings he thought he heard the steps again, closer this time. Why then didn't his light reveal the runner? And then he knew the answer, *saw the answer* in the flat wall ahead of him where the shaft broke into yet smaller shafts to the left and right.

At the wall he stopped again to listen. *On the right. The sounds were coming from the right-hand shaft.* He followed it a short distance. The shaft sub-divided again.

According to his calculations the left one should take him

closer to the North corridor which, he believed, couldn't be much farther away. Soon, though, the shaft split again. He should go back, he told himself, before he got in too deep; he took the right hand shaft, thinking *it* must surely connect to the North corridor. After several yards it dead- ended. The left shaft then—surely that one. He followed its uneven meander for several minutes before giving up.

There seemed no point in going on. He retraced his path by following his own footprints in the dirt. When he reached the second intersection he heard steps again in the shaft to his left. *Not far ahead*, he thought, *not far at all.*

The passage subdivided and he veered to the left shaft in pursuit, then right, then right again until there was no sound at all: nothing but the dry rasp of his own breath. He turned back, thinking that all he had to do was reverse the order of the three turns he had just taken and he would be close to the main West corridor, then one more left turn and he would be home free; but when he reached the second of the intersections there were footprints in every direction and he was thoroughly confused. He cursed the design of the grid. Morales was right. What kind of distorted vision had created the plans for such a maze? And what kind of lapse in corporate judgment had approved those plans? The sheer folly of it. Was this why Albright had seemed so uncomfortable discussing the tunnels?

He braced himself against one of the support beams and listened, hoping, *praying* for a sound: footsteps, *anything.* He flashed his light into the mouths of three shafts. Which one? *Which one?* And the panic that he had been fighting seized him so viciously he thought he might have a heart attack right then and there, his heart was thumping that hard. All that was needed now to complete his nightmare was to have the dimly lit faces of the boys calling out to him from the depths of the shaft.

He considered shouting for Eddie or Morales but he choked back the urge and stumbled into the shaft nearest him, unsure whether he had traveled this way before, moving not out of instinct so much as blind desperation. In the dirt there were overlapping footmarks: a smaller print and at least two sets of larger ones. The ground was too dry to determine which were his own. He was lost; he had failed the boy.

Light appeared unexpectedly: a dim glow beyond the reach of his flashlight. The shaft widened and he was jogging through it, the ground becoming hard and level beneath his feet. Soon he no longer needed his flashlight. The hall stretched into the distance in the familiar alternating pattern of shadow and light.

He stopped and bent forward with his hands resting on his knees. In ragged gasps he drew air deeply. Never, never would he have thought that barren concrete would bring him such joy.

Below the ceiling was an air vent covered with the familiar metal grate. A short distance ahead, at the intersection of a transverse hall, he saw the small green plaque that read *North*. He would make his way back to Falcone in the West corridor where they would wait for Morales; but no sooner had he begun walking in that direction when he heard footsteps behind him. He squinted into the patchwork of light and shadow. *The boy!* Far down the hall he was running away.

"Son!"

But Hutch had already turned a corner. Ramsey took off after him thinking, *Don't run, child, don't run.*

When he reached the transverse hall Hutch was gone. *Where?* He walked slowly as if he expected him to materialize out of the shadows. Simple fact: the kid had been too fast for him. Figuring he must have fled into one of the offshoot tunnels ahead, Ramsey ran until he reached the main West corridor. Maybe Falcone had found the boy, was keeping him safe and sound right now. The concrete ended a short distance ahead. Falcone was nowhere in sight.

He flashed his light into the blackness of the dirt tunnel beyond and his breath caught in his throat. The beam found the blood first: a smear down the wall of raw dirt and stone, uneven streaks drawn with bloody fingers; and below that, sitting slumped on the tunnel floor—*Jesus, Eddie, no!*— Falcone with his head fallen too far forward, nearly severed from the neck.

He barely had time to kneel beside the body and register

Philip Cioffari

the sad-eyed, startled look of his assistant—and the fact that the .38 was missing from his shoulder holster—when the boy's voice came from the darkness ahead. He flicked off his light and remained in a crouch, listening.

*****

Hutch was running fast, barefoot for secrecy's sake, his shirt flying open where it had been cut. A shadow, larger than his own, leapt up on the wall to greet him. The shadow's arm shot out; a hand clamped his wrist. He screamed, tried to twist free, but the hand held him tight. "Little Boy Blue," the priest said, a fevered light scorching the flat surface of his eyes. "I *do* love you."

Hutch thought: not *blue*. Not *blue*.

Blue was the color of Mary, Most Pure.

Red was the color of sin and blood. *His* sin. *His* blood. *Little Boy Red*.

*****

The scream was close—twenty-five feet, Ramsey thought, maybe closer. A light beam shone deeper in the tunnel and the boy was caught in its glare. Then blackness again: the boy and the light gone. Ramsey, afraid his own light would betray him, moved ahead in the dark using the wall to guide him.

He had not traveled far before his feet kicked something soft and spongy. His hand, feeling around in the dirt, touched a shoe—several inches beyond that, a second shoe.

Somewhere close by the boy screamed again. Words came muffled through the walls, followed by a laugh, a groan, running footsteps. The boy cried out; Ramsey thought this must be some kind of demented game, the hunter stalking his prey, the killer toying with his victim. Why else would the boy still be alive after all this time?

He passed the first of the unfinished transverse halls and heard nothing in either direction. Half-crouching, he edged forward close to the wall. The sounds were still ahead of him: scufflings, garbled words, heavy breathing. At the next intersection, he turned the corner and swung his light into the shaft.

In that split-second of illumination he recognized the man in the Majority Life I. D. photo, older now but the eyes' vacant stare and the sharp line of his nose were unmistakable. In the confines of the tunnel the man seemed unusually tall, thin to the point of emaciation. He held Hutch pinned against the wall; but somehow—the sudden intrusion of light perhaps, or Ramsey's shout—the boy managed to slip free. Cafferty lunged and grabbed his foot, Hutch turning in the air then hitting the ground hard. Ramsey stepped into the hallway and fired over the prostrate body. Cafferty's shoulder jerked back, his mouth contorted, the impact blanched his face.

The boy was on his feet, running.

Ramsey had to hold his fire and watch Cafferty, hunched over and holding his shoulder, retreat deeper into the tunnel. Luke Hutchinson, with his arms flung wide, fell against him and clung tight, Ramsey asking *Are you all right? are you hurt?*

As Ramsey carried him back into the lighted corridor, footsteps came behind them. He turned, struck suddenly by a blinding light. Before he could raise his gun, Morales shouted, "It's me, Tommy."

"Cut the light, goddamnit."

The tunnel went black. Morales' shadow moved in the dim light. "Sorry," he said. "I couldn't see what was going on."

Ramsey shielded the boy from the sight of Falcone slumped against the wall. He set him down on the concrete and crouched beside him. "You'll be all right now, son. It's over." The terror in the boy's eyes told a different story, however. Ramsey pulled the torn ends of his shirt together. He said, "In time you'll forget about what happened here."

He regretted the lie as soon as he uttered it, but the boy was still trembling and he didn't have the heart to amend it.

"Where *is* he?" Morales said.

Ramsey nodded toward the dirt passage.

"Dead?"

"I nicked his arm."

"We'll get Moriarity to send the storm troopers in."

Ramsey, still kneeling by the boy, stopped him with a hard flat stare. "No."

"Why the hell not?"

"I said *no.*"

"He's trapped, for god's sake. He's not going anywhere."

"Eddie's dead," he offered by way of explanation. "I don't want to lose anyone else." He got to his feet and checked his watch. "I've still got fifteen minutes."

The half-light lent to Morales' strong, tanned face an added urgency. He walked a short distance into the blackness and came back. "It's a goddamn lion's den in there."

"Take the boy back."

"And leave you here? Not a chance."

"He needs medical attention."

"We're partners, remember? I go where you go." He stood squarely in the center of the tunnel as if he might block Ramsey's way.

"Do it, Tommy. Do this for *me,* okay?"

Morales squinted into the dark tunnel. "It's the asshole of the earth in there."

"We can't leave the boy here. You know that. Take him back. Then come get me."

"Too fucking dangerous."

"One on one. Nobody else needs to get hurt."

The hard steely glint in his ex-partner's eyes made Morales finally back off. "You're making a big mistake, Ram."

"I'm good at that."

*****

He moved into the unfinished extension, using his light for guidance. He knew exactly where he had last seen Cafferty—in the second right-hand transverse hall—and he made his way quickly back there. At the T intersection he took the right hand passage. This was where the man had vanished. It was only a short distance to the second T and, approaching it, he thought he would have to guess, left or right; but his flashlight picked up blood stains in the dirt at the entrance to the left passage. He hurt Cafferty more than he'd thought.

Move slowly. Keep the light close. Keep it from reflecting off the support beams. He talked himself through the tunnel until he came to a wall, shafts running off to the left and right. No blood on the ground to guide him.

The passage he chose—the left one—dead-ended. He back-tracked to the right-hand passage and moved ahead without any light this time, feeling his way with his hands along the irregular walls. No support beams here.

The shaft smelled strongly of earth, the floor was strewn with chunks of rock and dirt, and he wondered if this was part of the original construction: this passage seemed too rough—even by the standards of the unfinished tunnels, too haphazard in the twists and turns of its design, too new. *Could it have been dug more recently?*

That was when the smell first hit him: the stench of corruption that grew more overpowering as he advanced.

He stopped to brace himself against the wall and nearly retched. No way he could hold the light and the gun and still keep the handkerchief pressed to his nose so he limited his breathing, drawing in what air he needed in quick gasps through his mouth. Then the homemade passage widened and his flashlight picked out the first of the bodies: the badly decomposed, almost unrecognizable remains of a child, a boy, and beyond that, propped against the wall, the bony frame of another child, boy or girl it was impossible to know; and farther along the wall the light passed over the skeletal bones of at least four other children before he found the bloodied body of Donald Seward.

Sick with the horror around him, he didn't see the flicker of movement to his left, catching up with it too late, *after* it had fluttered into the eye of the beam.

The cold edge of steel ripped down his arm and he reeled back against the wall, firing in a straight line across the darkness: four shots in succession. The flashlight hung limp from his hand. At the edges of its glow he saw a shadow shift along the wall. If he wasn't too old to believe in monsters, he would have suspected the hulking thing that hovered there had been resurrected from the terrors of his childhood.

A flash of light preceded the deafening ricochet of gunshots off the stone on either side of him. He dropped to a crouch and fired at the dark shape, emptying his final two rounds into the unholy being rising from the bones of the dead.

Despite the searing pain he managed to lift the light, its beam slapping Cafferty full in the face: the man's eyes wide and astonished, his face despite its sickly color looking oddly boyish and innocent, except for the lips which turned up at the edges in what might have been a mocking grin. Arms outstretched, he fell toward Ramsey, calling out, "Daddy. . . Heavenly Father . . . help me."

Chapter Seventeen

SUNDAY

The following Sunday morning he drove Krissie to Gate of Heaven. At Evan's grave she set a plastic vase in the dirt and arranged the dozen white roses. Kneeling, she prayed the way a child might pray: eyes shut tight, lips moving. Then she made the sign of the cross and stepped back to where he was standing on grass that shimmered a blinding green under the bright sun. "I asked him to forgive me. . . . If only he could."

"Evan wasn't capable of holding a grudge," he said. The unexpected simplicity of that made her cry. He held her until the spasms stopped. To an observer, from across the rows of headstones, they might easily have passed for husband and wife consoling one another.

She pulled away and stiffened her shoulders. The sun brought out the light in her eyes with such brilliance he lowered his gaze. He was not accustomed to her beauty in daylight. "I promised myself if you gave me this," she said, "I wouldn't ask for anything else. I know you have to try to work things out with your wife."

He was thinking: a child comes and goes, and the world is changed forever. He said, "We can't build a life around one particular person, one particular moment. There's got to be some larger principle, some belief."

"God, you mean?"

The past week, lying alone at night in the empty house, his imagination had been relentless, forcing back upon him the images from his dream: the boys, the darkness, himself at the center. He understood the dream now in a new way. It wasn't the boys who were lost and in need of help. It was himself.

"Some way of loving," he said, "larger than our need to be loved in return."

She cocked her head and forced a smile. "You know, this might be the most poetic way a guy's ever broken up with me." She bit her lip, shook her head and looked away. "I'll wait for you in the car, okay?"

She walked between the rows of stones, unsteadily but with determination, her shoulders thrust as a ballast.

There was too much on his mind to talk to Evan; that he would save for another time. Lifting one of the roses from the vase, he crossed to Eddie Falcone's grave on the far side of the willow tree. It was the first in a row of newly dug sites on the cleared field. No headstone yet. Simply a swath of broken earth.

On the open field, the sun beat down without relief. He removed his jacket and folded it over his arm, then leaned forward to lay a rose on the dirt. He thought he had been drained of feeling but grief chose that moment to show up unannounced. "You son-of-a-bitch, Eddie. You goddamn son-of-a-bitch. I was the one with the debt to pay."

The sun's reflection on the windshield hid Krissie from view. He seemed to surprise her when he opened the door because she turned away quickly and adjusted her sunglasses, brushing her fingers across her cheeks.

"You drive," he said.

"Oh, no, I couldn't. I mean, I haven't driven in a year—"

"That's right." He held out the keys but she made no move toward them. There was a cowering, little girl look in her eyes that he hadn't seen before.

"I don't think I should."

He stood there in the road, squinting in the sunlight, offering the keys. "I think you should."

She was tentative at first, as if she were a fifteen-year-old with a learner's permit: gripping the wheel too tightly, easing the car much too slowly into second gear. The cemetery road was narrow but uncrowded. Past hedges and tall oaks and the parked cars of mourners, she drove more cautiously than necessary, braking prematurely whenever someone stepped off the curb ahead. At the base of a hill that led to the cemetery gate, she pulled over and stopped.

She glanced at him: the plea as much in her eyes as in her voice. "I can't go out there."

"Course you can."

"I can't."

He thought if he kept looking at her the affection he felt would deepen into love and he would have to take her in his arms forever. Shifting in his seat he stared through the window at an ancient oak, its leaves hanging thick and heavy in the heat. The wind stirred and he thought he heard the leaves whisper, or was that another trick of his imagination?—anything not to hear the silence of the morning which seemed unendurable, reaching beyond them and far across the wide fields of the dead; and then the car was moving again, climbing the hill steadily toward the gate.

*****

Later that afternoon Ramsey showed up for the graduation ceremony at St. Jerome's. From the bleachers he watched the graduates, Mike Brody among them, file in procession across the school yard to row upon row of folding chairs. The air had cooled down, the sky a bright and glorious blue as Father O'Malley took the podium, his voice rising above the steady hum of parkway traffic, counting off for an interminable fifteen minutes the rewards of a Catholic education: the character-building results of hard work and discipline, the God-given strength to be derived from daily prayer, the ethical foundations that had prepared each of them for lives of moral responsibility.

"But most of all," he said in his conclusion, his voice choked with pride, his massive frame rising to its full height above the rows of graduates, "what you have learned here at St. Jerome's Academy, what you will take with you as you venture out into the highways and byways of the world is *a respect for one another*. You have learned to revere and cherish the differences among us that make us each, every last one of us, unique in God's sight, indispensable in His divine plan."

Yeah, Ramsey thought, wouldn't *that* be nice.

He stood now to watch the graduates come forward to receive their diplomas or, more accurately, the token slip of paper that substituted for the diploma they would receive eventually. The school—the physical plant of it, the personnel, even this ceremony itself—left a bitter taste in his mouth. Under interrogation, O'Malley had acknowledged only a passing relationship with Cafferty; he had no idea why a number of St. Jerome's boys had been targeted. According to O'Malley there had been nothing in the man's behavior as an occasional and part-time employee here to arouse suspicion of any sort. "Only God could understand a twisted mind like that," he told Ramsey. "Let's leave it in His hands, shall we?"

The priest's smug dismissal of the tragedies infuriated Ramsey, just as he was furious with Shannon for maintaining that only coincidence could explain why as many as four of the victims were members of the Order of St. Sebastian. As far as Farrell's evening visits were concerned, the priest would say only that the boy came for confession, and that the seal of the confessional prevented him from going into detail.

Whatever unholy alliances existed here would remain cloaked in secrecy. And what happened between Shannon and Arthur Farrell two Sundays ago, and how that might have contributed to the boy's death, was consigned now to the realm of speculation. Uncertainties of the maze, the mind's secret hallways.

There was no way he would crack the clerical wall of silence, but he stepped onto the field now so he would be in position when the procession passed by. He would make certain both Shannon and O'Malley saw him, he would force eye contact with each man. A small gesture, to be sure, but he would serve notice one more time: *I'm watching you.*

Catholic Boys   219

PHILIP CIOFFARI

Philip Cioffari holds a Ph.D. in Literature from New York University. He is Professor of English, and Director of the Performing and Literary Arts Honors Program, at William Paterson University in New Jersey. His collection of short stories, A HISTORY OF THINGS LOST OR BROKEN, won the Tartt fiction prize and was published by Livingston Press at The University of West Alabama in Spring, 2007. His short stories have been published widely in commercial and literary magazines and anthologies, including *Playboy, North American Review, Michigan Quarterly, Northwest Review, Florida Fiction, Italian Americana*, etc. His first independent feature film, LOVE IN THE AGE OF DION, which he wrote and directed, won Best Feature Film (on video) at the Long Island International Film Expo 2006. He has written and directed for Off and Off-Off Broadway. His work has been shown in New York at the Belmont Italian American Playhouse, the Chelsea Playhouse, American Globe Theatre, Pulse Ensemble Theatre, American Theatre for Actors, and elsewhere. He is the recipient of many writing fellowships and awards, including the New Voices Fiction Prize from the Writer's Voice in New York City.